The whims of a drunken fool . . .

"Glad to see you gents made it out of St. Alban's in one piece," he said, in a stage-whisper that filled the air around us with fumes of the liqueur he had consumed.

"What the devil are you talking about?" Jean-Claude snapped, annoyed in nearly equal parts at having his name mangled and at sacrificing his time to "the whims of a drunken fool," as he would say later, once we reached the welcome outdoors. "We have not even been to the school today. We were at Sloane's all morning, as you yourself might very well have been."

"Why, haven't you heard?" he asked, dumbfounded at our ignorance, but clearly delighted at the opportunity to disabuse us of it. "St. Alban's is under siege, or at least will be before the day is through."

I exchanged a knowing glance with Jean-Claude, and asked, in an attempt at a casual tone, "Under siege? By whom?"

Thomas cut his eyes back and forth. "By the whole bloody town, from the looks of things. Every damned peasant who could lay his grimy hands on a shovel or pitchfork is there, threatening to break down the front gate and dig the whole place up, looking for bodies."

ATTENTION: ORGANIZATIONS AND CORPORATIONS
Most Harper paperbacks are available at special quantity discounts
for bulk purchases for sales promotions, premiums, or fund-raising.
For information, please call or write:

Special Markets Department, HarperCollins Publishers,
10 East 53rd Street, New York, New York 10022-5299.
Telephone: (212) 207-7528.   Fax: (212) 207-7222.

HAL McDONALD

The Anatomists

HARPER

An Imprint of HarperCollinsPublishers

This is a work of fiction. Names, characters, places, and incidents are products of the author's imagination or are used fictitiously and are not to be construed as real. Any resemblance to actual events, locales, organizations, or persons, living or dead, is entirely coincidental.

HARPER
An Imprint of HarperCollins*Publishers*
10 East 53rd Street
New York, New York 10022-5299

Copyright © 2008 by Harold McDonald
ISBN: 978-0-06-144375-6

All rights reserved. No part of this book may be used or reproduced in any manner whatsoever without written permission, except in the case of brief quotations embodied in critical articles and reviews. For information address Harper paperbacks, an Imprint of HarperCollins Publishers.

First Harper paperback printing: April 2008

HarperCollins ® and Harper ® are registered trademarks of Harper-Collins Publishers.

Printed in the United States America

Visit Harper paperbacks on the World Wide Web at www.harpercollins.com

10 9 8 7 6 5 4 3 2 1

If you purchased this book without a cover, you should be aware that this book is stolen property. It was reported as "unsold and destroyed" to the publisher, and neither the author nor the publisher has received any payment for this "stripped book."

For Nancy, who believed . . .

ACKNOWLEDGMENTS

I would like to thank truTV, whose "Search for the Next Great Crime Writer" contest got me to start writing *The Anatomists*; HarperCollins Publishers, whose interest in the book spurred me to finish it; and my daughter Hillary, whose intriguing question during a leisurely ten-mile run gave me the idea that set the whole thing into motion.

CHAPTER 1

As Queen Victoria prepares to enter her fifth decade upon the throne, I stand poised upon the threshold of my own momentous milestone—namely, retirement.

Looking back upon my long and, I must humbly add, distinguished career in medicine, I cannot help but reflect on how very much my chosen profession has changed since I first entered into it nearly half a century ago. Techniques for the diagnosis and treatment of physical maladies have, of course, advanced considerably over the past several decades, but an even more substantial, if perhaps subtler, alteration has occurred in the public perception of medicine itself, and of those of us who practice it. What is today considered a respectable—nay, very nearly sacred—vocation to which to dedicate one's life was once viewed by the common masses with suspicion, and in some cases with outright antagonism, due to a variety of social dynamics far too numerous and complex to go into here. Suffice it to say that the early days of my career were fraught with difficulties, and even dangers, from which a physician starting out today is completely immune. Had I been in possession of a full foreknowledge of these difficulties as I initially contemplated the pursuit of medicine, however, I should not have veered one step from the path I actually followed, so very fascinating were the characters with which it brought me into contact and the adventures it afforded me. One such adventure befell me shortly after I first entered into the formal study of medicine.

Having completed my university studies at Oxford in 1824, I ventured to London and enrolled in St. Alban's Medical School, to pursue the course of study that would ultimately permit me to practice as a physician. Upon inquiring from the Registrar where I might find lodgings close by the school, the gentleman directed me to a dingy narrow house that commonly let rooms to medical students. Earlier in the day, he had directed another student to an apartment at that same address, and, the accommodation being intended for two inhabitants, thought we might wish to share the rooms, as well as the expenses.

I followed the man's directions through crowded, dirty streets until arriving at the designated address, where I climbed a torturous set of stairs up to the first floor and rapped upon the apartment door. In response to a vague, indistinguishable voice from the other side, I let myself into the apartment, where I encountered one of the most singular specimens of human mortality ever to walk the face of the earth. It was Jean-Claude Legard, formerly of Paris, but now a confirmed "Englishman" ever since arriving in Cambridge three years earlier for his own university studies. I shall never forget that first glimpse of him, for it was part and parcel of the man's entire character, as I would come to know it over the course of the next many years. He was sitting at a small table beside the cold empty hearth busily occupied in a game of chess—with himself! Sliding the chessboard 'round and 'round, he played first one player's move, then the other, all the while studying an anatomy book that lay open at his left elbow. He never so much as acknowledged my presence until he got himself into checkmate and turned over his king, punctuating this final move with a strange clicking sound from his tongue. Then he stood up, introduced himself formally with a slight bow, and immediately asked me if I cared to play a game of chess. It was to be the first of countless such games.

Our first year of medical study passed quickly, involving mostly theoretical bookwork along with great quantities of rote memorization. Jean-Claude, of course, excelled in all of this foundational study—his confidence in the synthetic powers of reason being second only to his monumental faith in his own capacity for wielding these powers. While not nearly as capacious as he in absorbing raw intellectual matter, I nonetheless handled myself adroitly enough to complete the first year without serious incident and advance to the second year, when we should finally be permitted to lay aside the books from time to time and venture into the operating theater for some practical firsthand experience with human anatomy.

To embark upon next this phase of our studies, it was incumbent upon us to procure our own anatomical specimen, or, in slightly less euphemistic words, a human body. There being in those days virtually no legal means of procuring such specimens, students of medicine reluctantly but almost universally resorted to trade with that seedy species of night-laborer known as "resurrectionists." Not to put too fine a point upon the matter, the resurrectionists were grave robbers for hire. If a medical student required a specimen, he sent word out "on the street," and sometime during the next few days would be approached by a beggar, urchin, or some other species of societal refuse announcing the imminent delivery of said specimen. And then, at the appointed hour and location, the resurrectionist would arrive with the grim fruit of his night's labor, take his money, and disappear back into the darkness from which he had emerged.

Like most students of medicine, Jean-Claude and I felt a natural and instinctive revulsion toward this evil practice, but realizing, alas, that it was a necessary evil, when our time came to produce a cadaver for our continued study of the human anatomy, we swallowed our repugnance and ventured onto the street. The agent of our brief intercourse with the trade turned out to be a surprisingly clear-eyed and energetic lad of fourteen named "Jimmy," whom we arranged to meet at a certain dark hour on a certain dark street corner two blocks away from St. Alban's. We arrived, as instructed, with a rustic wooden handcart, which we had "borrowed" from the school's maintenance shed. Bumping this cart through the virtually deserted street, fearing that every jarring cobble broadcast our nefarious mission to the whole of London, Jean-Claude and I felt alternately sinister and ridiculous. Just imagine for a moment, two respectable young medical students hauling an empty wooden handcart through the streets like some common day laborers. Sensing my emotional ambivalence regarding our current task, Jean-Claude dispelled my nervous gloom by concentrating on the ridiculous rather than the sinister element of our plight. For all his surface respectability and seriousness, Jean-Claude had a wickedly droll irreverent streak that was highly welcome on occasions such as this. "To market to market, to buy a fat pig," he quietly chanted, in that peculiar Anglo-French dialect of his. "I say, Jean-Claude," I replied in mock moral outrage, but with unmistakable relief in my voice. "Do have some respect for the dead." Had we not been strolling through pitch-blackness, I am sure I would have seen that familiar little curl that always appeared in the corner of his mouth when he was particularly pleased with something he had said. Our moment of levity was short-lived, however, for the faint light of a lantern up ahead soon revealed to us the gangly figure of Jimmy, leaning casually upon his own handcart.

"Good evenin', gentl'men," he greeted us in a matter-of-fact tone, as if it were a load of turnips he had in that cart instead of what had once been a living, breathing, rational human being. "Let's make this quick, now. Don't want to attract no attention, do we?" As much as I wholeheartedly agreed with this last sentiment, I couldn't help wincing at the less-than-discreet volume at which he pronounced it.

"The agreed-upon fee was four guineas, was it not," Jean-Claude interjected, clearly as eager as I to bring this transaction to a rapid close. He produced from his coat pocket a small purse of coins, which Jimmy tossed up and down a few times, as if checking the weight, then stuffed unceremoniously into his own coat pocket. And then, after threading his fingers together and giving his knuckles a good crack, as if he were getting ready to dig a ditch instead of . . . well, what he was about to do, he squatted down behind his cart, heaved a large canvas bag up onto his shoulder, and then deposited the bag into our own cart with an unforgettably sickening thud. "Come 'round again if you got any more business to do," he said casually, and turned and walked away. Following the dim light of his lantern with our eyes, we watched in curious disbelief as he strolled merrily down the street, parked his handcart before a row of run-down-looking houses, and disappeared into a door hanging none too securely on its hinges beneath a sign that read THE JOLLY FOX TAVERN.

"He appears to like his work, that lad," Jean-Claude observed, with that slight clicking of his tongue, though whether of disapproval or amusement, I could not tell. And then, patting the side of our cart with the flat of his hand, by way of invitation, queried, "Shall we?" Swallowing my repugnance and trying to adopt a portion of Jean-Claude's flippant bravado, I grasped one handle of the cart, he grasped the other, and we wheeled our dread burden back to St. Alban's.

Public anatomical dissections, for the benefit of student observation, were typically performed by veteran surgeons in the bright, spacious operating theatre of Sloane's Hospital, the institutional sponsor of St. Alban's. When the time came for the students to practice the surgical procedures we had observed in the demonstrations, however, we were herded into a close, dank common dissection hall at St. Alban's, where we worked elbow to elbow upon anywhere from four to eight cadavers at a time. In order to prolong the useful "life" of these dead bodies, dissections took place during the winter months only, but the perpetual chill in which we conducted our researches did little to quell the noxious atmosphere that is so natural and inevitable a feature of post-mortem existence. It was a dissection table in this charnel house for which our burlap-clad subject was bound, but first we had to perform a cursory private examination of the cadaver to assure ourselves that it was not already dismembered, or in an advanced state of decomposition—in short, to make sure we'd gotten our four guineas' worth.

Toward this end, we carried our evening's "purchase" into a defunct root cellar, upon whose dark earthen walls hung smoky torches whose feeble light had poorly illuminated countless precautionary examinations such as the one we were about to perform, and deposited the sack unceremoniously upon an ancient, smooth-worn, and rather disturbingly stained carving table there.

As horrifying as our dark endeavor had seemed to me while our "subject" was crudely and shapelessly wrapped in burlap, once we had him laid out upon the table, my professional curiosity to a large degree overcame my revulsion. We had, after all, been preceded in our labors by a whole train of anatomists, many of whom were held in quite high regard by polite society. Hadn't Leonardo da Vinci done many times what we were preparing to do tonight?

Thus morally and emotionally mollified, I took my place at Jean-Claude's side and gave my undivided attention to the poor fellow spread out on the table before us—a mustachioed man in his mid to late twenties who, aside from being dead, appeared the very picture of health.

"Hmm," I heard Jean-Claude mutter, significantly. Having grown up in the home of a Parisian gendarme, my friend had a more-than-passing acquaintance with violence and death, and as he stood there meditatively stroking his chin, I knew he must have noticed something amiss with our subject.

Having, not disagreeably, no prior experience with dead bodies myself, I nonetheless immediately suspected the meaning behind his speculative utterance. "The clothes," I ventured.

"Yes," he responded. For in truth, there was something quite odd about the departed man's mode of attire. "When the deceased is prepared for interment," he continued, "is it not the practice to attire him 'to the nines,' as they say? But this man here . . ."

"Yes," I said. "He looks as if he'd been playing cards all night long."

"*Précisément*," responded Jean-Claude, looking pleased with the analogy. "Playing cards, yes. And in genteel company."

This latter observation referred to the quality of the man's clothing, which was, indeed, that of a gentleman—expensive fabric tailored to a perfect fit, just the sort of clothing one might expect a deceased gentleman to be buried in. The strangeness of the ensemble lay, not in the suit itself, but rather in the general state of dishevelment in which we found the suit on first inspection. The coat, for example, was missing entirely. The vest, terribly wrinkled, gaped halfway open, and the unbuttoned collar and loosened black tie hung shapelessly about his neck. "Not exactly prepared to meet his Maker, eh Jean-Claude," I observed.

"We can know nothing of what happens when he meets his Maker," he replied, "but perhaps we can find out something about what sent him on his journey. And regardless of how strange his clothes may appear to us, we can discover little while he still has them on. To work!"

And with that sudden exhortation—of the kind, by the way, Jean-Claude was extremely fond of uttering—we set about undressing our gentleman. Being of a slightly more robust physical nature, I grasped him underneath his arms and lifted him to a seated position, while Jean-Claude worked at removing his vest and shirt. After a few minutes of this labor, I began to gain a new understanding of the word "deadweight," for my shoulders and back began to ache under the prolonged strain. "I say, Jean-Claude," I groaned, "do get on with it."

"I am working as rapidly as I can, my friend. You see, I already have the vest and tie, and here comes the shirt . . . But what is this?" he exclaimed as he removed the collar. *"Mon dieu!"*

Seeing that Jean-Claude had succeeded in removing the man's shirt, and having reached the end of my physical endurance, I allowed our subject to return to his original prone position and stretched my cramping shoulders and back.

Paying absolutely no heed to my physical distress, Jean-Claude held the shirt collar in front of my face, and said, "What do you make of this, my friend?"

For a moment, I could make out nothing but the shadow of my own head, so very uneven was the lighting, but after shifting my position and blinking away the sweat that had trickled into my eyes during my recent exertion, I saw it. There in the dead center of the back of the collar was a single rust-colored spot about the size and shape of a single halfpenny. "It looks like blood," I said, somewhat stupidly, having not fully recovered my composure.

"Of course it is blood," he responded, a bit too

excitedly for my tastes, given the circumstances. "Do you know what this means?"

I had been acquainted with Jean-Claude for over a year at this point and had long since become accustomed to these impromptu dialectical sessions. Nonetheless, I always seemed to be one step behind him in his chain of reasoning. "I have my own theory," I said, trying to appear guardedly knowledgeable, "but why don't you tell me yours first?"

"*Zut!*" he exclaimed, rolling his eyes, and raising his hands as if in supplication to the ceiling. "How many dead men have you ever known to bleed? This man, however—a gentleman, by all appearances—bled after he was placed in these clothes, presumably his burial clothes. *Regarde,* and from the dishabille of his clothes, he appears to have been quite mobile in them for some time before he died. The bleeding, and the wrinkled clothes—they can mean only one thing!" Here he paused, as if to permit me to provide the conclusion to the premises he had patiently laid out before me. Fortunately, before I had to venture a guess as to where he was headed with all of this, another thought occurred to him. "Quick, turn him over! We must see."

Together, we rolled our gentleman over onto his face. Jean-Claude lifted the man's hair and peered closely at the back of his neck. "A torch!" he commanded. "*Tout de suite!*" I reached for the brightest flame on the wall and illuminated the area that had so captivated my friend's attention. "Exactly as I thought," he said, with a hint of smug satisfaction in his voice. "Do you see now?"

I started to take exception to his emphasis on the word "now," but before I could formulate a proper defense, I did see. At the base of the dead man's skull, in the very center, was a small, perfectly round and perfectly lethal-looking hole. "This man has been murdered," Jean-Claude solemnly pronounced.

"Murdered?" I replied, sorely taken aback. "How can that be? I read nothing of a murder in the newspaper. And surely if a gentleman such as this had been murdered . . ."

"Do you really not see, my friend? How could the murder have been in the newspaper, when you and I are the first to know of it?"

"What do you mean?" I said, giving up all pretense of following his logic. "A gentleman such as this is stabbed to death, and no one takes notice? I know the wound is somewhat out of the way, but we found it. And surely someone else would have bothered to take a look. The man's wife, for example. Or the men he was playing cards with, if that's what he was doing. Or the undertaker, for heaven's sake."

"Do I have to draw you a picture?" he said, grasping his own hair by the roots—a gesture, by the way, with which I was to become extremely familiar over the next few years. "There was no undertaker, for this man was never taken under! He was never buried. He did not come into our hands from the ground. He came to us directly from the street."

"But who . . . ?"

Jean-Claude did not even allow me to finish my question. "I very much fear that the agent of delivery in this case, was also the agent of death."

"You mean that lad . . . what was his name."

"Jimmy, I believe it was. *Précisément.*"

"My God," I gasped. "But whatever for?"

"Why, for money," he explained. "Four guineas for a gentleman's life." Jean-Claude paused for a moment, reflectively, and then continued. "It is not without precedent. Someone relies upon the trade of fresh bodies to make a living. The graveyards supply the fruits of his trade, but sometimes the harvest is scarce. The money runs out, and he must find his bodies somewhere else. In desperate situations, he seeks his dead among the living."

"So you think that boy . . . Jimmy . . . ?"

"I think that if he killed this man, it shall go hard with him. But there is only one way to know for certain. We must go directly to the source. And if he has not ventured back out into the night, I believe we will find him at . . . what was it? Ah yes, at the Jolly Fox. Come, my friend."

For the second time that night, we ventured out onto the streets. This time, however, since it was illumination we sought rather than cover of darkness, we carried a lantern, and thus made far greater haste than we had on our first such journey. In less than half an hour, we arrived at our disreputable-looking destination, where we found the handcart still parked out front.

The scene that greeted us upon opening the

door reminded one of something from the deeper circles of Dante's *Inferno*. Smoke hung heavily in the air, dimming the already feeble light thrown off by a few dirty lanterns. Men and women from the very lowest rung of society's ladder lounged about the place in various postures of dissolution, eating greasy food and drinking stale beer and cheap gin. My stomach turned within me, and every fiber of my being screamed to be released back into the fresh night air. Jean-Claude, however, appeared totally impervious to the noxious atmosphere and merely searched the smoky enclosure until his eyes came to rest upon Jimmy, leaning casually against the bar, drinking a tankard of beer and laughing over some story the barkeep had just related. What a depraved specimen of humanity, I thought to myself, to have such a light heart after executing such a dark deed.

While I stood transfixed to the spot, I saw Jean-Claude stroll resolutely toward the lad and engage him in conversation. As they spoke, I watched the levity flee from Jimmy's face, to be replaced by a gravity that bespoke a full awareness of the import of what my friend was saying to him. After a few moments of such deep discussion, Jimmy set his mug upon the bar and followed Jean-Claude across the room and toward the front door, leaving me alone in the tavern until I hastened to join them outside.

As I approached the two in the quiet darkness outside, I heard Jimmy vociferously protesting his innocence. "I'm tellin' you, Cap'n, I never laid eyes on 'im before I dug 'im up. And 'e was just as dead then as 'e is right now."

Jean-Claude's childhood in a police officer's home showed very clearly now, as he pressed his suspect for a full disclosure of the truth. "It is very simple then," he said calmly but pointedly. "If it is as you say, then you should be able to take us to the empty grave. If you cannot, however, show us the grave, we will have no choice but to conclude that the body came, not from the ground, but from the street. And as dead men do not, as a custom, walk the streets, we will have no choice but to conclude that he was not dead until you encountered him. And as such lethal encounters are not permitted by the law, we will have no choice but to turn you over to the authorities."

I could not help shuddering a bit at the cold calculation of my friend's treatment of the lad, but the chilly inquisition produced an instantaneous result in his auditor. "I'll show you!" Jimmy said, with a desperate earnestness. "It's not 'alf a mile from 'ere, the graveyard—right beside the All Souls Church. Just give me a minute to grab me shovel."

"You may, as you say, 'grab' your shovel," Jean-Claude said sternly. "But we shall accompany you in your grabbing." It turns out we did not have to accompany him far, because the shovel was lying in his handcart.

Thus supplied with the means for unearthing the truth, whatever that truth might have been, the three of us set out into the dark streets in the direction of All Souls Church, or more accurately, toward the cemetery immediately thereby. Our journey could not have lasted more than ten minutes, but it provided ample time for reflection on the nature of our current dark purpose. The evening had begun strangely enough—with Jean-Claude and me heading out into the streets of London to purchase a dead body from a resurrectionist—but here we were now, scarcely two hours after that first expedition, traipsing to a cemetery to dig up a grave! Truly a macabre twist to an evening that was already the stuff of nightmares.

When we arrived at the side gate to the cemetery, Jimmy shuttered the lantern to permit a mere sliver of light to escape. "The night watchman," he whispered, explaining his precaution. "He didn't see me the first time tonight, and I don't fancy 'im seeing me this time."

We followed our guide through a gap in the fence where some ironwork was missing—whether by natural or human agency, I had my own opinions. Picking our way among the graves, and barking our shins on more than one headstone, we finally came to a stop at an unmarked, freshly dug patch of earth. "This is the one," Jimmy whispered. "Now you gentl'men listen out for any noise that ain't one of the three of us, while I get busy."

Without further prologue, Jimmy began quietly and expertly moving aside the freshly dug earth. As quickly as he worked, however, the prospect of being accosted by the night watchman made Jimmy's progress seem unbearably slow. Jean-Claude and I both batted our eyes into the darkness and

strained our ears for anything out of the ordinary—
out of the ordinary for a graveyard at midnight,
that is—until suddenly Jean-Claude exhaled an
nervously energetic "Ah!" and left my side. In the
dim lanternlight, he had spied a shovel propped
against a nearby tombstone and, wasting no time
in taking advantage of the opportunity to hasten
this unbearable process along, joined Jimmy in
the rapidly deepening hole to make quicker work
of the job. Visibly relieved to be doing something
rather than nothing, Jean-Claude could not resist
an attempt at humor. Grasping a large clod of mold
from the pile at his feet, he addressed it, "Alas poor
Yorick." I, for one, was not amused.

Finally, after what seemed an eternity of waiting, we heard the resounding and unmistakable
thud of metal upon hollow wood. Jean-Claude's
shovel had struck the coffin lid. I joined the two of
them in the hole, and we all three worked rapidly,
removing the remaining earth until we had cleared
a space around the coffin lid. Jimmy and I worked
our fingers down through the loosened earth, trying to get a purchase on the lid, while Jean-Claude
held the lantern directly above our heads. "The
proverbial moment of truth," he said, moving his
gaze back and forth between Jimmy and me, very
much like a cardplayer trying to determine whether
or not his opponent's wager is a bluff.

And then, finding the seam for which we were
searching, we lifted the lid and tossed it onto the
scattered mold beside the open grave. As Jean-
Claude lowered the lantern into the hole, my

hands quivered, both out of fatigue from the past half hour's strenuous exertion and from nervous anticipation as I considered the possibly lethal consequences of this project for the young lad standing between us. I shifted, to move my shadow from in front of the lantern, and the beam of light fell starkly upon the interior of the open coffin in which we beheld . . . absolutely nothing! The grave was, indeed, empty!

"Well, my young friend," Jean-Claude addressed Jimmy, visibly relieved at the outcome of our search, "it appears you have escaped the gallows. Nevertheless, you would perhaps be well advised to seek for yourself another occupation—one that does not involve dead people."

Jimmy, clearly relieved at having escaped the cloud of suspicion that had hung about his neck, but also feeling somewhat smug, in spite of himself, at having thus been proven "right," stroked his fuzzy chin for a moment, then ruminated, "Funny you should mention a change of career, 'cause I've been looking about me of late, you know, considering me options. Would you gentl'men happen to know of some respectful employment for an industrious fellow such as myself?"

Jean-Claude stole a quick glance at me, and even in the dim lamplight I could see an amused twinkle playing about his eyes. "Hmm," he pondered, with feigned gravity. "Perhaps we could find some situation. It would depend upon the skills you have to offer and the type of experience you have had."

Jimmy's face lit up. "I'm quite a hand at dig-gin', as you gentl'men can attest to. And it ain't just graves, neither. You tell me something what needs to be dug up, and I'll have it done before the words are out of your mouth good."

Two or three times during the course of this tête-à-tête, I thought I heard the crunch of leaves, as if underfoot, but I couldn't be sure until the dis-tinct snapping of a twig shattered the black still-ness just outside our tiny circle of light. My suspicions were confirmed by the instantaneous cessation of conversation between my two com-panions. "I believe it would be a very good idea if we very quickly and very quietly vacated the premises," I whispered, as calmly as possible.

"We can't go now," Jimmy said incredulously, "without we fill in this hole we just dug up. That's one of the—what d'you call it?—nonnegotiative rules of my profession. You don't leave no evi-dence behind, and no one's the wiser, if you know what I mean."

"Honor among thieves," I heard Jean-Claude mutter under his breath. "As much as I respect a professional man's 'rules,' Jimmy," he continued, more audibly, "I am afraid my friend is correct in urging our immediate departure from this place. Unless, of course, you fancy spending the night in jail."

Jimmy opened his mouth—to protest, no doubt—but before he could utter the first sylla-ble, the night's stillness was shattered by a gruff, troll-like voice, and this voice was not whispering. "Stop right where you are, and don't move a muscle," the voice growled. And for a moment, we did exactly as we were commanded, being essentially blind beyond a distance of five feet, and thus completely ignorant of the strength of our new foe.

"It's the night watchman," Jimmy whispered.

"I gathered as much," replied Jean-Claude, in a fully audible voice. "And as for whispering, I think there is no longer the need for it. We have already been discovered."

"What shall we do?" said I, admittedly at a complete loss for ideas.

"The only thing we can do under the circumstances," Jean-Claude said, with a tone of resignation totally alien to his character.

"You mean just give up?" I said in utter disbelief. "Just let ourselves—two gentlemen—be arrested . . . for grave robbing?! We'll never live it down, Jean-Claude!"

"My friend," he returned, in a low whisper once more, "I have no more desire than you to be arrested. I also have no intention of being arrested."

"But . . ." said I, with a sense of helpless ignorance that was to become familiar to me in such situations, for try as I might to keep up, Jean-Claude always seemed to be one step ahead of me.

"We shall recruit the darkness to be our ally," he whispered, unnecessarily cryptically, to my way of thinking, until he explained. "The lamp you have in your hand . . . Keep it shuttered until our foe comes within two arm's lengths of us. When he is clearly visible, throw open the shutter toward his face, then just as suddenly close it again. He will be momentarily blinded, and we will seize that brief opportunity to escape. Jimmy will lead the way, since he is accustomed to navigating graveyards in the dark."

"Stay put now, or I'll shoot you where you stand!" the voice barked from the darkness.

"He is clearly armed, my friends," pronounced Jean-Claude, at a normal volume once again. "We have no choice but to stand here and wait."

From the darkness, we could hear the footsteps moving closer and closer for what seemed an hour, as our eyes strained to catch a glimpse of his. Finally, the faintest outline of a human form materialized, and then our would-be captor stepped into the small circle of light. His appearance was exactly consistent with the sound of his voice, for he looked very much like a troll—rude and unkempt, as if he spent his entire life out of doors. Cradled in his dirt-caked hands was an antiquated-looking musket, which he waved vaguely in our general direction.

"He can't do nothin' with that old thing," Jimmy whispered out of the side of his mouth, in a tone of amusement.

"I am not willing to wager my life upon appearances," Jean-Claude replied audibly. "We had better do as he says." But under his breath, he muttered, "Wait until I give you the signal," and when our would-be captor was quite literally close enough to smell, shouted, "Now!"

I opened the shutter as I had been instructed, and the pitch-black cemetery was suddenly bathed in lamplight. The watchman threw his hands before his eyes, dropping the musket in the process, and we took the opportunity to set off toward the front gate as quickly as our legs would carry us. The sound of footsteps immediately behind us reminded me of the second part of Jean-Claude's instructions to me, and I quickly closed the shutter on the lamp, plunging the graveyard into darkness once more. Almost immediately I heard the dull thud of flesh and bone meeting solid wood, followed by a series of stinging French epithets, most of which I had never before heard, even from Jean-Claude.

We continued on in the darkness, four sets of footsteps, dodging the large tombstones, barking our shins on the small ones, and generally flailing about in chaotic confusion, until the three of us somehow managed to find our way back to the street, where our pursuer left off his chase and returned to his grim demesne.

Not before we had left several hundred yards of cobbles between the three of us and the graveyard did I finally unshutter the lamp and restore our sense of sight. And a sorry sight it was, too. Jean-Claude sported an angry-looking bump above his right eye and was missing his hat. Thorns and brambles completely covered my own suit, the left coat sleeve of which was but a few threads away from falling off entirely. Even Jimmy, who presented a fairly sad spectacle to begin with, was somewhat the worse for wear. Observing the altogether-disreputable spectacle we presented, and feeling the relief of our narrow escape, I could not help but laugh, and I was soon followed in my mirth by Jimmy, who likewise appreciated the utter ridiculousness of our situation. Jean-Claude, on the other hand, was less amused. "Perhaps you would both like to return to the cemetery for another encounter with the night watchman," he said, with a disapproving pucker around the corners of his mouth, "so very much did you enjoy that one."

"No, Jean-Claude," I replied, stifling my laughter, "my appetite for midnight graveyard chases is quite satisfied for the moment. It's about time we started back for St. Alban's, anyway."

"Yes, it is about the time," he said curtly. "Let us go." Then, recovering his composure sufficiently to remember his manners, he addressed Jimmy. "Adieu, my young friend. I am happy that you proved our suspicions to be in error."

"Likewise," he replied, and turned to leave us, but paused briefly to express a thought that was troubling him. "I really wish we could have got that box covered up before the watchman found us. The law kind of looks the other way, so long as we fellows go about our work with . . . what'ya call it? . . . discretion. But leaving that gentl'man's grave open like that, for all the world to see . . . that's a bad job, and it's likely going to make things difficult for us . . . for the people what practice my trade."

Jimmy's professional misgivings proved to be disturbingly prophetic, for the headlines of the next evening's *Gazette* virtually screamed out the results of our late-night churchyard expedition.

BODY SNATCHERS STRIKE ALL SOULS CEMETERY. Jean-Claude and I had spent the entire day carrying out our researches on the cadaver that had already caused us no end of difficulty and would be the source of even greater trouble in the days to come. Having determined not to introduce our unfortunate fellow into the general butchery of the common dissection room—realizing that identification of the corpse would be impossible within a few hours of his arrival there—we embarked instead upon a limited postmortem examination strictly to determine the exact cause of death. It was, as had appeared from the first, a puncture wound to the base of the skull, administered with rather concentrated violence by a sharp object passing unimpeded through the muscle and tendon at the back of the neck, between the atlas and axis vertebrae, and directly into the medulla, producing an undoubtedly instantaneous death. Having satisfied our curiosity on this point, at least, we returned our gentleman to his burlap shroud and hid him underneath a pile of coal until we could deliberate with clearer heads how best to proceed from there.

After spending so many hours underground, I craved a breath of air and strolled out into the street, where I immediately encountered the troubling headline regarding our night's labors. Purchasing a copy from the vendor nearest the school, I carried it back inside to share the "news" with Jean-Claude. Reading the story aloud, I could not help reddening with embarrassment at my familiarity with the entire scene—the scattered earth, the open coffin, the discarded shovels—but my embarrassment vanished in an instant, to be replaced by a far more complex emotion, when I came upon the identity of the deceased person whose remains were currently in our possession. An exacerbating, and sensational, element of the story involved the social stature of the deceased— who was well connected with a rather prestigious name—but prestige had very little to do with our . . . surprise, in the matter. Our surprise lay solely in the identification of the deceased's name: *Mrs.* Alfred Darcy.

CHAPTER 2

"Rather than scratch our heads over what we do not know, let us concentrate for the moment on what we do know, shall we?" Jean-Claude was pacing the floor of our sitting room, with determination both in his footsteps and upon his face. Realizing that I was, quite literally, scratching my head, I removed my hand from my temple and imprisoned it in my lap, to prevent it from wandering once again. "But what is it that we do know, Jean-Claude?" I queried. "This whole episode is one confusing mess as far as I'm concerned."

"That is all a matter of perspective, my friend," he replied, halting in his tracks immediately before me and fixing me with his keen gaze, made even sharper by the intensity of thought going on behind it. "Look at that chessboard," he said, giving a quick nod toward the table where we had left an unfinished game to wander out onto the deserted streets of London the night before. "Is what you see there meaningless confusion?" I let my eyes wander over to the chessboard, trying to imagine what Jean-Claude was up to now, and observed an arrangement of pawns and bishops and knights that together portended, all too clearly, my imminent checkmate.

"No, it's not confusing at all," I answered, somewhat irritably. "You were about to beat me . . . again."

"Of course that is what you see," he said, a bit more smugly than I thought appropriate. "That is because you understand the rules of chess and know that, confusing though the board may appear to someone unfamiliar with the game, there is a finite number of moves that could have resulted in this particular configuration of pieces. Had we time enough, and motive—that is, if it really mattered to us—we could reconstruct the entire game, in reverse, one move at a time, no?"

"I suppose so," I said, growing more confused by the moment. "But I fail to see . . ."

"That is just the problem, *mon ami*. You fail to see. You fail to see, because you refuse to see. *Regarde*. Here is a game of chess. It is unfinished, but we can easily see how it came to this point, and how it will end, just by looking at the pieces on the board at this moment. Now consider the game laid out for us on the carving table at St. Alban's." He paused briefly here to allow me to fully appreciate the cleverness of his analogy. "It is in its late stages, *certainement*, but there are moves yet to be made. We examine the pieces on the table, work our way backward to determine how this configuration came to be, then anticipate our opponent's next move."

"Opponent?" I said in disbelief. "You don't mean . . . ?"

"Yes, I do mean, my friend," he interrupted, with a look of gleeful anticipation spreading across his face. "There is a murderer roaming the streets of London. And we are going to catch him—checkmate—before he can kill again."

"Don't you think we ought to leave that up to the police, Jean-Claude?" I asked, incredulous, but somehow not entirely surprised. I had known Jean-Claude just long enough to anticipate the madness out of which, eventually, some method would inevitably emerge. "Perhaps you've forgotten, but our trade is with the living—wounded or sick, granted, but living. Don't you think we should leave murder to the police?"

"Perhaps *you* have forgotten," he said, "but the police have no idea a murder has taken place. All they know is that a woman died, of natural causes, and that her body was stolen from its grave, no doubt for use in the medical school. Such theft is an outrage, yes, but it is not a crime the police will bother themselves with. The public is another matter, however. They do not look kindly upon the robbing of graves. And if we go to the police with our knowledge of the murder, the public will surely learn of our involvement in 'the desecration of the dead,' and storm the school. You remember what happened in Glasgow, no?"

"All right, Jean-Claude," I said, literally throwing up my hands in exasperation. "You have me in check. To get me in checkmate, though, you'll have to convince me that there's actually anything we can do about all of this . . . confusion. I'm still of a mind to just plant the unfortunate chap out in the yard with the others and wash our hands of the whole bad business."

"Ah, I knew you would come around, my friend," he said eagerly, his mind already racing down the various twisted paths of probability. "Let us begin with what we know about the case."

"With the chess pieces on the table," I said, satisfied with my grasp of Jean-Claude's metaphor, even if I was completely in the dark about every other aspect of our "case."

"*Bien*," he said, clearly delighted in my participation in his game. "Let us examine the board and see what pieces lie before us. First, we have a man, of unknown identity, and presumably not even reported missing, who is dead of a puncture wound to the brain. Second, we have an empty coffin, from which, if we are to believe our young acquaintance of the streets, the man's body was removed before it was delivered to us. Third, we have a woman, known to us only from the newspapers, deceased three days ago of natural causes, and then placed into a coffin—the very coffin from which our dead man was removed. Metaphorically, this woman is our queen, and the queen has been captured." He paused briefly, glancing over at the chessboard with the slightest hint of a wrinkle upon his forehead.

I took advantage of the silence to interject my own observation. "And I suppose our dead man is the king." My satisfaction with my own cleverness was short-lived, however.

"Have you not heard a word I have been saying?" Jean-Claude snapped. "All the while I have been talking, you have been sleeping, yes? Have I not said that the game is not over? How, then, can our king be dead?"

"It's just a metaphor, Jean-Claude," I said, a bit more defensively than I intended.

"Ah, but behind a metaphor often lies the truth," he replied, a bit more gently, having clearly sensed the edge in my tone of voice. "Our dead man is a key piece to the game, yes, but not the king. Which piece he is depends entirely upon his relationship with our captured queen. Was he a close acquaintance of the lady, or was he merely a pawn in a much larger game and only related to her by the unfortunate circumstance of being dead, eliminated by the same player who removed her from the board."

"And placed him in the same wooden box, don't forget," I offered, warming somewhat to the game, in spite of myself.

"Yes, my friend. That is what I said." He paused briefly, giving me one of those cryptic sidelong glances of his, then continued. "Whoever did the placing of our dead man, of course, did the removing of the dead lady. Alas, that is the crucial question, and we have no means of answering it at this point. The related question of who placed the lady in the box in the first place, on the other hand, is *not* beyond our limited means of comprehension. And answering the latter question will certainly take us one step closer to answering the former. Where is that newspaper, with the story of the 'scandalous' graveyard robbery?"

I produced the *Gazette* from the shadowy corner where I had tossed it in outrage and shame when I read the story of our late-night graveyard adventure, then unfolded it beneath a lamp on the table. I reddened once again at the all-too-familiar details of our all-too-close escape from the night watchman. Following the lurid account, however, was the summary of an obituary notice from the previous day's paper, covering the details of the deceased woman's life and describing the circumstances under which she came to be placed in the coffin from which she was so rudely snatched in the following night.

Mrs. Alfred Darcy, aged thirty-two years, died in her home on the Darcy Estate three days ago of a cataleptical seizure. The deceased woman was the widow of Sir Alfred Darcy, a renowned scholar of Oriental history and culture who had died in his sleep six months earlier, presumably from complications related to his advanced age. The "distinguished" Mrs. Darcy, it turns out, was not born into distinction at all, but began life rather ordinarily as Abigail Worthington, the youngest daughter of a wool merchant "of some pretensions." Her elevation in social class resulted from a chance encounter that led to Miss Worthington's employment as Sir Alfred's personal secretary—a position that had been filled and vacated with

some regularity throughout the duration of the
"temperamental" scholar's career. Miss Worthington held the position for a full year—twice the
duration of her most tenacious predecessor's
tenure—and when the terms of her employment
changed at the end of this period, it was not termination but marriage that changed it. Quite simply, Sir Alfred "fell" for his lively young secretary
and decided he absolutely could not live without
her as a partner in his life, as she had heretofore
been a partner in his work, and the two were
wed in an unpretentious garden ceremony on the
Darcy Estate. Following their union in holy matrimony, Sir Alfred and Mrs. Darcy maintained a
quiet, private existence for nearly a year until Sir
Alfred's unfortunate, but not necessarily untimely,
death, after which his young widow was joined
on the estate by her bachelor brother Peter
Worthington, and lived a solitary, respectable
widow's life until her own death—the result of
prolonged grief over her husband's death, by some
accounts—six months later. And then her mortal
remains were interred in the cemetery at All Soul's
Church, only to be unceremoniously removed
from her grave less than twelve hours later. But of
course we already knew that part.

"Quite a collection of pieces, eh, *mon ami*,"
Jean-Claude said, with what I felt to be an inappropriate relish, considering the circumstances.
"And what do you make of it? What is to be our
next 'move'?"

"I'm for burying our gentleman cadaver in the
yard and washing our hands of the whole affair,"

I replied, and then added, with a sigh of resignation, "but I don't suppose that's what you have in mind, is it, Jean-Claude?"

"Absolutely not. A murder has been committed, and we are the only people, save the murderer himself, who know of it. It is our duty as civilized human beings to bring the killer to justice."

"Without having ourselves exposed as grave robbers," I added. "Don't forget that part. So what do you propose? What is our next 'move' to be?"

"I am delighted that you agree with me, my friend. And as for our next move, there is but one logical possibility. We must return to the All Souls Church and make inquiry into the journey of the coffin from the front of the church, during the eulogies, to the churchyard, for the interment, and most importantly, to find out if perhaps it was left unattended at any point along that journey."

"Well all right," I begrudgingly agreed. "So long as we go through the front entrance this time, instead of climbing over fences in the dark."

CHAPTER 3

The next morning found us strolling through Southwark in the direction of All Souls Church, a walk that took us considerably less time than had our previous journey to the same destination, when darkness and an intentionally circuitous route had utterly disoriented the both of us. Today, however, we found the church with no difficulty, arriving, in fact, far more quickly than I would have preferred, being, as I was, still figuratively "in the dark" about what we were to say to whoever greeted us there. "I say, Jean-Claude," I protested, suddenly doubting the wisdom of our chosen course of action. "I do hope you've thought this thing through. I mean, what the devil are we supposed to say?"

"Do not concern yourself so gravely, my friend," he replied, with annoying confidence. "We are merely two devout Christians, coming to the church to say an early-morning prayer, and to light a candle for the soul of your dear, departed mother."

"Begging your pardon," I huffed, "but my mother is still very much alive, bless her. And as for the candles, the Church of England is Protestant, and doesn't go in for the 'purgatory' kind of thing."

"Very well," he said, far more unconcernedly than I felt at all appropriate for the situation. "We shall be travelers from the Continent, stopping at the church to admire the architecture. And as we speak to the vicar, if the subject of last evening's terrible theft from the graveyard just happens to come up, we will not dissuade him from speaking of it." Jean-Claude's amendment of our "script" came not a moment too soon, for we now found ourselves standing immediately before the church. "After you, my friend," he said, holding open the gate.

To approach the entrance to the narthex, we had to pass directly by the cemetery, scene of our recent midnight adventure. In the light of day, it appeared much smaller than it had seemed running through it in total darkness. As wrapped up as Jean-Claude was in his role of "tourist," I noticed that he, too, glanced at the cemetery as we passed, involuntarily lifting his hand to touch the bump upon his forehead. Try as I might, I could find no evidence of the "theft" that had created such a sensation in the *Gazette* barely twenty-four hours earlier—no scattered earth, no police, no angry townspeople. Perhaps the thing would simply blow over after all, I thought hopefully, and people would stop implicating St. Alban's, and its students, in the whole tawdry business. Of course, even in the unlikely event that the world forgot all about the theft of a "lady's" body, Jean-Claude had no intention of forgetting, even if we both wound up in jail for our efforts.

After the bright morning sunshine, our entry into the hushed dimness of the church unnerved me, given the thoughts that had just been set astir in my mind by our return to the cemetery, and when a deep booming voice addressed us from the darkness, I nearly jumped out of my skin. "Good morning, gentlemen!" the darkness said. "How can I help you this fine day?" I couldn't see Jean-Claude's face for the darkness, but if the tremor in his voice was any indication, the disembodied greeting had affected him in a similar manner to the way it had affected me.

"We have come to look at the architecture," he said abruptly, but after taking a deep breath to calm himself, clarified. "We are visiting London for a short time, and would like to see your lovely church." And then, having fully regained his equilibrium, he added, "An acquaintance of mine in Brittany recommended it to me after his recent visit to England."

During this brief exchange, my eyes adjusted sufficiently to the darkness to permit me a shadowy glimpse of the person from whom the voice emanated, and my initial impression was that we were in the presence of a large bear—a bear wearing ministerial cloth, yes, but a bear all the same.

"By all means make yourselves at home," the

bear boomed from less than five feet away. "I'll be more than happy to show you gentlemen around the place. And your friend from Brittany is absolutely right to recommend All Souls to you gentlemen, for it is true gem of a church."

While he spoke, I became sufficiently accustomed to the darkness to make out the definite features of a man atop that mountain of black cloth—a man whose girth and stature were no less ursine for the human face at the pinnacle. His face was as broad as a platter, featuring bright red cheeks, a fleshy nose of a hue to match the cheeks, and a capacious mouth that appeared to be perpetually on the verge of an enormous grin. Crowning the entire mountain of flesh was a shapeless mop of tightly curled hair of a dark but indeterminate hue. "It was built exactly ninety-one years ago, in the style of Christopher Wren, as you've no doubt already noticed." So saying, he took us each by the elbow and led us through dark-stained oaken doors into the church's interior, pausing at a niche containing a marble slab whose surface featured the reclined form of either a priest or an astrologer—it was difficult to tell. "Here lies the body of Josiah Hooke," he said, in an altogether-unsuccessful attempt at deep reverence. ". . . who expired shortly after the church moved into this new structure. And if you'll be so kind as to follow me down the aisle here," he continued, leading us deeper into the church, "I'll show you a chapel dedicated to the memory of all the brave soldiers who sacrificed their lives during the American Uprising."

For the better part of an hour, we followed this man up one aisle and down the other, pausing occasionally to behold some ecclesiastical "treasure," and all the while listening to an exhaustive, not to mention exhausting, narrative history of "this grand edifice." At long last, having covered every square inch of the church's interior, he led us out onto the church grounds, and we found our opportunity to broach the subject that had actually brought us here in the first place. As we walked through a rose garden bordering on the cemetery, Jean-Claude said, "Please excuse my forwardness, but is this not the cemetery from which a prominent lady's body was recently stolen? I read something in the newspaper."

For a moment, I felt that perhaps Jean-Claude's question had been too abrupt, and might strike our guide as somehow irreverent, but my fears were quickly dispelled. The man's demeanor certainly altered in response to the question, but rather than taking on a wounded or an indignant air, he became newly animated in a way that could most accurately be described as conspiratorial. Shifting his eyes back and forth, as if to see if anyone were nearby who might listen in, and lowering his tone to what, for him, must have been intended to pass for a whisper, he said, "That's right. Two nights ago, it was. Thieves came in here and snatched her right out of her grave! My brother nearly caught the devils, too—he sometimes keeps watch over the graves, of a night. He heard voices, and the distinct sound of shovels, which, in a graveyard after dark, can only mean one thing." I kept my eyes locked on our host, fearing that an exchanged glance between Jean-Claude and me would have the undoubted appearance of guilt about it. "Oh, we've been hit before, but usually you find the evidence in the morning, after the thieves are long gone. There'll be some disturbed earth, sometimes several paces away from a grave, where the devils have tunneled their way in, so as not to be too obvious. Other times, it's dirt that's been piled just a little too high over a new grave, or sunk a little too low, or maybe a shovel that's been left behind. Once"—he leaned closer to us, making a couple of exaggerated sidelong glances— "we found a small portion of a broken coffin lid, where they had dug just enough to get to the head of the coffin, snapped the lid in half, and dragged the poor fellow out by a rope around the neck. Dreadful!" he said, pausing briefly to permit us to appreciate the depravity of the scenario. "But never," he continued, "until two nights ago, have we actually caught them in the act!"

"So your brother actually saw the . . ." For a rare moment, the appropriate word eluded Jean-Claude. ". . . the perpetrators," he finally said, trying to keep our host's story from wandering, while at the same time not appearing unduly interested in it. "What exactly did he see?"

"There were three of them standing beside the grave, although he thinks there must have been one or two that got away, since the men he saw were not carrying the body. Well, two of them appeared to be 'gentlemen,' if you can call people gentlemen who make a practice of digging up respectable people's graves, and hauling off the dear departed for heaven knows what purposes. The third was a young lad—a swain, from the looks of his clothes. He appeared to do the lion's share of the manual labor, while the others stood by and looked on." At this remark, I could sense Jean-Claude's neck stiffening with indignation as he recalled the many shovelfuls of earth he had personally removed from the grave.

"And how is it that these scoundrels were able to get away from your brother?" he said, in a less-than-civil tone, to which our host seemed completely oblivious. "Was he not armed in some way?"

"Oh, he had a rifle, but for all the firing it was capable of, it might has well have been a walking stick. It belonged to my father, from when he did his national duty in the Irish Revolt. And even if the gun were functional, the thieves overpowered him before he could so much as pull the trigger."

"They what?!" I found myself saying, with entirely inappropriate heat, angered at the insinuation that I would ever resort to "overpowering" anyone. But then, reining in my choler, I added, "Good heavens, I hope he wasn't injured."

"Oh, just a few bumps and bruises," he replied. "He's quite a rugged old fellow. But these three ruffians assaulted him, leaving him stunned for a few moments, while they managed to escape the church grounds."

"And then he went to the authorities to report the 'attack,'" Jean-Claude said, once again involuntarily rubbing a fingertip over his bruised forehead.

"Why, of course. It isn't just every day that someone of Abigail Darcy's social stature is buried here at All Souls, and to have her body snatched, quite literally under our noses . . . Well, it just doesn't look good. The church and its grounds are sacred property, and anything committed to its premises is a sacred trust. That's why my brother takes his watching so seriously. He considers it a sacred duty." I couldn't help thinking of the low wages such a "job" must bring, and wondering if the man performed this "sacred duty" because he wasn't fit for anything else.

"You said that people of Mme. Darcy's 'social stature' are not commonly interred at All Soul's," Jean-Claude said, trying to divert our host's narrative into a more productive channel. "What sort of people are typically buried here?"

"Oh, members of the church, almost entirely. And there's not a whole lot of nobility among our ranks," he said, chuckling slightly. And then added, as if out of habit, "As precious as they all are in the sight of the Lord."

"How then did the lady come to be buried here?" Jean-Claude asked.

"Now it's funny you should ask that," he replied, conspiratorial once again, ". . . for a number of us around here asked the same question when we first learned she would be coming to spend eternity in our midst. Everyone knew about the death, of course. It was in all the newspapers. But when my brother told me that All Souls had been contacted by the lady's family, and that her funeral would be right here, in my church . . . !

Well, to say I was surprised would be a gross understatement."

"So the funeral was a large affair?" I asked, trying to keep my hand in the game, but instead of an immediate reply, the only reaction my question elicited from our host was more eye-shifting and a lowered tone of voice.

"For me, that's the strangest part of this whole thing," he finally said, leaning in even closer to where we stood. "For all the attention her death received from the papers, the lady's funeral was performed before a virtually empty church. Aside from a few museum folks, most of whom appeared older than any of the exhibits in their collections, it was mostly church staff in attendance. There were a couple of the Darcys' servants here, and the lady's brother, of course. It's my understanding that it was he who first contacted All Soul's and made the funeral arrangements."

"But why here?" I asked. "Surely there was a family vault somewhere."

"I'm sure there's a family vault in *Mr.* Darcy's family," he said. "But *Mrs.* Darcy's family was not of the same social standing—a tanner, I think her father was. Or is. Who can be sure? The brother was the only representative from her family. Apparently he had some connection with the church, to cause him to make the arrangements here. I don't really know."

"Did you not speak with him before you conducted the ceremony?" Jean-Claude asked. "Surely he provided some details about his rationale for bringing his sister here." For the first time since we began conversing with him, our host suddenly appeared less than cheerful. In fact, to say he appeared "crestfallen" wouldn't be a bad description of his change in demeanor.

"Well, actually," he said, looking down toward the ground, "I didn't preside over the funeral. You see, I'm not the head vicar here. That would be the Reverend Holloway." He paused, trying to think of what to say next, and then, just as suddenly as it had turned gloomy, his face brightened. "I assisted in the proceedings, though."

Overlooking the good reverend's sudden but brief attack of diffidence, Jean-Claude pressed him further for more details about the funeral. "So the only family member present was this brother?"

"Yes, the brother. His name was Worthington." And then another pause as he searched his bushy eyebrows for the brother's first name. "Peter, yes. Peter Worthington. And from the looks of things, he must have been very close to her, the poor thing. He seemed to be taking the death very hard. Wouldn't let the coffin out of his sight, in fact." I sneaked a quick glance at Jean-Claude, to see if he had registered this interesting detail, but if he noticed anything unusual, he didn't let on.

"Was he with the coffin when it arrived here?" Jean-Claude asked.

"No. As matter of fact, he arrived alone, just as the service was beginning. It's really a pity, too, for he would have been quite useful as a pall-bearer. As it turned out, the coffin had to be carried into the church by four of those museum folk. It's no job for the elderly—carrying a coffin," he observed, reflectively. "Why, they very nearly dropped the thing three or four times on the way to the grave. I must tell you, I breathed a big sigh of relief when she was safely in the ground." Another small cloud passed briefly over his features, as he recalled what a short time the lady actually remained in the ground, but Jean-Claude quickly set him right by diverting his mind to other matters.

"In my own experience," he said, ". . . it has often been the case that loved ones are particularly distraught upon the closing of the coffin—that final moment of separation from the dear familiar face. I have even seen family members physically restrain the undertaker as he attempted to lower the lid. Did Mme. Darcy's brother have a similarly difficult time with this moment?"

"I couldn't tell you that," he said, frowning with disappointment that he couldn't be more helpful. "We don't make a practice of putting the dear departed on display like that. Besides, the lid was already nailed down when she arrived here. Closed or not, though, I thought he was going to follow it into the ground. And then he stayed beside the grave during the burial itself. Usually the family leaves while that's going on, but this fellow stayed until the last shovel of earth was in place, poor chap." He stared silently at the spot, as if reliving the moment, but then suddenly—almost startlingly—he returned to the present moment. "Just listen to me, going on about that

grim business," he boomed, "when all you gentlemen wanted was to see the church. Do please excuse my lapse of hospitality."

"No apologies necessary," Jean-Claude assured
him. "You have been a most gracious host, and a
most helpful guide. Now, I am afraid, we must be
on our way. My friend in Brittany insisted that
I see the Tower of London, and there are, after
all, only so many hours in a day."

After exchanging a few rounds of "good day"—
our host clearly disappointed that we could not
remain longer and see some of the many other
"treasures" of All Souls—we made our way back
into the church, down the gloomy central aisle,
and out onto the front walkway. As we proceeded
into the street, I made a casual, final glance back
toward the church, and noticed our host still
standing on the front steps. Without slackening
my pace, lest he should remember "one more
thing" he simply had to share with us, I threw up
my hand in a wave, and we strolled through the
morning sunshine without looking back.

"Nice fellow, that vicar," I said, involuntarily
chuckling at the thought of the good-natured
and garrulous parson.

"*Assistant* vicar," Jean-Claude corrected, also
smiling. "Yes, very pleasant. And more importantly," he added, ". . . quite informative."

"Wasn't he, though," I concurred, recalling the
torrent of words from which we had just emerged.

"About a good many things, yes. There was
certainly plenty of—how do you say—chaff in

his talk. But buried in this mountain of chaff, *mon ami*, we also find some wheat."

"Come again," I said, wondering if perhaps one of us was not a little "off the mark" in our use of the English idiom. "Do you mean that bit about the burial."

"I mean," he said, suddenly serious, ". . . that we must pay a visit to Mr. Peter Worthington. And if I am not very much mistaken," he added, consulting his pocket watch, "a mail coach headed toward Darcy leaves from the White Stag Inn within the hour. That will give us just enough time for an early lunch."

CHAPTER 4

Our journey to Darcy, or more accurately to an inn just over half a mile from there, lasted barely an hour, during which time we deliberated precisely what it was we intended to do when we finally arrived at the estate. I was for posing as deliverymen of some sort, simply arriving at the front door without any knowledge of the tragic death, and ignominious "theft," that had befallen the house in recent days. I believed that as ignorant passersby, simply happening upon the house of misfortune, we would arouse less suspicion than we might if we appeared to have some prior knowledge of the events, and thus learn more from the house's inhabitants, who, eager to talk about the tragedy, as people in such a situation typically are, would completely unburden their souls to strangers whom they had never seen before and would never seen again. As I should have expected, however, Jean-Claude did not see things my way. He observed that, having nothing to deliver, we would make for pretty poor deliverymen and arouse unnecessary suspicion by appearing to have something to hide. The direct approach struck Jean-Claude as the more fruitful, and since he preferred it, the direct approach was the one we adopted (he always seemed so all-fired sure of himself that one found oneself agreeing with him for no other reason than his own belief that an idea or opinion was correct). We would simply call at the front door, and tell whoever answered that we were "investigators" (which, in essence, we were), seeking information regarding the missing body (which is, in fact, what we sought), in order to locate the remains and return them to the bereaved family (which we would certainly do, if we happened to find the body, even if this was not our primary motive).

All too quickly, it seemed to me, we found ourselves standing on the front landing of the Darcy House, trying to habituate ourselves to the personas we were about to adopt. As we pulled the bell and waited for someone to arrive, my mind went completely blank as I groped about for something—anything—to say when the door opened. Jean-Claude, however, was completely "in his element." An experienced amateur actor, having trod the boards of theatres in both England and France, he had arranged his bodily posture and facial expression to conform to his mental image of the role he was about to perform. When the door finally opened, however, he was as dumbstruck as

I when he beheld the figure standing before us. For what seemed like a full minute, we both stood there in gape-mouthed silence, as if we'd both suddenly been turned into pillars of salt. Or, to adopt a still-more-appropriate simile, we stood transfixed, as if we'd seen a ghost. For that is precisely the impression we both had as we, quite literally, and quite impolitely I must say, stared at the man who opened the door. The gentleman standing before us looked like a ghost. With his tailored clothes, his dark hair, and his elegant mustache, he was the spitting image of the unfortunate gentleman hidden under a pile of coal in the root cellar back at St. Alban's.

"May I help you?" he asked, in a voice that sounded reassuringly as if it emanated from the physical rather than the spiritual realm. I soon recovered my senses sufficiently to feel greater discomfort at our prolonged silence than superstitious fear of the "spectral" presence before us, and resolved to speak. Having regained my resolve, alas, I had not yet recovered my wits sufficiently to remember my own role, and when I opened my mouth to speak, what came out was, "Good day. We are here to make a delivery." The gentleman's understandable puzzlement was short-lived, because my own faux pas had the effect of cold water in Jean-Claude's face, bringing him immediately around to the lines his character was supposed to deliver.

"We are here to deliver our deepest condolences over your recent loss," he said deliberately, casting an unmistakably disapproving glance my way in the process, ". . . and to offer our assistance in recovering the remains of the deceased lady so that they may be buried with the respect and . . . permanence . . . to which they are entitled."

The gentleman paused momentarily, shifting his gaze back and forth between Jean-Claude's expectant face and my own. So inscrutable was his visage that I felt it equally likely that he would either invite us in for tea or throw us bodily into the street. Finally, he appeared to arrive at some sort of internal conclusion, and his expression softened into a polite smile. "Won't you come inside?" he asked, nodding somewhat formally toward the interior of the house.

Soon enough, we found ourselves seated in an elegant parlor, and while not offering us tea, the gentleman conversed more amicably than either Jean-Claude or I had initially expected. "It's all been a terrible shock to the system, you know," he began. "First, the sudden unexpected death of my dear sister . . . I feel as if she could walk into this room at any minute." Here he paused, and gazed sadly at the doorway leading into the next room. Suddenly, his expression changed, and his eyes flashed as though with fire. "And on the heels of that great loss, to suffer the outrage, the ignominy . . . There aren't words strong enough to describe the depravity of such an act. It's simply barbaric. These hospitals should all be razed to the ground, and their medieval inmates—the 'surgeons'—should be thrown into a dungeon."

Throughout this understandable outburst of

emotion, I shifted about uncomfortably in my cushioned chair, feeling every stinging word hit home as I recalled my all-too-intimate, albeit indirect, contact with the source of this man's grief. Sensing my extreme discomfiture, and perhaps concerned that it might in some way lead me to reveal our true purpose here, as well as our actual identities, Jean-Claude attempted to redirect our host's energies into a more productive channel. "So the deceased was your sister?"

"Why yes," he replied, regaining control over his turbulent emotions. "I assumed you knew. Abigail is . . . was . . . my older sister. Oh, how I shall miss her."

Sensing another imminent display of emotion, Jean-Claude quickly stepped in. "I must apologize for my lack of manners. We have not formally introduced ourselves. I am Detective Christophe Dubres, and this is my assistant James." I couldn't help throwing a quick, withering glance in his direction—"assistant," indeed. Of course, he pretended not to notice, and continued with his "introductions."

"I am originally from Paris, but am now an agent with the police of London."

Our host appeared somewhat skeptical, but replied politely enough, "My name is Peter. Peter Worthington. Originally from Shropshire, of course, like Abigail, but I've since called nearly every major city in Europe 'home,' if only for a time at least. I've been something of an habitual wanderer, I'm afraid, never quite able to put down roots in any one place. All that changed when I moved in here, however. Living here with my dear sister gave me a sense of place and belonging such as I'd never known before."

"When did you take up residence here with your sister?" Jean-Claude asked gently, not wishing to induce another display of emotion.

"Six . . . no, eight months. Eight months ago. I came here after Abby's husband Alfred died. Initially, I meant only to help her tidy up the . . . her late husband's affairs. Stay for a few days. But then days turned into weeks, and weeks turned into months. I'm so happy to have been able to spend this time, her final days, with her. But who could have imagined . . . ?"

"Yes, I know it is difficult," Jean-Claude interjected, occupying the silence as our host's gaze once again drifted longingly toward the doorway. "Are you alone here?" he continued. "Do you have no one with whom to share your period of mourning?"

"What's that?" he asked, returning once again from his brief mental sojourn. "Oh, yes. I'm alone, save for the groundskeeper and the cook. After Alfred's death, Abby and I released the majority of the staff, since it was just the two of us, and we live . . . lived, quite simply."

While he spoke, I permitted my gaze to wander about the room at the Oriental artifacts that occupied virtually every wall, cabinet, and tabletop. If this was "simple" living, I don't know what you'd call the Spartan existence Jean-Claude and I endured at our cupboard of an apartment.

"Of course, now I rather regret letting everyone go," Mr. Worthington continued. "It's so infernally quiet all the time . . . nothing to do but sit and think. Thank heaven Madeline will be here in a few days."

"Madeline?" I asked, heeding Jean-Claude's visual summons for my more active engagement in the interview.

"Yes, Madeline. Oh, do please forgive me. You'd have no way of knowing. Madeline is my sister . . . my other sister. She lives in Amiens. A bit of a wanderer like myself, I'm afraid, but she's stayed put in France for nearly a year now. I've written to her about poor Abby's death, and expect her here any day now."

"How long has it been since you last saw your sister Madeline?" Jean-Claude asked, with suddenly heightened interest. Feeling somewhat "out of the game," I resumed my role as silent observer.

"Hmm," he pondered, as his eyes drifted toward the ceiling. "I should say at least two years. We last ran into each other in Rome. She was studying the Italian language, and I was busily occupied pursuing the attentions of a lovely Italian contessa." He paused here briefly, allowing himself a slight smile at the obviously fond memory. "Madeline and I saw each other several times over a period of weeks, but then an Italian painter captured my contessa's attentions, and I moved on. To Naples, and then Greece."

"And you expect her here within a matter of

days?" Jean-Claude asked, overly eager it seemed to me. Our puzzled host remained silent until I clarified,

"Your sister, Madeline. You say she will arrive soon?"

"Oh, Madeline. Yes. Any day now."

"Would you mind terribly if we visited you again after your sister's arrival?" Jean-Claude continued, somewhat abashed at his momentary lapse in theatrical professionalism. "I should very much like to speak with her."

Mr. Worthington raised an eyebrow in a attitude of either uncertainty or displeasure, it was difficult to tell. "I suppose," he said, somewhat hesitantly. "Although I fail to see how she could be of any assistance to you. She hadn't laid eyes on Abby in five years or more."

"Nonetheless, we would like to see her," Jean-Claude returned. "With your permission, of course."

"I shouldn't think there's any point in it, but if you absolutely must, try again next week. That ought to give her time to get here." And then, shifting in his chair as if about to stand, "Will that be all, then?"

Jean-Claude and I exchanged uneasy glances, realizing that our interview was about to conclude without broaching the actual subject of our visit. "There is one question we must ask of you," Jean-Claude quickly asked, before our host had time to get out of his chair. "It is a difficult question, but I assure you it is of the utmost importance if we are to locate your sister's . . . Mrs. Darcy's remains."

Mr. Worthington did not speak, but settled back into his chair, encouraging Jean-Claude to continue. "When was the last time you saw her?"

"I left her reading a book by the fire, after lunch. When I returned an hour later, I found her lying on the floor, unconscious."

Jean-Claude's brow wrinkled, and he shook his head slightly. "No, no, monsieur. When was the last time you saw her *after* she perished?"

"You mean when did I last see her body?" Worthington asked incredulously. "Don't you think that's rather an indelicate question?"

"Yes, I know it is difficult," Jean-Claude said uneasily, fearing as I did that our interview would end before we found out what we wished to know. "But since it is your sister's body that is missing, any information we can have about the time between death and burial might be useful."

"I fail to see how it's in any way relevant," Worthington said irritably, "but if you must know, Abigail's body was prepared for burial by the undertaker, and he and I placed her in the coffin. I sat up all night with her—you know, watching—until early the next morning, at which time the hearse arrived to carry her to the church. I rode on ahead, to discuss some matters with the vicar, but she . . . they, arrived shortly after I did. Then the funeral was performed, and Abby was buried. I was standing by the grave when the undertaker covered the poor thing with earth. And there she remained until . . ."

"Very well," Jean-Claude interrupted, narrowly averting another display of emotion from our distraught host. "I simply wanted to verify that no one had access to the body *before* it was buried—the gardener, perhaps, or even one of the undertaker's men. Now we know, as we suspected all along, that our thief is most likely a typical, anonymous grave robber, and that the body is, as you yourself suspect, in one of the hospitals nearby. Which is where we will begin our search. James," he said to me, although it took me a moment to remember my "name," ". . . let us trouble this man no further. Good day, Mr. Worthington. We will show ourselves to the door."

CHAPTER 5

"Well, Jean-Claude," I said, as we made our way toward the inn from which we were to take the evening mail coach back into the city. "Or should I say, 'Christophe'? What do you think of Mr. Peter Worthington?"

"I think, *mon ami*, that something is rotten in the state of Denmark," he replied, quoting his beloved Shakespeare.

"Something rotten, indeed," I heartily concurred. "Why, he was the very twin of our cadaver. I must say it took me aback when he first opened that door. It threw you a little off your stride too, eh, Jean-Claude?"

"I will not deny that this Mr. Worthington's appearance rather startled me," he said, sniffing ever so slightly and cocking his head to one side, a sure sign that I had touched a sore spot. "But I would not describe the physical similarity between him and our Mr. Smith as that of twins."

"Oh really?" I said, somewhat perturbed by Jean Claude's splitting of hairs to find fault with my observation. "And precisely how would *you* describe the similarity?"

"Mark, my friend. Have you ever actually known any identical twins? Even if they were to wear the same type of clothing, there are always many distinguishing marks, clearly visible to the *attentive* eye." I cleared my throat, preparing to protest the insinuation, but he continued before I had the chance to speak. "No, the similarity of appearance between our two specimens is far too exact to be a result of nature. Such exact duplication can only be the work of artifice."

"Yes, I see. But how . . . ?"

"I do not know the 'how,'" he interrupted. "If we knew the 'how,' our game would be almost finished. The 'why,' however, is a matter of much greater clarity. *Regarde*, did you not watch the man's eyes, the way they shifted about each time he spoke of his 'sister' Madeline? And the way he kept looking toward the doorway, as if expecting, or fearing, that someone would walk through it at any moment?"

"He did strike me as excessively uneasy," I agreed, trying to imagine what the devil he was getting at. "But that's not entirely unexpected, considering the circumstances. His sister's just died, after all, and her body's been stolen."

For an uncomfortably long time, Jean-Claude simply gazed at me in silence, with a look of genuine amazement on his face. And then, just about the time the hopeful thought occurred to me that perhaps I'd unwittingly made a brilliant observation, he immediately disabused me of my optimism.

"You have been studying the human anatomy for a full year now, and are thus fully aware of what is supposed to occupy the inside of a skull, no? It is three pounds of gray flesh we call a brain. But inside your skull, what do we find? Wool! No, my friend. This man's 'sister' was not stolen."

"But where is she, then?" I blundered on.

After giving his hair a good long tug, he took a deep breath and willfully regained his composure. "I did not say that Mrs. Darcy was not stolen. I merely said that our host's sister was not stolen. That is because, if I am not very much mistaken, our host is not the brother of Mrs. Darcy."

"Then who the devil is he?" I asked, giving up all pretense of following his logic.

"He is an imposter, posing as Mrs. Darcy's brother," he continued. "And it would surprise me very much indeed if Mrs. Darcy's 'real' brother were not at this very moment slowly decomposing in a cellar at St. Alban's."

"Good God," I literally gasped. "So you think that man back there is a murderer? That he killed the real Peter Worthington?"

"Yes, my friend. And placed the body in Mrs. Darcy's coffin to dispose of the evidence." He paused for a moment, deep in thought.

"But if he put Peter Worthington's body in Abigail's coffin," I interjected, taking advantage of the rare silence, "where, may I ask, is the lady now?"

"I do not know, my friend!" he snapped, clearly

annoyed at not having all the pieces to the proverbial puzzle in hand. "Perhaps she really is in a common grave at some hospital," he ventured. But then, narrowing his eyes a bit, as if for greater focus, he continued in a calmer vein. "Or perhaps she is somewhere on the Darcy Estate, in one of the gardens, for instance."

"Yes," I agreed, finally beginning to see a pattern emerge from all of the seemingly unconnected arabesque shapes he'd been sketching for my mind's eye. "With no more of a staff than live on the estate, that would be possible. And depending on how familiar the real Peter Worthington was with the domestic servant and . . . what did he say . . . groundskeeper? Depending on how much interaction he had with them, they might not even notice the substitution. The similarity *is* rather remarkable." I thought once again of the disheveled gentleman who emerged from a canvas sack two nights before, and held the image side by side with the visage of the man with whose company we had only just parted. "Yes," I mused aloud. "Most remarkable."

My reverie was of brief duration, however, for Jean-Claude abruptly, and I must add quite vigorously, clapped me on the back, and said, with inexplicable delight, "Please forgive me my friend. I have grossly underestimated your powers of deduction." I nodded, silently, mystified as to the source of my friend's rare compliment but more than happy to accept it. "The staff may very well not notice the substitution of an imposter for the real Peter Worthington," he continued. "But a sister . . . even one he had not seen in—what did he say . . . two years . . . ? A sister would notice the difference."

"So you think . . ." I ventured cautiously.

"I think it will be very interesting to see what happens when Miss Madeline Worthington arrives from Amiens. I would very much like to be present at that reunion."

"Yes," I agreed, "to see how she acts when she sees him."

"To see the reaction, yes," he replied. "But also to protect her from harm. If the false Peter Worthington is indeed posing as a man he has murdered, and there is but one person who can expose the fraud, what is to prevent him from killing one more time, just to maintain the security of the illusion?"

CHAPTER 6

We arrived back at St. Alban's just after midnight, and found ourselves perched uncomfortably upon the horns of a dilemma. The subject of our indecision was none other than the dead body hiding in the root cellar—Peter Worthington, if Jean-Claude's theory was correct. The question we had debated throughout the last half hour of our journey back to the school was, simply, what to do with the man. We had purchased the body for the sole purpose of performing a dissection, from which to glean direct human anatomical knowledge necessary for becoming physicians—our ultimate goal for studying at St. Alban's. Having established the necessity for keeping our cadaver essentially intact, for purposes of identification if and when we ever pieced together who the man actually was, and how he came to be in Abigail Darcy's grave, we had forgone the customary practice of introducing him to the common dissection hall. Having also established the imprudence of immediately notifying the authorities of the murder, fearing that such a move would draw the wrath of the public at large, confirming as it would a connection between the medical school and the grave robbery at All Soul's, we opted not to turn the body over to the police. In short, we found ourselves, like it or no, the temporary guardians of a dead man's body. And despite the chill of the cellar in which the body was concealed, nature was well on her way to reclaiming the body for her own. Our question of what to do with the body, then, was anything but hypothetical, or casual. Something had to be done with our man, and soon. But what?

Reflecting back upon the burial practices of other civilizations than our own—the Egyptians, for example—we arrived at an expedient that resolved all the considerations of the problem we faced, for the immediate future, at least. One way to slow down the natural decomposition of a dead body, we knew, is to remove the internal organs. A systematic removal of these organs could also provide us with the human anatomical knowledge for which we secured the body in the first place, at no small expense to ourselves, I might add. An abdominal dissection, then, would help to preserve the body and advance our medical studies, both at the same time. Thus resolving to "kill two birds with one stone," we unearthed our cadaver from his shallow grave of coal, removed the burlap sack, and laid him out upon the table.

For the next several hours, we were quite literally "up to our elbows" in the grim business of abdominal dissection and organ removal. Pausing periodically to draw sketches or take notes—and more than once to retch at the intense sights and smells of our work—we proceeded from one organ system to another until our notebook was full and the cadaver's abdominal cavity was quite empty. The sun's first rays, trickling in through a grimy window just below the ceiling, found us placing linen rags where organs had once been, and stitching our man back together.

"A long night of work, eh, *mon ami*," Jean-Claude said, washing his hands in a basin of water. "And now, without so much as a single wink of sleep for refreshment, we must bask in the presence of the imminent Dr. Freidrich Keimer for three hours as he talks about the proper diagnosis and treatment of membranous croup, *mon dieu*! Please promise me this—if I begin to snore too loudly, you will give just the slightest nudge, in order to stop the disturbance, without interrupting my slumber."

I acknowledged his comment with a quiet smile, feeling as if perhaps laughter were not entirely appropriate in the presence of our unfortunate guest, spread out thus unceremoniously upon the table between us.

As it turned out, Jean-Claude had been conservative in his estimate of the duration of Dr. Keimer's lecture, for it was half past noon when he finally released us from captivity. Having eaten nothing that would remotely qualify as a meal since the previous afternoon's repast at the White Stag, we ventured immediately toward the Blacksmith, where we dined heartily on generous portions of kidney pie, washed down with an enormous beaker of Madeira.

Thus fortified, we ventured on foot toward the offices of the *Gazette*, where we searched through the archives for information regarding Sir Alfred Darcy. In this, as in all the other cases we would pursue together over the next many years, it was Jean-Claude's unshakable creed that we "begin at the beginning," which is to say, to seek out first causes, and in this situation the beginning appeared to lie somewhere in the direction of the deceased husband of the deceased Mrs. Alfred Darcy.

A quick perusal of the last year's issues of the *Gazette* turned up an obituary of the late scholar containing a quite thorough biography. Alfred Darcy was the only male descendent of a long and illustrious branch of a centuries-old family tree, much distinguished for its history of philanthropy and erudition. The latter virtue appeared quite remarkably early in Alfred, who, while but a mere lad of ten, decided his life's vocation was to be that of clergyman. To that end, he pursued a rigorous course of classical studies, which led him to an early graduation, with distinction, from Christ's College, and then on to Germany for more specialized study of Kantian philosophy. While at university in Cologne, a course he took with a professor of Eastern theology convinced Alfred that his true scholarly interests lay in Oriental history and culture, so he at once abandoned his pursuit of the ministry and dedicated the entirety of his indefatigable energy and a not-insubstantial fraction of his large family fortune to accumulating knowledge of, and artifacts from, the empires of China and Japan. His interest in Japan, whose contact with the Western world was at that time confined to a limited trade with the Dutch, made Alfred an almost permanent resident of Holland for a number of years, during which time he mastered the Dutch language and interviewed Dutch sailors who had journeyed to Japan. The project in which he was engaged at the end of his life was an English translation of the journals and ledgers of a Dutch trading company operating in Nagasaki. It was this translation project, in fact, that first brought him into contact with his wife, now widow, Abigail Darcy, who served as Alfred's amanuensis for several months before their marriage, and throughout the single year of their marriage until Alfred's death, at the age of seventy-two years.

The obituary concluded by observing that Alfred, having not embarked upon the state of matrimony until an advanced age, left behind no heirs, and was thus survived only by his young widow.

"Who is herself survived," Jean-Claude interjected, "by her 'brother' Peter Worthington. How very convenient."

"Yes, isn't it though," I agreed, having finally sniffed out the convoluted path Jean-Claude's mind had been following. "But who the devil is this fellow, anyway?"

Jean-Claude pursed his lips pensively. "And how did he have such close access to the real Peter Worthington and the body of his sister? Yes. These are indeed very intriguing questions, on a growing list of intriguing questions. And I believe our best avenue for answering them will also perhaps take us in the direction of finding Mrs. Darcy's body, if she is buried on the estate as I suspect she is. We shall—how do you say?—kill the two birds with one stone."

"What do you have in mind, Jean-Claude?" I asked, feeling distinctly uneasy over the prospects that came to mind.

"We must return to the estate, of course, to do some 'sniffing around.' We shall be the blood-hounds!" Jean-Claude said, entirely too eagerly for my tastes. He was warming altogether too quickly to an idea—a "scheme"—of which I had absolutely no desire to be a part.

"But 'sniffing around' someone's property, without so much as a 'by your leave,' " I observed, trying to bring to light the full implications of such precipitate behavior. "Isn't that what most people would call 'trespassing'? We've already been chased off private property one time this week, in case you've forgotten."

"You worry too much, my friend," he replied. "I am no more eager than you to be apprehended for trespassing. I am merely suggesting that it would perhaps be very enlightening to stroll the grounds of the estate."

"But . . ." I tried to interrupt, annoyed by such fine semantic distinctions in a matter of such serious potential consequence. He, of course, paid me no heed—or appeared not to, and continued talking. His line of reasoning, however, took a distinct turn in the general direction of common sense.

"And perhaps we do not have to put ourselves in harm's way, after all." He mused, stroking his chin and pursing his lips. "What would you say if I told you we could search the grounds of the estate without leaving the comfort and security our own rooms, eh, my friend?" His face brightened with growing approval of whatever idea it was he had just hatched. "We shall play a game of chess."

I found it impossible to conceal my baffled annoyance. "Would you mind very much, Jean-Claude, explaining what the devil it is you're talking about?"

"We shall hire someone to be our eyes and ears—no, our nose—on the estate, by proxy. What was that lad's name? Ah, yes. Jimmy. We must talk to Jimmy."

CHAPTER 7

That night found us returning to a certain dark and dreary street I'd never expected, and most certainly never hoped, to see again. Just about the time I half feared, yet half hoped, that we'd lost our way and were wandering in hopeless circles through an uninhabited labyrinth, Jean-Claude broke the stillness by exclaiming, far more brightly than the circumstances warranted, "Ah, the Jolly Fox Tavern. We have arrived."

"Indeed," I muttered, and followed him through the low, questionably stained doorway into the dank Dantean world that had literally haunted my dreams since our last visit. Totally unperturbed, Jean-Claude sauntered to the counter and fetched two tankards of ale, for the world as if we'd simply dropped in for quick dram. Then we situated ourselves at a table whose surface was a veritable hieroglyphic of knife marks and sat in wait for the lad in whose company we had all too recently passed a very busy evening.

"Cheer up, my friend," Jean-Claude said, clapping me on the shoulder. "You have such a long face, like someone has died."

"At the risk of stating the obvious, Jean-Claude," I observed, resisting his attempts at jollity, "someone *has* died, and we've managed to get ourselves involved in it. You can do as you please, but I'm leaving this opium den in five minutes, whether we see the lad or not."

"This is no opium den," he replied, calculatedly missing my attempt at hyperbole. "And you do not have to leave, for there is our lad!" I followed Jean-Claude's gaze toward the door, through which Jimmy had just entered, scattering random greetings among the assembled mass of humanity seated in various postures of dissolution throughout the infernal place. Jean-Claude leaped from his chair and joined the lad at the bar, buying him a drink and inviting him to join us at our table. When he seated himself beside me, I found it difficult to maintain my gloom, despite all my best efforts.

"Good evenin', gentl'men," he said happily, as if we were just the people he'd been hoping to see. "And to what circumference do I owe the pleasure of your company?"

Jean-Claude sneaked a quick sidelong glance at me, for the world as if he feared I might say the wrong thing, and then told Jimmy the purpose of our visit. "Actually, my friend, we are here on business. We would like to enlist your valuable services for a short time."

Jimmy's brow furrowed, and his gaze drifted down onto the table. "I don't go in for grave robbing no more," he said in a quiet, somewhat troubled voice, then looked Jean-Claude in the eye. "Just like you said. Remember, you told me to find a new line of employment, and I done it." Then he paused briefly, and corrected himself. "Well, I ain't exactly found me nothin' new yet, but I'm through with body snatching."

Jean-Claude silently searched Jimmy's face for a moment, and then burst into laughter. "I am delighted to hear that, my friend," he said. "You are too bright a lad to be engaged in such an unsavory trade. And having encouraged you to abandon it, we would never ask you to become involved in it once again. No," he continued, glancing at me, "we have employment of a different nature in mind. It is a temporary 'job,' of brief duration, but we will pay you handsomely for it."

Jimmy's face brightened. "In that case, I humbly offer my utmost services," he said, and then bowed formally. We briefly informed the lad of some—if not all—of the developments of the past couple of days, and our suspicions attendant upon those developments. Then we asked him, as delicately as possible, if he would consider taking an informal, but thorough, tour of the Darcy Estate, taking note of the residents of the house—their comings and goings and such—and of anything on the grounds that appeared in any way out of the ordinary. "Such as a spot of freshly disturbed earth," I added, for clarification, at which innocent remark Jean-Claude glared at me. "What?" I couldn't help saying, growing annoyed at his whimsical prejudices regarding the subject matter of our conversations. He simply ignored me and addressed our young companion.

"Yes, we are very interested in the grounds of the estate, but as you are a very observant lad, we will simply trust your discretion to note *anything* out of the ordinary. Are you interested?"

Jimmy stroked the light fuzz of his chin and stared thoughtfully at the ceiling for a moment. "That sounds like a respectable mode of employment," he said, then quickly qualified the terms of his accord. "So long as you don't expect me to lift nothin'. I didn't give up body snatchin' to become a petty thief."

"No, no, my friend," Jean-Claude reassured him, gently patting the boy's forearm. "You will 'lift' nothing but your own mental impressions of the place. Observe, and remember. That is what we wish you to do. And so, I repeat, are you interested?"

"I can do that," he said brightly. "It'd be a nice change of scenery—much nicer than graveyards at midnight, eh, gentl'men," he added, giving me a quick, knowing wink, and a slight jab with his elbow.

"Splendid!" Jean-Claude replied, clapping his hands with satisfaction. "We will bring a carriage around for you tomorrow morning just after dawn."

"Oh, there's no need for that," he said, pushing

his chair back from the table and folding his arms across his chest in an attitude of smug satisfaction. "One beneficiary of my former occupation is that you learn how to get around—from the country to the town, wherever's needed. You gentl'men just tell me where it is, and I'll take care of the rest."

We provided Jimmy with directions to Darcy— he was well acquainted with that "gen'ral vicinity," it turns out—and a general description of the portion of the property with which we were familiar. Then, after giving him directions to our apartment and arranging for him to meet us there the next evening, we sent him on his way, literally whistling through the darkness of the night.

CHAPTER 8

The next morning found Jean-Claude and me in the operating theatre of Sloane's Hospital, observing the amputation of a gangrenous leg. A middle-aged man had impaled his thigh upon a fence while fleeing the scene of a burglary, and the wound had become hopelessly infected. Throughout the operation, I couldn't help thinking of Jimmy and imagining the coincidence to be a bad omen.

"Nonsense," Jean-Claude said later that afternoon, over a jug of claret at the Blacksmith, where we had repaired for drinks in a vain attempt to force the poor patient's guttural shrieks from our memory. "Jimmy is far more agile that the unfortunate housebreaker who forfeited his leg to the surgeon today. Additionally, and more importantly, it is not a housebreaking we are speaking of here. A simple trespass is the only crime of which our young friend will be guilty. And trespassing pales in comparison with murder, would you not agree, my friend?"

I agreed, of course, as I did in virtually all such discussions. Jean-Claude was so perpetually sure of his own opinions, one had an extremely difficult time resisting such confidence, even if the point under discussion appeared at the outset to be hopelessly flawed. "But do you not think it makes him vulnerable to capture, or even worse?" I added.

"By whom? The Darcy Estate is home to but one 'gentleman' and two servants, unless one counts the deer that no doubt roam the grounds. I'm sure that, even if spotted by Mr. Worthington, the domestic, or the groundskeeper—or all three together, *mon dieu!*—our lad's fleetness of foot would easily carry him out of harm's way. You have, perhaps, forgotten our midnight jaunt through All Souls churchyard, yes?"

"No, I haven't forgotten," I said, recalling our harrowing flight from the night watchman, and how much more quickly Jimmy gained the street—and safety—on that occasion, than the two of us had.

"He will be perfectly safe. And we, I hope, shall be a great deal wiser for his visit. In the meantime, *mon ami*, we must not allow the moss to grow upon our own stones." He paused, to allow me to appreciate his facile grasp of the English idiom. "I have been thinking we would perhaps be well employed in making one more visit to the offices of the *Gazette*, to add some knowledge of the late Mme. Abigail to the considerable amount we have in our possession regarding her late husband."

I drained the dregs of my glass, and we began to make our way toward the door. Before we could make our exit, however, we were hailed—although "detained" would perhaps be a more accurate description—by one Thomas Bailey, a classmate at St. Alban's, who spent the vast majority of his waking hours in a state of profound inebriation. "Edward, John," he greeted us, far more audibly than was either necessary or desirable. I couldn't help stealing an amused glance at Jean-Claude, who was, as I expected, wearing upon his face an expression of extreme indignation, in response to the Anglicization of his name.

"Thomas," I replied, in a measured, although-not-unfriendly tone. I couldn't help feeling just the slightest bit grateful to him for the brief entertainment he had provided me at the expense of my friend's Frankish pride. "How are you?"

Our hope that our classmate's overture was but a passing, casual greeting was dashed when he gesticulated in what he took to be a discreet manner for us to join him at his table. As it was obviously too late for us to feign ignorance of his presence there, we grudgingly made our way to the dark corner of the tavern where he was encamped and seated ourselves at his table.

"Glad to see you gents made it out of St. Alban's

in one piece," he said, in a stage whisper that filled the air around us with fumes of the liqueur he had consumed.

"What the devil are you talking about?" Jean-Claude snapped, annoyed in nearly equal parts at having his name mangled, and sacrificing his time to "the whims of a drunken fool," as he would say later, once we reached the welcome outdoors. "We have not even been to the school today. We were at Sloane's all morning, as you yourself might very well have been."

"Why, haven't you heard?" he asked, dumfounded at our ignorance, but clearly delighted at the opportunity to disabuse us of it. "St. Alban's is under siege, or at least will be before the day is through."

I exchanged a quick knowing glance with Jean-Claude, and asked, in an attempt at a casual tone, "Under siege? By whom?"

Thomas cut his eyes back and forth, as if everyone in the place were waiting with bated breath to hear what he had to say. "By the whole bloody town, from the looks of things. Every damned peasant who could lay his grimy hands on a shovel or pitchfork is there, threatening to break down the front gate and dig the whole place up, looking for bodies." He paused dramatically, looking around him once again at the people who couldn't care less what he was talking about, and then leaned in closer to us. "It's because of those three fellows who dug up that grave in All Souls."

"Now you know as well as I, Thomas," I said, in

a poor attempt at a casual tone, "that bodies are rather routinely exhumed from graveyards throughout the entirety of England—an unfortunate fact, yes, but a fact nonetheless. Why should an angry mob single out St. Alban's?"

Thomas leaned even closer, until his chin practically rested upon the tabletop. "It's because two of the grave robbers were gentlemen—that's what the night watchman said—and since the graveyard was so close to St. Alban's, everyone's claiming that it had to be students from there. If that mob were to find the chaps who did it, I do believe they'd hang them on the spot." His eyes twinkled in a most inappropriate way, at the prospect of a little "excitement" to season his otherwise-bland existence. Neither my eyes, nor Jean-Claude's twinkled at this prospect, however. My eyes, I'm afraid to say, moistened with an altogether-different emotion—raw fear, and I found myself suddenly speechless.

Sensing my attack of aphasia, Jean-Claude rose above his own conflicting emotions to continue the interview. "And what are the authorities doing about this . . . this . . . state of anarchy? It is most insupportable." Even with the serious stakes involved in the matter of our conversation, I noticed he couldn't help reddening slightly at the awkward manner of his contribution to it.

Thomas didn't appear to notice, however, and simply continued where he left off. "I'd say there are a hundred or more of them, beating their shovels on the ground and shouting 'Pull down the bloody walls,' 'Kill the devils,' and such like. It's total and complete . . . anarchy," he said, delighted at the word he imagined himself to have pulled from thin air.

"But the police," Jean-Claude tried again. "Are not the authorities doing anything to halt the violence?"

Thomas blinked his eyes and stared at Jean-Claude, as if noticing his presence for the first time. "The police!" he said incredulously. "You must be joking. The police would like nothing better than to see St. Alban's pulled to the ground. Why they're no different from that mob standing outside the gates there, and if it weren't for the uniforms they're wearing, they'd be standing at the gates with their own pitchforks. Sure they look the other way, with grave robbing, but that's only because the grave robbers are peasants like themselves, just trying to earn a living, even if not exactly an honest one. You needn't expect any help from that quarter." Thomas paused, either from deep reflection or at the onset of imminent unconsciousness. Jean-Claude and I took the silence as an opportunity to excuse ourselves, and once again made our way toward the door, this time successfully gaining it.

Once outside, we both inhaled an immoderate dose of fresh air in an effort to clear our heads of the troubling thoughts that had nested there during our interview with the sodden Thomas. We walked for several blocks in no particular direction, completely silent. Jean-Claude was the first of us to venture upon speech. "An unwelcome complication indeed," he replied, to the thought I hadn't yet found words to utter. "Perhaps it will, after all, simply blow over."

"And then again, perhaps it won't," I said, trying to suppress the wave of panic rising into my voice. "I told you we had no business breaking into cemeteries in the middle of the night, digging up bodies."

"We did not 'dig up' bodies," he replied, regaining control over his emotions as the "little wheels" in his mind found some other grist to mill. "The box was empty, as you will no doubt recall. And even if we had 'snatched' a dozen bodies from the cemetery that night, we would be in no immediate danger of discovery. The watchman saw 'two gentlemen,' and while the illogical mob has amazingly drawn the logical conclusion that the gentlemen were students at St. Alban's, we are but two among many students. So do not worry yourself about being hanged—at least not for *this* offense." He looked at me with a raised eyebrow and a mischievous smirk, once again in full possession of his customary equanimity. "And the interruption in our lecture schedule that this flurry of mob rule will doubtless produce could very well be a blessing in masquerade."

Now it was my turn to raise an eyebrow at him. "Don't you mean 'disguise'?" I corrected. "A 'blessing in disguise.'"

"However you care to mask the blessing," he huffed, "or otherwise conceal it, we may very well find a temporary cessation of lectures to be a welcome development, providing us, as it would, uninterrupted time in which to engage in other more pressing matters. Such as"—he paused, for dramatic effect—"solving a murder."

CHAPTER 9

The route we followed to the *Gazette* offices took us considerably out of our way, but having little desire to be in the vicinity of St. Alban's at that particular moment, we found a circuitous route vastly preferable to the more direct one, which passed in front of the school. Besides, the weather was fine—sunny and mild—and before we had time to reflect upon the length of our journey, we found ourselves strolling into the chaotic interior of the newspaper's front office.

In times of mental duress, I have often found relief in intense mental activity, busying my mind to keep it from wandering into paths better left untrodden, such as reflections on being hanged by an angry mob of Londoners. A detailed foray through two years of *Gazettes* provided my troubled mind with just such a welcome diversion. We were searching, you will recall, for information regarding Mrs. Abigail Darcy, née Worthington.

Our afternoon in the archives provided us with far more material than we expected at the outset, the "common" young woman's marriage to the elderly gentleman having been something of a local scandal at the time, and thus offering a fecund source of editorial speculation. The earliest mention of Abigail Worthington appeared in a brief story about the opening of a Japanese exhibit in the British Museum. Alfred Darcy loaned a small but not insubstantial portion of his vast collection of artifacts to the museum, and made a rare public appearance to dedicate the temporary exhibit. Accompanying the "distinguished" scholar to the event was his young assistant, who appeared to be present as part of the collection rather than as a guest, for she was bedecked in "traditional" Japanese women's fashion—a silk "kimono," white face paint, and a complex ornamental hairpiece featuring a set of carved tortoiseshell combs.

While Alfred himself was mentioned in the *Gazette* a number of times, for a variety of different reasons, during the next several months' issues, no further reference to Abigail occurred until the lengthy, and none-too-flattering, account of their marriage, a small ceremony attended by a small handful of servants from the Darcy Estate and members of the British historical community— the bride's family sent regards, and regrets. The garden setting in which the couple married was described as "unadorned to the point of drabness," the only token attempt at decoration being the bride herself who, as on her previous public appearance, sported Japanese attire. In addition to the brief account of the ceremony, this particular issue of the *Gazette* featured a "society" piece in which the prominent scholar's union with the "lowborn schoolgirl" was excoriated for the extremely poor judgment, not to mention taste, that it displayed Sir Alfred's part. Of course, involuntary poor taste can be far more readily forgiven than a willful attempt to subvert the natural order of society, and the new Mrs. Alfred Darcy was spared not one drop of vitriol from the editorialist for her "crass presumption" in pursuing a matrimonial union that was as "unnatural as it was untimely." Following these accusations of impropriety —if not worse—was a brief biography of the "young" bride, included solely for the purpose of underscoring her common genealogy. The youngest of three children, Abigail was the daughter of a wool merchant from Shropshire. As a child, she had attended Miss Medlin's School for Girls, receiving a "typical" education in grammar and mathematics. After leaving school, she performed domestic duties in her family's household until introduced, by a former school acquaintance, to Sir Alfred, who was at the time deeply engaged in a work of scholarship and greatly in need of an assistant. The "clever girl" immediately presented herself to the gentleman, and he, greatly impressed by her youthful energy, enlisted her services as his amanuensis, until the completion of his much-anticipated work, or its premature termination, should his health require it.

The writer of the article expressed some doubt as to how far Sir Alfred's work advanced in the following months of Miss Worthington's employment, but ventured to predict that it would most certainly advance no further now that the two were married. "An incalculable loss to the British historical community," was his summation of the matrimonial union.

As chilly as was Mrs. Darcy's initial reception by British society, as represented by the editors of the *Gazette*, subsequent articles throughout the following months indicated a slight thawing of the public heart in regards to her. For several weeks after the marriage, neither Sir Alfred nor Mrs. Darcy was seen off the estate and received very few guests, almost all of whom were members of the historical community. But just as the couple, and their marriage, were on the verge of public oblivion, a soiree at the British Museum, intended to raise funds for the construction of a permanent "Elgin Room" in which to display the famous Parthenon marbles, drew them out of hiding and initiated a veritable flurry of similar public appearances. Widely known for his eccentric and unpredictable style of public speaking, Sir Alfred's presence on these occasions was cast into the charming shadow of his young bride, who, much to everyone's delight proved herself surprisingly adept at exuding charm and a seemingly unaffected sophistication that largely "won over" the other guests attending these functions. Throughout the next several months, until just before Alfred's death, the Darcys' name appeared almost weekly in the *Gazette* for their appearance at this or that public affair, and with each subsequent reference, the tone in which Abigail was mentioned became increasingly tolerant, quite nearly to the point of fondness. Of particular note was her tendency, at first openly ridiculed, then grudgingly admired, to appear in public dressed in Oriental attire—the same type of silk "kimono" and ornate headpiece in which she accompanied Sir Alfred to that first dedication ceremony at the museum. Given her husband's reputation for erudite eccentricity, Abigail's "odd" choice of clothing quickly came to be seen merely as an extension of his personality and endeared her all the more in that it appeared an involuntary sacrifice of good taste on her part.

Upon Alfred's death, the general consensus was an apologetic approval of the young widow, and the not infrequently expressed opinion that she "had shone a ray of morning sunshine into the twilit chambers of her husband's life and work." The dignified manner in which she comported herself during the period of mourning—scarcely venturing outside the house, much less appearing in public—only served to increase the public's regard, so that when she all too suddenly died, a mere six months after her husband's passing, one could easily have imagined that it was she, and not her husband, whose life had been distinguished by an international reputation for historical research. The brief announcement of a small private funeral would most likely have "closed the book" on Abigail Darcy, had it not been for the shocking crime that had been perpetrated against her mortal remains, mere hours after they had been committed to the earth.

"And of course we know far more than we'd care to about that particular detail," I said, thinking of the angry mob massing outside St. Alban's.

"Yes, we know a great deal about it," he responded, ignoring the tone of frustration that had crept into my voice. "But there are so many things about it that we do not know." Jean-Claude paused with deeply knitted brow, clearly wrestling with one of these unknowns. "For example," he finally spoke, ". . . why was Mme. Darcy buried in the All Souls churchyard in the first place? The vicar himself said that people of her social standing are rarely buried there, having access, as most do, to a private family cemetery or vault. I am sure that the Darcys must have such a place, so why was not the lady buried beside her husband?"

"Well the obvious answer is that her body was stolen from the coffin before it could be buried." I chuckled with admittedly wicked delight at my friend's rare lapse of precision with detail, but quickly moved on, not wishing to antagonize him needlessly and arouse his own rapier wit. "But more to the point would be the fact that her husband wasn't buried at all."

"Pardon?" he said, raising an eyebrow as he watched me thumb through three months' worth of *Gazette*s.

"Ah, here it is." I folded the newspaper into a single column's width and placed it upon the desk. "Eccentric to the end, Sir Alfred instructed, via his last will and testament, that his body be burned upon a ceremonial pyre, and his ashes scattered across the surface of a pond in the garden of his estate."

"Of course! The Oriental temperament. A scholar spends his life studying Japanese customs, and in his death he wishes to follow the Japanese custom."

"I can understand why she wouldn't want to be cremated, even if that's the way her husband went—the prospect doesn't exactly please me either," I said, with a slight involuntary shudder. "But why was she buried in All Souls? I'd say that six months' marriage with the old gentleman surely entitled her to a proper burial in the Darcy family cemetery. All Souls is so"—I searched for the right word, then simply said the one that first came to mind—"so common. It has all the charm of a pauper's graveyard."

"Do not let our friend the vicar hear you say that," Jean-Claude scolded, raising an index finger in mock admonishment. "But perhaps you forget, *mon ami*," he continued, thinking aloud, ". . . that the lady's burial was not of her own choosing. She was young, yes, and had little reason even to have an opinion on such matters, let alone put the opinion into writing. No," he said, tapping his fingertips lightly together, "the decision of a place of burial was that of someone else. And the only 'someone' who remains an active player in our little game of chess—at least on the other side of the table—is Monsieur 'Peter Worthington.' "

"Yes, it always seems to come back to him, doesn't it?"

"*Certainment*," Jean-Claude said resolutely, sliding the newspaper across the table in my direction—a clear sign that he felt the *Gazette* had provided us all the information of which it was capable, and the time had come to move on to other sources of enlightenment. "I shall be very eager to speak with young Jimmy, upon his return from Darcy."

CHAPTER 10

When we carefully and discreetly passed St. Alban's on the way to our apartment that evening, we were relieved to find that the angry mob had dwindled to a moderately disgruntled handful. The gathering dusk and a dense misting rain seemed to have blunted the edge of the crowd's righteous indignation, turning their thoughts instead to a warm hearth and a shepherd's pie. I must admit that I was more than happy to return to our own hearth, where I wasted no time in producing, Phoenix-like, a roaring blaze out of the glowing embers from our morning fire. A dinner of toasted cheese and brown bread, washed down with a lively jug of claret, took the evening chill out of my bones and altogether repaired the broken spirits I had dragged home from the *Gazette*.

Jean-Claude, whose spirits were virtually impervious to fracture, casually perused an edition

of *King Lear* he had purchased from a bookseller
we passed on the trip back to our rooms, while I
gathered a few remaining crumbs from the table
and threw them into the fire. Absentmindedly
watching the blackening grains, I stumbled onto
an odd stray thought. "You don't suppose," I ventured, "that this Peter Worthington fellow—the
second one, I mean—cremated Mrs. Darcy's
body, after he replaced it with that of the murdered man? There was, after all, a precedent right
there within the family."

Jean-Claude silently finished the passage he was
reading and looked up from his book. "No, I do not
suppose," he said, somewhat hesitantly. "I will admit to you, however, that the same possibility had
crossed my mind. It would explain a lot, yes? The
mysterious disappearance of the lady's body, 'into
the thin air.' But then we must ask ourselves a
question. If someone, a cold-blooded killer, for instance, goes to the trouble of burning one body,
why not burn two, while the fire is hot? You have
not forgotten, *mon ami*, that the coffin was not
empty when young Jimmy first unearthed it?
There was a body inside the box, even if not the
correct body. And while we are asking questions,
we must consider why someone would take the
trouble of burning a body, when burying it would
be so much easier. It takes a great deal of heat to
reduce flesh and bone to ashes. If you were to dig
through the remnants of last night's fire, for example, in addition to being horribly burned . . ."
He paused briefly, his lip curling in amusement at
the mental image of me unaccountably rifling

through the blazing fire before us. ". . . you would most certainly find, completely intact, the chicken bones you commended to the flames after dinner. And if little chicken bones can endure the fire, how much greater resistance would human bones offer to the flames. You recall the size and density of the tibia, no? And the femur? Not to mention the skull, and three pounds of brains inside."

"Yes, I recall," I said, unenthusiastically, recalling the many dissections we had witnessed in the operating theatre of Sloane's, and our own recent, albeit limited, experience with human dissection. "But burying a body in one's garden is not exactly child's play, either, especially if one doesn't wish for evidence of the burial to be visible."

"We do not know that the body is buried in the garden," he corrected. "That is one of the reasons we sent Jimmy to Darcy, *n'est ce pas?* And even if the body turns out to be in the garden—or in the front parlor, *mon dieu!*—that would provide the answer to but one of a great multitude of questions. There are still quite a few pieces remaining on our chessboard."

Jean-Claude's metaphorical reflection was brought to an abrupt and welcome halt by a loud, insistent knocking at our door.

"Good evening, gents," said Jimmy, strolling into our sitting room as if he were the host, and we his guests. "Ah, there's a nice fire." Without further prologue, he planted himself before the hearth and held his red-knuckled hands toward the flames.

"By all means make yourself at home," Jean-

Claude said, sending an amused glance in my direction. "It is turning cold outside, no?"

"It ain't so much the cold as the wind," the youth replied, rubbing his hands together. "A horse on the open road kicks up quite a breeze."

"I trust you had a pleasant journey, excepting the cold," I offered.

"'Deed, I did. It's nice getting out of town once in a while, riding through the country." While he talked, Jimmy's eyes drifted insistently toward the cupboard. "It really sharpens a fellow's appetite."

Jean-Claude chuckled and walked toward the cupboard, removing the remnants of our evening meal. "Please help yourself to some bread and cheese." For the next few moments, the only sounds in the room were the ticking of the clock, and the grinding of Jimmy's teeth, as he reduced our pantry to a gnawed cheese husk and a few stray crumbs. Comfortably seated by the fire, enjoying a glass of claret, the lad could have been a magazine illustration of aristocratic ease. He was just short of drifting off to sleep, in fact, when our impatience to discover the results of his visit to Darcy finally compelled us to interrupt his reverie.

"Did you find the estate without difficulty?" Jean-Claude asked matter-of-factly, not wishing to appear as eager as we actually were.

"No difficulty at all," he replied, draining his glass and setting it on the table. "I used to hunt rabbits in a wood near there, so I'm quite knowledgeable of the area." He resumed his silence, as if in assuring us that his journey to and from the Darcy Estate had been a pleasant one, he had satisfied the full extent of our curiosity.

A moment more of utter silence was finally too much for Jean-Claude's fragile patience. "And the residents of the house, did you find them to be happy and in good health?" he asked, in a voice dripping with sarcasm, which Jimmy either willfully ignored or rather remarkably did not notice. The question itself, however, appeared to remind him of the reason for his evening visit to our rooms.

"Oh, the Darcy folk," he replied, seeming almost surprised by the question, but willing to discuss the matter nonetheless. "Yes, well, let's see now. I got there about midday, I guess it was. Of course, I didn't ride my horse right up the front door, but I tied him in a patch of trees about half a mile from the front gate, so they wouldn't see me approaching the place."

"Very clever of you," Jean-Claude said, still not the model of sincerity but in a better humor. "And what did you do when you arrived at the estate itself?"

"I came up upon the house from behind, through the woods, which wasn't difficult, believe me. It's a big place, the estate, but most of it's all grown up, like, with trees and all, so you don't know you're in civilization until you're practically in the garden."

Jean-Claude's sarcasm vanished in an instant. "Ah, the garden," he said eagerly. "Please tell us what you saw there."

"Well, like I said, I kind of stumbled into it. The woods gave way to a patch of bamboo, which ain't easy to walk through, believe me. I was pushing and twisting my way through those wooden poles, and all of a sudden found myself in a clearing."

"The garden," Jean-Claude said, literally sitting on the edge of his seat.

"Of course, the garden," Jimmy continued. "But not like any garden you ever saw before. For one thing, it's got a church in it."

"A church?" I couldn't help asking.

"A small one, yea, but a church." He paused for a moment, my incredulity clearly causing him a moment of doubt. "At least it looked like a church. It didn't have a steeple, or a dome—nothing like that—but it was all decorated, like a chapel. Yea"—he brightened—"like a chapel."

"Please describe this 'chapel,' " Jean-Claude directed, trying to keep the lad's thoughts moving in one direction for more than a moment.

"Well," he said, closing one eye tightly in an apparent attitude of deep concentration. ". . . it was about four feet wide—I told you it was small—and ten feet tall. Three stories tall, it was, with wings, like, sticking out from the corners. Quite odd." He paused thoughtfully, and continued, clarifying his description. "Beautiful, but odd."

I grew increasingly confused with every detail of the account, so it was with no small amount of vexation that I noticed Jean-Claude nodding knowledgeably, for the world as if he knew precisely what Jimmy was talking about. "A pagoda," he said.

"A what?" Jimmy said, giving voice to the exact question that hung upon the tip of my own tongue.

"A pagoda," he explained. "And you are not very far amiss in calling it a church, because it is a type of holy place, or a shrine, in the Orient. Its presence in the garden is not unexpected, given Sir Alfred's devotion to the Eastern culture. Nor is the forest of bamboo, through which you passed with such great difficulty, particularly surprising, since it, too, is indigenous to Asia."

"It may not strike you as extr'ordinary, having a church in your backyard, but I find it mighty queer, myself," Jimmy said, in a tone of forced annoyance, but actually quite pleased with himself for having been so nearly correct in his description of a pagoda as a church.

"Continue describing the garden, if you please," Jean-Claude urged.

"Well, about a stone's throw from the house, there's a little shed, with a bridge leading over a stream that runs onto a pond. Now this pond . . . it's got a waterfall on one side and lily pads floating all over it." I couldn't help thinking of the newspaper article about Sir Alfred's cremation, and reflecting on what else might be floating on the pond's surface. "Swimming around in the water," he continued, "there was all kind of fish—big ones, little ones, orange ones, black ones, and some you couldn't hardly see, 'cause they was the same color as the water. Those people are mighty fond of their

fish, make no mistake." Pausing, as if he'd just
made a mental connection that had heretofore
eluded him, he leaned toward us, alternately fixing our eyes with his, to assure himself that he had
our full and undivided attention. "They even keep
some inside the house."

"What do you mean, 'inside the house'?" I said
incredulously, sending a quick accusatory glance
toward Jean-Claude. "Your instructions were to
explore the house from the outside only. Entering
the house itself exposed you to far too great a risk
of discovery."

"There's no need to have a fit, gove'nor," he responded, with a look of amused smugness spreading across his face. "Nobody 'discovered' me. My
former line of work taught me a great deal of—
what do you say?—discretion. Why, more than
once I've crept into a house and snatched a body,
while the people inside were right in the middle of
a wake!" He reflected silently for a moment, while
a look of pride spread across his face. "Get discovered?" He chuckled, shaking his head. "Not bloody
likely. I'm very discreet, see, so you needn't worry
about me being such a careless chap as to go and
get myself caught." Here, he paused, chuckling
once again at the absurd prospect. I, however, was
neither as amused, nor as assured, as he. Jean-
Claude, on the other hand, appeared to be of one
mind with Jimmy.

"Was there anything else of note in the garden?" he asked the lad. "Anything that appeared
to have been recently moved or disturbed?"

"Not that I noticed," he said, apparently taking a

quick mental inventory. "From the looks of things, nobody's been in that garden for a long, long time. There's a stone path from the shed to the rear entrance of the house that's so overgrown—with grass, you know—that you can't see the stones unless you're right on top of them. Them folks is in dire need of a gardener."

Jean-Claude's eyebrow wrinkled slightly, as if a stray thought were struggling to work its way from the depths to the surface of his mind, but he quickly relented and allowed it to sink back whence it had come. "So you entered the house," he said, fully attentive to the moment again. "Tell us what you saw there—something about fish, you say?"

"That's right." Jimmy's eyes brightened. "Just when you come in the rear entrance, there's another garden, like, *inside* the house. In a big room with a glass roof."

"A winter garden," I offered, but Jimmy simply went on.

"And in this room, there's a big pond, like the one outside, but a bit smaller. And swimming around in this pond," he said, lowering his voice and shifting his eyes back and forth, as if concerned some invisible person might be eavesdropping, "were some of the strangest-looking fish you ever saw."

"What was so peculiar about them?" Jean-Claude asked.

"Well for one thing, they were all ugly. I've seen a lot of fish in my day, and some of 'em haven't been none too pretty, but these were the ugliest by far. Some of them were long and flat, kind of like snakes that've been stepped on. And there were some other ones, even uglier—gray and fat, with no particular shape at all, kind of like swimming rocks. But the shape wasn't the queerest part." He looked side to side, watching out for the invisible people once again, then spoke in a low, secretive voice. "It's what they do when you touch 'em."

"You touched one?" I said, completely aghast at the license this lad had taken with the instructions we gave him.

"Yeah I touched one," he replied matter-of-factly. "And do you know what he did?"

"What did he do?" Jean-Claude asked, with amused interest.

"He blew up like a balloon, and just rolled around there in the water. I sure would like to have me one of those things," he said, his face growing dreamy at the prospect. "Imagine what the lads down at the Jolly Fox would say."

Jean-Claude struggled to hide a sense of great amusement with the lad's narrative, which I, quite frankly, did not share, such needless peril had he exposed himself to in thus roaming about the interior of the house. "Peculiar," Jean-Claude finally said, intruding upon Jimmy's fond reverie, then attempted to guide him back onto the path of his story. "And was there anything else noteworthy in this 'room'?"

"Not really," Jimmy answered, thoughtfully stroking the light fuzz just barely visible upon his chin. "A few green statues along the wall, some trees planted in big clay pots, a couple of chairs . . . nothing else really notable—except for that pond, like I said."

"So you continued on into the main house, I assume," Jean-Claude said, refilling the empty glass that Jimmy had placed, none too subtly, upon the table where we were sitting.

"Right," he answered, holding the glass in front of the fire to admire the deep red color of the claret. "I continued to the main house." Then, after taking a grateful draught and smacking his lips in contentment, he suddenly thought of something. "Have you gentlemen ever been to the museum?"

"Do mean the British Museum?" I asked.

"I suppose that's the one," he replied, frowning slightly. "Is there another?"

"Yes," Jean-Claude intervened, to keep Jimmy from drifting off track. "We've both been there a number of times."

"Well then, you know just what this house looks like on the inside. It looks like the British Museum. There's statues everywhere, and suits of armor, and swords, and paintings on the wall. That's in a couple of the biggest rooms. Then when you move on toward the front of the house, there's another room—not quite as long, but taller, much taller—that's nothing but books, books, and more books, all the way from the floor to the ceiling. I never seen so many books in my life. And that was all on the ground floor. When I went up the stairs, the main hallway had some statues and pictures and such, but mostly it was just ordinary bedrooms, and most of them ain't used anymore, from the looks of it."

"Throughout your grand tour of the Darcy House," I said, somewhat sarcastically, "did you happen to see any people?"

"I saw a gentleman and a lady—the masters of the house, I assume."

"A lady?" I said, looking at Jean-Claude in surprise and meeting a similar expression on his face.

"This lady," Jean-Claude asked, ". . . could she have been a servant—the cook perhaps?"

"Cook?" Jimmy repeated incredulously. "Why would you think that? Didn't I say a 'lady.' And a gentleman, too, that appeared to be her husband, based on the looks of it."

"And what were this gentleman and lady doing?" Jean-Claude continued, in a tone that only hinted at the puzzlement we both felt at the revelation.

"Talking," he replied. "Just talking."

"What were they talking about?" I asked, somewhat more impatiently than I intended.

"At first I couldn't tell, 'cause they was several rooms off. Then I moved closer—discreetly, though, so as not let on I was there—and I could hear them better, but it wasn't until I got right outside the room they were in that I could make anything out. It was the front parlor, I think it was, and I situated myself so I could see them in the hall mirror. He, meaning the gentleman, was sitting in a chair by the fire, and she, meaning the lady, of course, was declining on the sofa. She seemed a bit agitated about something, and he was trying to calm her down."

"Why did she seem to be upset?" Jean-Claude asked, giving voice to my own pressing curiosity.

Jimmy pursed his lips and closed one eye, clearly trying to recall what he had heard. "The best I could make out was it was something about money. Oh, and some man. Yeah, there was a man's name came up a few times. A funny name." He closed both eyes, for even greater concentration, and apparently found the answer on the back of his eyelids. "William . . . that was it," he said proudly. "William Testament."

Jean-Claude flashed an amused, knowing glance in my direction, and I had to divert my face to hide my own mirth. Realizing there was little benefit to be gained from pressing the issue, however, we both maintained our silence and permitted him to continue.

"That's right. She was angry about this William, and the gentleman kept telling her not to worry herself about it, saying that what William did was . . . how did he say? 'Common and lawful,' that's it. Whatever William did was common and lawful, so they—meaning, I suppose, the gentleman and the lady—wouldn't have to pay for it."

"Pay for what?" I asked, more confused than I cared to admit.

"No need to ask me, 'cause I can't tell you." He shrugged his shoulders in a gesture of resignation. "About the time I was starting to understand—you know, getting into the rhythm of their conversation—the gentleman stood up and disappeared from the mirror. Fearing he might just reappear in the hallway beside me, I took the opportunity to make my way to the rear of the house—through the kitchen this time—and out the back door into the garden. Then it was through the weeds, into the woods, and back to the road."

"Are you sure no one saw you?" I asked, concerned. "One of the servants, perhaps?"

"Didn't I already tell you there was no gardener, nor other outside servant—the weeds and all, you know?" he returned irritably. "And there wasn't another living soul in that house besides the lady and gentleman, not unless someone was hiding in one of them dark rooms upstairs. Which I, frankly speaking, don't find likely, do you?" He ceased his narrative, positively glowing with self-satisfaction at thus having the final word, and disabusing us both of our wild surmises. "One of the servants, indeed!" his expression said.

With neither Jean-Claude nor I seeing any advantage in pressing the lad further for knowledge that clearly was not in his possession, we paid him his agreed-upon fee, gave him a handful of biscuits from our pantry, and sent him back into the deepening night.

Glancing out the window to make sure Jimmy was well out of earshot, Jean-Claude turned to me and said in a tone of mock solemnity, "And so, another player enters the game. Tomorrow, we must seek out Mr. William Testament."

"Indeed," I replied, bursting into long-restrained laughter. "In-deed."

CHAPTER 11

Having slept no more hours over the past few days than I could practically count on one hand, the very last thing I felt like doing after Jimmy left was to trek through the rainy darkness to St. Alban's and bury a dead body on the grounds, but trek we must and trek we did. Dr. Edmonds's exhortation for all students to "see to your carrion, lads, so's to avoid a second resurrection," customarily enigmatic though it sounded, was clear enough to a pair of future surgeons who were at that very moment concealing a dead body, with a sackful of rapidly decaying organs alongside, under a pile of coal in the cellar. With local public sentiment running so strongly against the medical profession at the moment, in wake of the recent body-snatching incident at All Souls, about which Jean-Claude and I knew entirely too much, one did not require an inordinate fund of imagination to conceive what would happen if this public ventured onto the school grounds and stumbled upon our specimen, or the half dozen others laid out in various stages of dismemberment in the common dissection hall. Some rather ugly confrontations had occurred in Scotland during the past year, pitting the medical community against the public at large. In one such incident, two medical students were caught transporting a man's body—seated upright between them on a coach, of all things—and ultimately had themselves locked up in the local jail in order to escape the angry mob's wrath. With such an unpleasant prospect all too clearly in our minds, Dr. Edmonds's warning provided more-than-adequate impetus to send us all scurrying through the dark to the common burial field behind the school.

Venturing back into the cellar, our makeshift dissection room, we found our gentleman right where we had left him, under a pile of coal. As strongly as the now-familiar subterranean den smelled of mold, by the time we arrived that evening it was beginning to smell strongly, and distinctively, of another odor entirely. A lack of sleep over the past few days, and less-than-regular eating habits, had left my stomach in a somewhat weakened state, and it was only through an act of iron will that I kept down the meal I had consumed earlier in the apartment.

"Your dinner did not sit well with you, *mon ami*?" Jean-Claude said cheerily, trying to lure my mind away from our immediate circumstances. "Perhaps it was the cheese. It did taste a bit over-ripe to me."

"Yes," I replied, grateful for the distraction, and for the offering of a respectable excuse for my sudden fit of indigestion. "It left quite an unpleasant aftertaste."

Eager to be out of doors as soon as possible, we worked quickly, laying aside the coal and retrieving two burlap sacks, one considerably smaller, and less sharply defined, than the other. This sack, the one containing the organs, we placed upon the surface of the larger sack—in the approximate location of the dead man's chest—and then, both of us holding our breath, we lifted the body from either end, and carried it through a long, dark hallway, up a winding rickety staircase, and out onto a shapeless plot of earth known throughout the school as the "compost heap." In actuality, of course, the isolated patch of ground served as the final resting place for unfortunate souls whose last contribution to the civilized world was the advancement of anatomical knowledge.

It was common practice, on visits to the "heap," to drive a wooden stake a few inches into the freshly turned earth above a new arrival, in order to prevent other students from unearthing the remains when they came to bury their own specimens. Given the necessity for us to be able to recover our gentleman, if and when we should ever determine how he came to be in such a state in the first place, we took extra care to bury him a bit deeper than usual and to clearly mark the location of his grave so we could easily return to it when circumstances required. The smaller sack, on the other hand, we heaved into an open pit and covered with a few square feet of loose soil, greatly relieved simply to have it well beyond the reach of our visual and olfactory senses.

Safely back in our rooms, seated comfortably in front of the fire, I consumed an immoderate quantity of brandy, both to cut the chill that gripped my limbs and to mute the images that troubled my mind's eye. After nearly an hour of fighting to keep my eyelids open—fearful of the dreams that lay in wait for my consciousness to go off duty, I finally drifted into a restless but welcome slumber, from which I did not emerge until the first gray light of dawn filtered weakly through the window.

CHAPTER 12

Upon stepping out the door into the street next morning, we were most rudely assaulted by a vicious western wind, which, in a fit of wintry malice, hurled handfuls of sleet directly into our faces. My head ached from the previous night's libations, and the bitter cold exacerbated my misery to such an extent that all I could think of was burying myself in the covers of my bed and escaping the entire day through slumber. It was not a bed that awaited me this fine day, however, but a seat in the lecture hall where we were to spend the entire morning observing and practicing the delicate business of setting broken limbs. Wound thus tightly in a cloak of my own profound discomfort, I found myself irritated nearly to the point of violence by Jean-Claude's obvious and unapologetic enjoyment of the "bracing" and "invigorating" foretaste of winter weather. While I spoke intermittently and with great reluctance, loath to remove the scarf from my numbed lips, Jean-Claude chattered like an excitable schoolboy throughout the duration of our journey, continuing his side of the conversation we had begun over breakfast.

"No cook, no gardener," he yelled, over the biting wind. ". . . no servants in the entire house. What else could it mean?"

"They decided to try going it on their own?" I ventured, halfheartedly.

" 'Going it on their own?' *Mon dieu!* The cold has perhaps frozen your brain, yes?" To which challenge he received no reply. My brain wasn't frozen, but my face most decidedly was, and I felt no inclination to crack it open for his amusement. "It means," he continued nonplussed, "that the plot is far more sinister than we at first imagined. In addition to a murderer, we also have an accomplice, not to mention a partner in fraud."

"How so?" I mumbled, growing vaguely interested in spite of my physical misery.

"*Regarde.* Mme Abigail dies. Her body is, presumably, placed in a coffin, where it lies throughout the night awaiting a ceremony and burial. Keeping watch over the body, according to custom, is a surviving family member—the brother, Peter Worthington. Sometime during the night, the brother is killed, and his body placed in the coffin. What becomes of the lady, we will not concern ourselves with for the moment. Our killer, already a close facsimile of the brother, attires himself in such a manner as to complete the transformation. And then, sealing the coffin himself, he takes the bereaved brother's place and awaits the dawn arrival of the undertaker, who conveniently carries away the evidence of his crime."

"But we've already established that," I said, irritably. "What's this new 'sinister' element you referred to?"

"When we paid a visit to Darcy, the alleged Peter Worthington mentioned two servants, a groundskeeper and a cook, yes?" Jean-Claude's eyes sparkled, both with the cold, and with delight at the added complication our "chess game" had thrown in our way. I simply nodded in reply. "And who would have more direct access to the contents of the house—bodies included—than the two servants who live on the estate? Now the thought had entered my mind," he said, punctuating his observations with a pedantically raised index finger, ". . . that this groundskeeper may very well be the killer of, and poseur for, Peter Worthington. But there were two problems with this theory. First, with only two servants on the entire estate, would not the domestic immediately recognize the groundskeeper beneath the 'mask' of Peter Wellington? And second," he added, marshaling his middle finger to stand at attention beside his index finger, "even if the domestic were sufficiently deaf and blind not to notice this bold substitution, the arrival of Peter Worthington's sister would greatly embarrass the groundskeeper's attempt to maintain the façade."

"Of course," I replied irritably through my scarf. "Hence our concern for the sister's safety upon her arrival. We've already said . . ."

"Ah, you have gone straight to the heart of the matter, my friend—to the 'rub,' as Hamlet would say. The sister does arrive, and does meet with the false Peter Worthington, but does she expose his fraud? And does he harm her in retaliation? No! Quite to the contrary. Jimmy finds the man and the lady conversing with great familiarity, like a real brother and sister, yes?"

"And what the devil if they actually are brother and sister, Jean-Claude," I snapped, as a gust of icy wind whipped the scarf from my face, allowing a blast of sleet to abrade my frozen skin. "He's Peter Worthington, and she's . . . Margaret, or whatever the name was—the sister from France. Maybe everyone is telling the truth, and we're simply suffering from an overactive imagination." I regretted the words the instant they came out of my mouth, not wishing to offend Jean-Claude, even if he was a source of occasional irritation. I needn't have troubled myself, however, for, when thus in the grips of a logical conundrum, he was totally unflappable.

"Have you forgotten the dead man whose body provided us with a subject for anatomical study, hmm? He was no 'flight of fancy,' nor was the hole in his brain."

"Very well, then. Proceed," I said, fully aware that he would most certainly proceed, whether I gave him leave or no.

"*Regarde*, on the very occasion when Jimmy sees the gentleman and lady—presumably strangers, according to our first theory—conversing in a manner that is anything but strange, he also notes the complete absence from the house of anyone else, servants included. We begin with four people in the house, and we end up with two. So I ask you"—he paused, as the wind once again ripped the scarf from my face—"where are the servants—the groundsman and the cook?"

"On holiday?" I guessed weakly, unable to think much about anything save a warm fireplace in the lecture hall.

"They have gone nowhere," he announced, snapping his fingers, by way of prologue to the denouement that was sure to follow. "The cook and the groundskeeper are still very much in residence at Darcy House, only they are no longer serving in the capacity of servants. They are posing, respectively, as Peter and Madeleine Worthington, brother and sister of the deceased Abigail."

"So you think . . ." I asked, trying to assemble the oddly shaped puzzle pieces Jean-Claude had just laid out before me.

"Yes. The groundsman, or even the cook, *mon dieu*, killed Peter Worthington, and together they placed his body in the lady's coffin. When the evidence was out of the house and safely under the ground, *voilà*! They assume the roles of the deceased widow's brother and sister—sole heirs to the Darcy family fortune."

"I say," I reflected aloud, forgetting the cold temporarily, or perhaps simply numbed to such an extent as to be impervious to it. "There is a certain logic to that. Yes. One thing still troubles me, though," I added. "Why go through all the bother of taking Mrs. Darcy's body out of the coffin and replacing it with Peter's, when all their efforts still left them with a body to dispose of?"

Jean-Claude pursed his lips, silent for the first time since we left our rooms. "I am afraid," he finally said, "that we shall have to explore that question at another time, for we have arrived at our destination." And in truth, our plodding footsteps had led us, once more, to the gate of St. Alban's, a place of which I had, quite frankly, grown weary during the past few days. I found myself involuntarily drawing back from the entrance, but when I considered the prospect of retracing the icy way back home, a few hours of bandaging "broken" arms and legs suddenly seemed quite attractive, and giving vent to an ambivalent sigh, I gratefully stepped through the door and out of the cold.

When we walked into the hall, we found most of our colleagues already seated, arranged in ascending tiers from a central "stage," upon which sat James Lear, an extremely self-conscious-looking first-year student who, based upon his "privileged" location in the center of the hall, had fallen prey to the legendary persuasive powers of our head of school, Dr. Edmonds, and "volunteered" to serve as a subject for the day's demonstration. Seats near the fireplace having long since been spoken for, we settled ourselves as far from the drafty doorway as possible, and prepared to learn all there was to know about setting broken bones.

A few moments after our arrival, the casual chatter of eighteen men in various stages of thawing, suddenly died down as our lecturer, Dr. Clarke, strode in from the wings carrying what appeared to be enough splints, cloth, and gauze to mend the fractures of an entire Roman legion. A general rustling sound, not unlike the winter wind through the dried brown leaves outside the window, ensued as students throughout the hall thumbed through their notebooks in search of a fresh page on which to record the day's proceedings. Without so much as a "good morning" by way of preface, the good doctor laid into his reluctant volunteer, setting and bandaging virtually every bone in the poor man's body, until by the end of the proceeding he resembled nothing in the world quite so much as an Egyptian mummy.

Having thus thoroughly immobilized his patient, Dr. Clarke invited us to proceed in an orderly fashion to the floor of the theater, where we could more closely observe his handiwork, and secure splinting and bandaging materials with which to practice upon each other. We did as instructed, and spent the next three hours tying hopeless knots around limbs twisted into assorted inhumane positions until the session finally came to an end, not because we had mastered the required technique of setting broken limbs but because we had endured just about all we could as subjects of it.

Throughout the last hour or so of this session, we rather unconsciously became aware of a muffled roar emanating from outside the lecture hall. Sounding initially like a rising wind—a not-unexpected phenomenon, given the season— the roaring gradually increased in volume and

intensity, until by the time we tidied up and prepared to retire for a late luncheon, it had reached a
rather alarming pitch. And when James, gratefully
freed from his state of mummification, stepped out
into the courtyard to get a breath of air and find
out whence the sound originated, alarm proved to
be an entirely appropriate response. No sooner had
the poor man walked out the door than he ran
back inside, his face grown white as a sheet.

"What the devil is wrong with you, man?"
asked Thomas Bailey, sober now, as he typically
was during the daylight hours before noon.

"We're under attack!" replied the terrified man.
"There's hundreds of them. Maybe even thou-
sands. We'll all be killed!"

"What's this about an attack?!" roared Dr. Clarke,
as he strode through the cluster of students gathered at the door. "Get ahold of yourself, man.
You're positively hysterical." With this exhortation still ringing in the air, he threw open the
door to see what all the fuss was about, and the
sight that greeted our eyes indicated that our fright-
ened classmate was not terribly far off the mark in
his assessment of our situation. However one cares
to define the term, "attack" was not a bad description of what was going on outside—although
"siege" might have been a little more precisely
accurate—for massed at the front gate of the school
were at least a thousand people, some of whom
were armed, and all of whom were angry. Dr.
Clarke closed the door, considerably less self-
assured than he had been before he opened it, and

said in a husky low voice, "Someone go fetch Dr. Edmonds, quickly!"

In truth, looking out the door at the angry mass of humanity, having multiplied at least tenfold since yesterday's "call" at the school, we were all painfully aware of what the spectacle meant, since similar scenes were all too frequent an occurrence throughout Great Britain in the days before the Anatomy Act provided a legal, reliable source of human subjects for anatomical study. Schools had been ransacked, physicians' homes had been burned, and students and surgeons had been violently attacked, because of the uneasy but necessary alliance between the medical profession and the resurrectionists, among whose well-organized trade our friend Jimmy was but an apprentice, and fortunately for him, a retired one. It took but a spark to ignite the smoldering public resentment against our profession. Perhaps a dog unearthed a bone from a hospital yard and dragged it home to his horrified master. Perhaps a careless grave robber left behind obvious evidence of his night's work. Or even, perhaps—as was not at all an uncommon occurrence—a disgruntled resurrectionist tossed a putrefying corpse at the front gate of a medical school during the night, as punishment for nonpayment of services, and the morning sun rose to confirm in the people's minds that, so long as the medical schools operated, death and burial were but minor inconveniences compared to the fate that likely awaited them once "safely" underground.

Alas, it is all too true that bodies were exhumed by the scores for the purposes of medical study, but how many thousand lives have been saved by medical advances arising from this anatomical study? These people massed at our front gate, however, were not thinking about medical advance as they angrily waved their pitchforks, guns, and shovels above their heads. All they could see when they looked through those iron bars were the fiends who "snatched" their dear husband, or their child, or their aunt Martha, and we "fiends" knew that we were all in serious trouble.

It took several minutes for Dr. Clarke's envoy to find Dr. Edmonds—he was in the archives searching for a letter describing a surgical procedure performed in Scotland the previous year—and by the time he arrived in the lecture hall, the crowd had grown visibly larger, and angrier. As angry as the crowd was, however, the scarlet hue spreading across Dr. Edmonds's broad forehead hinted that the anger at the gate very possibly had a rival on this side of the door.

"Did I not tell you," he roared, in his thick Scottish brogue, "that such would be the result if you 'gentlemen' went messin' around in graveyards? 'Leave the body snatchin' to them that knows what they're doin',' said I. 'We mustn't let it be common knowledge that our sacred profession relies heavily upon the professional traffickin' of dead bodies,' said I. 'Heaven only knows what'd happen if it were one of you butchers got nabbed in the graveyard.' Didn't I say it? If I said it once, I said it a hundred times. And now look out there!" With this exhortation, he threw open the door, exposing us all to the nearly palpable gusts of wrath emanating from the crowd. "I'll tell ya this," he growled, sweeping a flashing eye and an accusatory finger around the room, making sure to include everyone present in the scope of his mounting anger, "if I had so much as an inkling which of you it was went diggin' around the churchyard at All Souls the other night, I'd grab ye by the collar and throw ye to them wolves out yonder." He closed the door, and appeared to regain some small degree of his composure, his face now merely bright red, instead of the deep purple shade it had worn during the initial blasts of the storm of his indignation. Of course, throughout the entire speech, I writhed in mortification at knowing far more than I cared to about the late-night episode to which he referred, and literally quaked at the suspicion that it was only a matter of time before someone read the guilt that must be clearly written upon my face. I don't know how Jean-Claude was comporting himself during this display, for I dared not look at him, fearing that our complicity would ring out across the entire hall.

"But since," he continued, in a slightly more measured tone, "I do not know who it was that dug up the lady in All Souls, I have no choice but to face the crowd myself—try to talk some reason into the irrational beasts." At this statement of his intentions, a collective gasp went out from the lot of us, for we all believed that such a confrontation would undoubtedly end in the good doctor being torn apart limb from limb. When I saw the iron determination fixed upon his face, however, I had to conclude that if there was anyone in the world who was the equal of such an unequal match, it was Dr. Edmonds. Clutching the iron handle, he pushed open the door and took one step outside. Then suddenly, poised, as it were, upon the threshold between two worlds, he roared out a final, parting vow. "If anyone of you has that lady, or any other human body that's not livin' and breathin', on these premises, I'm comin' back here, if it's the last thing I do, and dissecting your quiverin' body with my own bare hands!" The door slammed shut behind him, leaving us all quivering indeed.

We stood in complete stony silence for a full minute, listening for an alteration in the pitch or intensity of the crowd's fury as he approached them, until one of us—a third-year student from Lancashire—found the breath to speak. "I'm sure glad it wasn't me who took that lady. I'd far rather confront that mob out there than stand face-to-face with Dr. Edmonds, if and when he should return, and confess that it was I who managed to get us all into this mess. By the time this whole thing is over, St. Alban's, and Sloane's Hospital, too, for that matter, could very well be reduced to a pile of smoldering embers. Dr. Edmonds has poured his heart and soul into this place, and to think that a single careless act should bring all those decades of hard work to naught."

The already oppressive air attained an even

greater density during this heartfelt panegyric, and every word of it pierced my guilty heart like a dagger. The lecture hall in which we stood seemed to contract around me, squeezing the breath out of my lungs. So terribly constrictive was the grip my guilt had upon me, that I was just before screaming out a confession, when a familiarly sardonic voice pierced the heavy silence.

"Are you daft?" said Thomas Bailey, rescuing me from myself, just in the nick of time. "It's not because of the bloody hospital that he's so angry. Oh, sure, he's not delighted at the prospect of having the place pulled down around his ears, but what's really got his choler up is something a little more personal."

"What do you mean, 'personal'?" asked the third-year from Lancashire, in a wounded tone, clearly offended at having his dramatic moment thus interrupted. "What could be more personal than a man's lifetime of work."

"You *are* mad," replied Thomas, with an incredulous grin on his face that soon proved contagious, despite the dire circumstances. "If I thought that, after six or seven decades of life upon this earth, the only thing that could arouse my passions was my work, I'd just as soon be shot right now, because there would literally be nothing left for me to live for. Bloody work!" he huffed, and then chuckled in derision.

"I'll tell you what's got the old man's ire up," he continued. "It's that woman, the Darcy lady, that was snatched from the graveyard. There's the sore spot."

"That's what I said, you fool!" Lancashire retorted, in a tone that belied his apparent self-assurance.

"You said nothing of the sort!" sneered Thomas. As befuddled as our colleague typically was "after hours," he was a fairly formidable rhetorical opponent if one happened to catch him before he had had the chance to get very far "in his cups." "*You* said it was the peril to the hospital that angered him about the incident. And *I'm* saying it was the theft itself, or rather the object of it, that's got the good doctor so red about the temples. Don't you know who that woman was?"

We all glanced around at each other in confused silence, knowing full well the identity of the "stolen" body, but suddenly sensing that this knowledge barely scratched the surface of a much more elaborate story, no one dared to say anything. For the first time since Dr. Edmonds stormed into the hall, I felt my intense guilt evaporate in the heat of an even-more-pressing interest. Sneaking a glance at Jean-Claude, I saw that he was as riveted to Thomas's "oration" as I.

Sensing he was in full, unchallenged possession of the "floor," Thomas paused dramatically before satisfying the curiosity he had aroused. "He was acquainted with her, you see," he began, ". . . through her husband, Sir Alfred. The old man and our Dr. Edmonds went way back, to university days, in Cambridge. They studied there at the same time, Sir Alfred having gotten rather a late start, due to the time he spent traveling the globe in search of 'treasures.' When they completed their studies, and each embarked on a distinguished 'career'"—he paused over the word, and glared sardonically at Lancashire—"they corresponded frequently, Dr. Edmonds from London, and Sir Alfred from all over the world. When Alfred finally 'retired' here, to work on his endless translations, and catalog his vast collections, the two of them, along with several other scholars of note, formed the Atheneum, a philosophical society."

"Yes, I know that," Lancashire offered eagerly, happy to have found a thread in the narrative to which he could catch on. Thomas ignored the interruption.

"Officially a 'club of mutual improvement and collegial collaboration,' the Atheneum is also known for a tradition of rather riotous festivities, with more than one meeting in their illustrious history having begun with serious philosophical debate, and ended with a smashed punch bowl and broken furniture. When Alfred first hinted at his intentions to marry, it was less the fear of how the marriage would affect his work that bothered the other members than the prospect of losing such a jovial drinking companion."

Thomas's surprising account of Dr. Edmonds's extracurricular activities was interrupted by a sudden surge in the noise from the crowd outside. "What's happening out there?" asked a saucer-eyed first-year student. "Can anyone see?"

"He's at the gate," replied Jean-Claude, who had moved to a window on the opposite end of the hall. "There appear to be some officers of the militia. Yes. The doctor is speaking with them. The gates, for the moment at least, appear to be holding back the barbarians."

"As I was saying," Thomas snapped, more annoyed at being interrupted by the rioters than fearful of being attacked by them. "When the wedding actually came off, the whole 'gang' was in attendance, raising glass after glass in the couple's honor until dawn forced them all to crawl back home and sleep it off. From that evening on, Alfred rarely darkened the door of the club, so very preoccupied was he with his 'research.'" Thomas raised an eyebrow at Lancashire, and then continued.

"Shortly before his death, however, he dropped in on the club one evening to share a bowl of punch and to discuss plans for donating his vast collection of jade statuary to the museum. One bowl gave way to two, a third followed, and before long it was a typically merry evening at the Atheneum. The merriment was to be short-lived, however, for a chiming clock reminded Alfred of his domestic duties, and he prepared to bid everyone farewell. Just before he left, never again to be seen alive by anyone in the company—although none of them knew this then, of course—his manner grew serious, and he expressed his avowed wishes that, upon the occasion of his death, whenever that inevitable day should arrive, his body be placed upon the top of a wooden bier and burned until all that remained was ashes, which were to be scattered upon the surface of a pond on his estate."

"I had read he was cremated," I offered, recalling the story in the *Gazette*. "Because of his admiration for Oriental culture, wasn't it?"

Now it was my turn to be fixed in Thomas's sardonic stare. "No . . ." he said, with an exaggerated show of patience, much like a parent with a child who asks one too many foolish questions. "It had nothing to do with the Orient." I looked at Jean-Claude for support, but he merely shrugged his shoulders. "It was for public health. In addition to all the frivolity that goes on at the Atheneum, the club does have a serious agenda, and one item near the top of it is the perpetual risk of widespread contagion posed by our overburdened church cemeteries. One proposed remedy, of course, is the creation of public cemeteries, but the Atheneum advocates, in addition, an organized system of cremation—it was Shelley's beach cremation that gave them the idea, I believe—and Sir Alfred wanted to set an example.

"So, when word of his untimely death spread to the various members of the club, they gathered quickly to formulate a plan for carrying out their colleague's final wishes. Our Dr. Edmonds, as the club member having the longest history with the old man, was sent to Darcy as an envoy, to carry the group's intentions to Sir Alfred's young widow. Dr. Edmonds expected resistance from that quarter, the idea being admittedly unorthodox, to say the least, but was delighted to find her in complete accord with her late husband's wishes." Then lowering his voice, as if the doctor out there at the gate might hear him above the roar of the crowd beside which he stood, he added, "And based upon the report of a very reliable messenger, the lady's accord was not the only thing about her that delighted Dr. Edmonds. In fact, one might even go so far as to say that he was fairly smitten."

"You're not serious," I said, trying to imagine the crusty old man keeping company with an exotic woman less than half his age.

"Oh yes," he replied. "Unlike some human icebergs I know—" once again, glaring at Lancashire— "Dr. Edmonds is a creature of flesh and blood. Why, he was even married once, long ago, but his wife died of cholera before their first anniversary. The fact that he never married again, rather than indicating a lack of feeling on his part, quite to the contrary shows how very deeply his feelings run, his first loss paining him so badly that he avoided experiencing such loss again. But, I will admit, that is a bit of speculation on my part.

"What is not speculation, however, is the fact that, two days after Alfred's death, the members of the Atheneum arrived at Darcy, fetched the man's body, then traveled in procession to a predetermined secluded location where they had constructed an enormous bier, as instructed. Placing the body upon the dry wood, they ignited the pyre, and stood watch until the flames reduced his remains to ashes, which, when sufficiently cooled, were gathered into a jade urn and transported back to the Darcy Estate, where they were scattered upon the surface of a pond, as instructed.

"In the weeks following this ceremony, Dr. Edmonds visited the widow at Darcy two or three times—merely to assure himself of her well-being during the stressful period of grief, of course—but after the lady's brother took up residence at the estate, he made it quite clear that the doctor's services were no longer required. As far as I know, Dr. Edmonds never laid eyes upon her again, until called to Darcy one morning several months later to attend to her as a patient, apparently suffering from a cataleptical seizure. By the time he arrived, however, the only service left for a physician to render was the official declaration of death."

Upon this final remark, Jean-Claude and I instantly locked eyes, transfixed with the same thought. "By whom was the doctor summoned to the estate?" Jean-Claude asked, making a poor attempt to strike a tone of "casual" interest. The question clearly struck Thomas as somewhat "off-subject," for instead of answering immediately, he pondered silently for a moment, with a slightly bemused look upon his face, before finally venturing, "By the lady's brother, I would assume. It was a hired man from the estate who actually brought Dr. Edmonds the summons."

Before either Jean-Claude or I had time to formulate our next question, the discussion was brought to an abrupt and final halt by a cry from the platter-eyed first-year, stationed before the window formerly occupied by Jean-Claude. "They're coming!" he shrieked, in a voice quaking with terror at the thought that his end had surely come. And while perhaps not quite as visibly shaken as this poor fellow, we were all, to a man, ready to leap through the nearest window and flee the premises, should circumstances warrant. Before making such a desperate exit, however, someone had the presence of mind to open the door slightly, in order to see precisely who "they" were.

Standing practically on top of one another, in order to get an eye close to the narrow vertical opening, we were somewhat puzzled by what we saw, and didn't know whether relief or fear was the more appropriate response. Striding purposefully across the courtyard, shoulder to shoulder with an officer of the militia, was Dr. Edmonds, and immediately behind him were ten individuals from the hoarded angry mass of humanity at the gate. To our relief, the ten men were unarmed and appeared altogether to have been thus plucked from the bosom of the mob, for the indignant fury that was etched across the crowd en masse had completely deserted the faces of their individual members thus isolated, to be replaced by an expression far more closely akin to embarrassment. As the group approached the door behind which we stood huddled like so many curious children, we all scattered to different locations throughout the hall and pretended to be busily occupied with various tasks associated with the study of medicine, as if a mob siege were a regular part of our daily routine. Momentarily, the door burst open, revealing Dr. Edmonds and his motley retinue in tow.

"Gentlemen," he addressed us in his formal "lecturing" voice, "there seems to have been a

terrible misunderstanding. As a result of the hei-
nous and shocking crime perpetrated at All Souls
Church last week, a terrible rumor has been set
abroad among some of the good people of London." He paused here to close the door behind
two stragglers, who were clearly having second
thoughts about leaving the safety of the crowd
outside. "It seems they have the mistaken impression that we practitioners and students of medicine routinely scavenge the local graveyards for
newly buried bodies, which we bring back here to
the hospital and desecrate in all manner of un-
godly ways. In order to dispel this gross untruth,
I have invited some representatives from among
their substantial number to thoroughly examine
the premises of our respectable institution, and
satisfy themselves, and those out there at the gate
whom they represent, how very mistaken—albeit
entirely sincere—these concerns are."

Throughout this bit of theatrical oratory, everyone in the room, with the exception of Dr. Edmonds himself, writhed uncomfortably where he
stood. It would be difficult to say who felt greater
consternation at the prospect of a stray dead body
actually coming to light, the envoy who had entered the hospital with the expressed intention of
finding such a damning piece of evidence, or we
students who had gone to great lengths to hide
any such evidence. Before anyone from either
party had very much time to reflect upon the implications of such an unwelcome discovery, however, Dr. Edmonds set the school into a flurry of
activity. "Make yourselves at home, gentlemen!"

he ordered the cowed envoy. "And you students, put yourselves fully at their disposal! Show them around the whole place, and let them see what an entirely respectable facility we operate here." In this final directive to us, the students, I detected a subtle emphasis of the word "around," and we thereby proceeded to lead the ten mystified men throughout the premises of the school, making sure to divert them "around" anything that might validate their suspicions.

The entire tour went off without incident, our accusers acting positively apologetic as they neared the conclusion, and we were just on the verge of escorting them out the door and into the gathering evening, where they could report our innocence to the crowd, and everyone could return to the divers and scattered household fires from which they had been lately snatched by a collective fit of vindictive hysteria. We were on the verge, that is, until Thomas, grown overbold with a sense of imminent safety, threw open a closet door to reveal how very little we had to hide, only to reveal a human skeleton that we had moments before gone to great pains to hide. The air grew suddenly thick with tension, as we all stood looking eye to socket, as it were, with the mounted skeletal remains of "Captain" Jack McBride, a notorious murderer executed at Newgate some ten years earlier. Accepting the legal alternative to a murderer's fate of "hanging in chains" after death until his body fell into pieces, which hungry dogs would transport to the four points of the compass, he had given his body over for dissection, which was carried out here at St. Alban's within hours after his death. Following the dissection, his bones had been cleaned, boiled, and mounted, and the skeleton had stood dutifully in the corner of the lecture hall ever since, a perpetual exhibit of osteological study.

"What's that?" asked one of the men, suddenly losing his diffidence in the face of this apparent confirmation of the mob's worst suspicions. "Or should I say, *who*'s that?" he added, with rising heat. The other nine members of the party moved to stand at his side, and the afternoon's drama threatened to take a tragic turn. But then a very familiar voice pierced the veil of tension with a steady, assured common sense.

"That is a plaster model of a human skeleton, of course," explained Jean-Claude, in a tone that utterly belied the duplicity of his remark. "It is used to teach the framework of the human body, and to assist in the instruction of setting broken bones, such as you yourself might suffer in an accident— a violent fall from your horse, for example. Such models are very common—expensive, yes, but not at all difficult to attain." He folded his arms, warming to his role. "It is one of the technical advancements of medical study."

The ten men stood in silent uncertainty for an uncomfortably long minute, looking alternately at the remains of Captain McBride in the closet, and into each other's anxious faces. Finally, a man who had yet to say a word since entering the door, chose an opportune moment to break his silence. "If it's just plaster . . ." He hesitated, suddenly aware that he had moved to "center stage," "I don't suppose there's any harm in it." And with that timid observation, thirty men breathed a collective sigh of relief, and the halted procession to the front door resumed once again.

The delegation returned to the waiting mob at the gate to report what they had, or more importantly had not, seen inside the school, and within ten minutes the whole assembly had scattered like so many cockroaches under a lantern. Some years later, when a mob of twenty thousand angry townsfolk raided a medical school in Aberdeen and, finding three cadavers in various stages of dissection upon tables in the operating theater, assaulted the students and burned the place to the ground, I couldn't help breathing a belated sigh of relief at the violent fate we had so narrowly escaped that day.

When the threat of danger had retreated with the mob, we all chattered giddily and nonsensically for some moments, intoxicated with the sudden release of nervous energy. Even Dr. Edmonds, typically immune to such frivolity, engaged in a bit of verbal sparring with some of the bolder students, clearly as relieved as any of us simply to have four sound walls around us and a roof over our heads. Finally, having spent its fuel, the impromptu celebration sputtered out, and students began making their way out into the evening, which many if not most would measure out, not in hours, but in tankards of ale or beakers of wine.

As Jean-Claude and I moved toward the door

and prepared to follow our colleagues' example, Dr. Edmonds arrested our forward progress by planting his substantial form squarely before the exit. Initially fearing that he had, after all, somehow deduced our role in the All Soul's "incident," and was preparing to confront us with charges to that effect, he quickly set our minds at ease with a broad grin and a genially proffered right hand, which we gratefully grasped, each in turn. "That was a quick bit of thinking there, Mr., eh . . ."

"Legard," Jean-Claude assisted him. "Jean-Claude Legard."

"Yes, Mr. Legard," the doctor continued, ". . . a very dexterous maneuver. You likely saved us all a great deal of trouble."

"It was nothing, really," Jean-Claude demurred. "I have great respect for this institution and would have hated to see any harm come to it, especially as a result of public ignorance."

"But that's the devil of the thing," said Dr. Edmonds, running a hand through his unruly gray hair. "Because it's not ignorance, really. They know what goes on in here, at least most of them do. They just don't like to be reminded of it—to have it shoved in their faces. Which is just what an episode like that spree at All Souls does. It shoves it in their faces, and they simply can't let it pass without staging some sort of protest. But all's well that ends well, I suppose, and you certainly did your part in helping it end that way," he concluded, slapping Jean-Claude heartily on the shoulder.

"I was happy to do what I could," he replied, wincing slightly under the pressure of the good doctor's meaty hand. And then, spying an opportunity to gain some information—to capture a vulnerable pawn—Jean-Claude subtly diverted the drift of the conversation. "At the risk of appearing intrusive, sir, I would like to offer my heartfelt condolences for the pain your personal involvement in this situation must have caused you. You were acquainted with Mrs. Darcy and her husband, no?" I questioned Jean-Claude's forwardness, wishing simply to drop the subject of Abigail Darcy altogether, fearing that prolonged discussion of the matter would arouse Dr. Edmonds's suspicions regarding our interest, and involvement, in it. So relieved was he still to have been thus yanked from the jaws of almost certain disaster, however, that he appeared not to notice the non sequitur.

"It's kind of you to say so," he replied, nodding reflectively. "She was a dear thing, almost like a daughter to me." I couldn't help noticing the slight emphasis of the word "daughter," and a furtive, almost defensive expression drift into his face, and just as quickly fade. "I felt it was my duty to look after her after Alfred's death—she was so vulnerable, you know, and I did what I could to help her. But then that brother of hers entered the scene . . ." He hung upon the thought, quite literally scowling, and continued speaking, as much to the floor as to Jean-Claude and me. "I shall never forgive myself for letting him run me off like he did. He was a wastrel and a dissembler, I could tell the first time I laid eyes on him. And if he didn't have something to do with her death, I'm a fool instead of a doctor—a young thing like that, in the very flush of health and vigor. What a jolly laugh she had." A lengthy, pensive silence ensued, which Jean-Claude was ultimately compelled to break.

"It was you who made the official pronouncement of death, was it not?" Jean-Claude asked quietly, not wishing to divert Dr. Edmonds from the current productive drift of his thoughts. "That must indeed have been a painful office to perform."

"I was summoned to Darcy to *treat* Abigail," he hissed, growing angry at the memory, "not to sign her bloody death certificate. On my way out there, all I could think of was finally gettin' to see her again after all those months—to be able to help her in some way, after leavin' her to shift for herself for so long. 'From this day forward,' I vowed, 'I shall look after her, whether Mr. Peter Worthington likes it or no.' Little did I know what I'd actually find when I arrived at the house." Another pause ensued, during which Jean-Claude and I quite literally leaned forward, awaiting the sequel to this comment.

"And you found . . . ?" Jean-Claude prompted.

"She was dead, plain and simple. Laid out on the bed with her hands already folded upon her chest. I tell you, that man couldn't wait to get her under the ground. At first, I refused to believe my eyes. 'She's just sleepin',' I said, 'or perhaps feelin' a wee bit faint.'" Silence again, and then a deep sigh. "But when I made my examination, there was no denyin' the truth. Abigail was dead, and mark my word, that man—that monster—was somehow responsible. I thought of poisoning, of course, but when I looked for visible evidence—melanosis of the gums and tongue, that sort of thing—I could find nothing. 'We shall have to make an inquest,' I said. 'I shall take her back to the hospital.' 'You'll do nothing of the sort,' said that beast. 'I'll not have my sister cut into pieces as if she were a side of beef.'

"I knew right then I'd have to get some help from the authorities, if I was to find out what killed her. But it's a tricky proposition, as you gentlemen saw today. The police are no quicker than the public to approve of dissection, so for them to force a man to give over the body of his dear departed sister, for the purposes of bein' cut upon . . . Well, I knew I faced an uphill battle. I was willin' to take it on, though. And I walked out of the house with the intention of comin' right back, just as soon as I found somebody with a strong enough arm—whether it be of the law or no—to get him out of the way so I could find out why she died." A flush spread across the doctor's temples, and skin over his jaw muscles rippled as he gnashed his teeth.

"But on my way back to London, who should I meet making a beeline straight for Darcy? Simeon Rupp, jack of all trades, the most notable—and the most profitable—being the funeral business. That Worthington creature had summoned the undertaker with the same messenger he sent to summon me! And the next thing I know, Abigail is lying six feet underground in the All Souls graveyard. I barely found out in time to make it to the funeral. Even with that disheartening turn of events, however, I didn't abandon my plans to find out how she died. I even bandied the possibility of hiring a resurrectionist to fetch her to the hospital, so I could examine her. But then . . ." He grew silent again, as the rage inside him forced his jaws together.

"Then someone stole the body before you could get to her," Jean-Claude completed the thought.

"Yes," he replied quietly, then added. "And the crowning insult is that it may very well have been one of you men who took her." Jean-Claude and I were both startled by the sudden insinuation, especially considering how close it hit to home, and we clearly did a pretty poor job of concealing our discomfiture, for Dr. Edmonds quickly clarified the nature and direction of his suspicions. "Oh, I don't mean the two of you, of course. You've always comported yourself too much like true gentlemen to be involved in such as that." At this remark, an acute sense of guilt rose up within us to vie with our anxiety for primary control over our emotions. "But I can't say the same about some of your colleagues. There are three or four men here at the school that I shall be keepin' under a very close watch in the coming days, to see if they'll lead me to Abigail's body so I can find out what killed her. It'll gall me till my dyin' day if I don't make that man pay for what he did." The doctor looked frantically around the room, as if he might find the body right there if he only tried hard enough, then blinked his eyes several times, like someone just waking up from a restless sleep.

"Just listen at me," he said in a sad, apologetic tone, ". . . goin' on and on like that in front of you gentlemen, when all you did to deserve it was the simple courtesy of offering your condolences. You shall think twice before striking up a conversation with the old man again, I'll wager."

"Not at all," we both protested in unison. "And if there is anything we can do to help you," Jean-Claude continued, ". . . please do not hesitate to ask."

"I just might do that," he responded pensively. "I just might."

Bidding each other a good evening, we parted company, and Jean-Claude and I passed into the welcome fresh air outside. Pausing in the courtyard, I couldn't resist glancing back through the window into the lecture hall, where Dr. Edmonds still stood on the very spot where we had left him, searching the room with frantic, reddened eyes.

CHAPTER 13

"The doctor was a bit more forthcoming than we expected, yes?" said Jean-Claude, placing my king in check. After dinner and drinks at the Empty Horn, where we rehearsed the day's dramatic events with no fewer than ten of our colleagues, who had likewise repaired to the bustling, noisy tavern, we had returned to our rooms and immediately begun a fresh game of chess. As usual, Jean-Claude had me on the run from the first move.

"We certainly got a good deal more there than we bargained for, I must say." I moved my king out of immediate danger, but by that time the handwriting was on the proverbial wall. "For a very uncomfortable moment, there, I feared he was going to be as good as his word and—how did he say it?—'dissect our quivering bodies with his bare hands.' I do believe he was capable of it, angry as he was."

"I am sure we were not in any danger," he replied thoughtfully, placing my king in check once again. "But I cannot say that he would not be capable of killing someone, given the right, or shall I say, the wrong, circumstances."

"You mean Peter Worthington," I guessed, pleased to have arrived at the same deduction as Jean-Claude, at virtually the same instant. "I thought exactly the same thing while he was talking. All that stuff about 'making him pay,' and so forth. There's a man who'd better watch his back."

"Perhaps you have forgotten, *mon ami*, but it is a little late for Peter Worthington to 'watch his back,' having already suffered a fatal wound from that quarter."

"The fellow masquerading as Peter Worthington, then," I corrected, freeing myself from check with an ingenious block using my remaining knight. "*He'd* better watch his back. As far as Dr. Edmonds knows, he's the genuine article, and I can quite easily imagine him going after the man in order to 'make him pay.' He has no way of knowing that the actual Peter Worthington has already paid all he's capable of paying . . . in this life, at least."

"And has he really no way of knowing this?" Jean-Claude asked, in a tone indicating that any attempt at an answer on my part would be entirely superfluous.

"I don't see how he could," I replied. "Since the only people who know he's dead are you, me, and Jimmy. Oh, and the murderer, of course."

"Précisément," he said, moving a bishop that appeared to have no relation to the state of siege under which my king suffered. "The murderer."

"Good heavens!" I exclaimed, forgetting the chessboard for a perilous moment. "You don't seriously think our Dr. Edmonds killed that man, do you? I mean, anger is one thing. But to actually take a dagger, or a stiletto, more like, and ram it through another man's skull . . ."

"Through the cartilaginous tissue at the base of the skull," he corrected.

"Cartilage or bone, Jean-Claude, it's an act of extreme violence we're talking about."

"And it was a man with an extremely violent temper with whom we discussed the matter earlier this evening."

"Do you really think the old man could have done it?" I asked, then, spying a weakness in my adversary's defense, made a bold offensive move with my castle.

"I do not know what to think," he pondered, reviewing the board. "But let us for a moment play the advocate of the devil. Dr. Edmonds was personally involved with Abigail, of whom, as the widow of his friend of many decades, he feels extremely protective. A complete stranger, so far as Dr. Edmonds's awareness extends, suddenly enters the stage and cuts him off completely from contact with the lady. This angers him deeply, and the anger smolders for many months' time as he must sit by helplessly and long for the lady from afar."

"So you got the impression it was more than a

paternal affection he felt for the lady," I interjected. "I sensed that, as well."

"Paternal or otherwise, the affection, in the prolonged absence of its object, creates a sense of helplessness that greatly exacerbates his anger—adding more fuel to the fire, as it were. And just at the moment when his impotent rage is at a climax, the woman dies, and the doctor concludes that the man who has been the source of all his suffering for the past many months has now been the cause of the dear lady's death, thus making permanent the exile he had every reason to believe was merely temporary. In short, his anger turns into desperation, and his sole motivating principle—his *raison d'être*, is now bringing the killer to justice, for which object he must have access to the lady's body, in order to conduct the postmortem examination. But here Peter Worthington obstructs the way yet again, burying her before such an examination can be made."

"Ah, but Peter Worthington was already dead before the funeral," I corrected him. "Before Dr. Edmonds had any way of knowing she was to be buried so shortly after her death. He barely made it to the funeral in time, don't you remember?"

"That is what he said, yes. But did he not also say that he passed the undertaker—Simeon Rupp, I think it was—on the road? He could most easily have inquired of the man what day the funeral was to be held, and would thus have known that he must act quickly if he wished to prove that the lady was poisoned, in order to implicate Peter Worthington in her death."

"I say, that does all fit rather nicely together," I agreed. "So you think that sometime during the night Dr. Edmonds returned to Darcy and killed the man, in order to get to the lady's body in time to prove what, or rather who, killed her. That would explain the disappearance of her body."

"Once again, my friend, I do not know. But speaking for the devil, I can easily imagine the doctor returning to Darcy later that evening to make a claim on the body, forcing the issue. It is, of course, doubtful that Peter Worthington would readily accept such a claim, so conflict would be virtually inevitable in the encounter. Whether or not Dr. Edmonds had violence in mind as he journeyed out there, for the second time in one day, it is as difficult to believe that violence of some kind would not have occurred in this situation, as it is to believe that a lighted match could be thrown into a powder keg without incident." As I recalled the deep purple hue of Dr. Edmonds's face at the hospital earlier that day, and his threat to "dissect us alive," "powder keg" was an entirely appropriate simile for the man's explosive temperament. "Letting the devil speak for himself, however," he continued, "we return to what we know without speculation. Sometime between Mrs. Darcy's death and the funeral service less than forty-eight hours later, Peter Worthington was murdered, and someone—presumably the murderer—removed the lady's body from the coffin and replaced it with that of Mr. Worthington. Regarding Dr. Edmonds's role in the affair, we can say no more with absolute certainty."

"So how do you propose we go about acquiring certainty," I asked, suddenly aware of how very speculative our discussion had been up to this point. Jean-Claude had a way of speaking of the most hypothetical scenario with such clarity and conviction that the afternoon newspaper seemed complete fiction beside it. "We can't very well simply stroll into Dr. Edmonds's office and, without so much as a 'good day' by way of preface, accuse the man of murder."

"Of course we cannot accuse him of murder," he agreed matter-of-factly. "Not yet, at least. For one consideration, he may have had nothing whatsoever to do with the death of Peter Worthington, in spite of the suspicious circumstances surrounding his relation to it. For another consideration, assuming the suspicious circumstances prove to be more than merely circumstances, he is now in possession of the lady's body. To prove the possession would be to prove the murder, a conclusion of which Dr. Edmonds would most certainly disapprove. If he were to believe he is suspected of this crime, it is quite likely that he would destroy the evidence in his possession—the body no longer being necessary for bringing Peter Worthington to justice since justice has already been dealt from the doctor's own hand. Finally, a third consideration involves the well-being of two people of whom I am extremely fond—namely, Jean-Paul Legard and Edward Montague. *Regarde.* Let us say he takes the practical course of destroying the lady's body, no longer having the need for it, and fearful that it will connect him to the murder of Peter Worthington. With this piece of evidence thus eliminated, he is completely above suspicion, because there is no evidence that a murder actually took place. Except, of course, in the unlikely event that someone should step forward and present the murdered body of Peter Worthington, assumed by the doctor to be quietly moldering in a lady's grave in All Soul's churchyard, until the afternoon *Gazette* makes the shocking revelation that the lady's grave has been violated, reportedly by medical students, no less. Well aware that whoever took the body knows that there is far more to this case that meets the eye, the doctor would likely go to great lengths to prevent these students from revealing their findings to the world. And these students just happening to be you and I, *mon ami*, we would do well to explore every other possible source of illumination before venturing into a direct confrontation."

"Isn't that what I just said?" I retorted, irritable at having to follow Jean-Claude's logical maneuvers on the chessboard and in the arena of verbal debate, both at the same time. "We don't dare confront Dr. Edmonds with our suspicions." With a nearly imperceptible elevation of his left eyebrow, Jean-Claude moved his knight. I searched the board, trying to decipher the logic behind this seemingly insignificant move, and a troubling thought entered my mind. "I say, Jean-Claude. What about the imposter—the man out at Darcy who claims to be Peter Worthington? If

Dr. Edmonds killed the real Peter Worthington, how did this fellow come into the game?"

"Ah, you have hit upon a central principle of science—the conflict between induction and deduction. Every solution to one problem breeds its own new set of problems to be solved. In our latest 'solution' to the problem of this crime, with Dr. Edmonds as the killer of Peter Worthington we neatly resolve the issue of the whereabouts of Mme. Darcy's body. It is in the possession of Dr. Edmonds. But at the same time we tie the loose threads on one side of the tapestry, we unravel some threads on the other side—namely, the connection between the faux Peter Worthington and the events surrounding the real Peter Worthington's death. Once again, we must resort to speculation in order discover a solution, hypothetical though that solution may be."

"And . . . ?" I said impatiently, blocking his knight with my bishop. "What is your 'hypothetical solution'?"

"Random chance, and opportunity. Consider, Dr. Edmonds kills Peter Worthington, and secures the body of Mme. Darcy. Perhaps he has the forethought to place the man's body in the now-vacant coffin, in order to avoid detection, or perhaps he carelessly flees the premises, leaving the body to lie where it fell. Now imagine a familiar of the house—a groundskeeper, perhaps—entering the parlor and happening upon the deceased Peter Worthington. This is random chance. But in thus happening upon the body, the familiar apprehends, in addition to a horrible crime, a quite convenient opportunity. Has he not been told many times how strong is the physical resemblance between himself and his late mistress's brother, now lying dead before him? What if he were to accentuate the similarity, with a trimming of the hair, a little wax on the mustache, and a proper suit of clothing, easily 'borrowed' from the dead man's chamber. There is but one living person on the estate—a housekeeper—who had known the brother well enough to notice the substitution, and with proper incentive, this housekeeper could possibly be persuaded to play a part in the deception. From this point on, everything remains as we initially suspected. The groundskeeper is transformed into Peter Worthington, the second, and the housekeeper is transformed into an entirely fictional character, the long-lost 'sister,' Mlle. Madeleine Worthington. As the sole living heirs of Alfred Darcy's widow, Peter II and Madeleine inherit the estate, and live happily ever after. Chance, and opportunity."

"That's quite a bit to prove, isn't it?" I said, suddenly realizing just how much of this theory was pure supposition. "You mentioned something about 'other sources of illumination.' Barring a direct confrontation with Dr. Edmonds, precisely what sources are you thinking of?"

"I am thinking," he said, scanning the board with an annoyingly casual eye, "that we would do well to pay a visit to the undertaker Mr. Simeon Rupp."

"Whatever for?" I huffed, waiting for him to make a move—*any* move.

"Ah, do you not see? With the exception of Peter Worthington himself, the two servants—the groundskeeper and the domestic—and now Dr. Edmonds, we know of only one other person who set foot inside the Darcy house after the lady's death."

"Simeon Rupp," I concurred.

"*Précisément.* And of what better person to make inquiry regarding a missing body than the person who prepared the body for burial, placed it inside the coffin, nailed the coffin shut, and transported it to the church. In short, a person who had access to the coffin on several separate occasions during the period of time in which the substitution of bodies occurred. It seems to me that there are many very interesting questions such a person might answer.

"For the moment, however," he added, standing up from the table and yawning broadly, "it is slumber and not illumination that my brain most requires. *Bon soir.*"

"But the game," I protested. "We're not finished."

"Ah, the game. Forgive me," he said, returning to the table and sliding his bishop across the board. "Checkmate."

CHAPTER 14

Following our nearly disastrous misadventure with the angry mob, Dr. Edmonds ordered a three-day hiatus in all activities at St. Alban's related to medical study, fearing a renewal of violence should our comings and goings happen to reawaken the public ire and precipitate a repeat of the previous day's performance. Jean-Claude and I gladly welcomed the brief vacation, being none too eager to face Dr. Edmonds anytime soon, and having several of Jean-Claude's "sources of illumination" to pursue. The first of these sources being Mr. Simeon Rupp, we made inquiries into the location of his shop and discovered it to be less than a mile from our apartment. Finding the weather mercifully mild after the bitter frost of the day before, we ate a bite of breakfast at Chowning's Tavern and took a leisurely stroll up the river toward St. Martin's parish.

Upon entering the street to which we had been

directed, we strongly suspected the innkeeper of having a good laugh at our expense, so utterly devoid of human life did the area appear. Had we stood in the weed-choked rat-infested heart of Rome during the Middle Ages, we could have had no stronger a sensation of absolute solitude than we felt here in this lost corner of London. Structures that appeared to have once housed apartments and places of business were literally falling in upon themselves, passively giving up the ghost to the relentless onslaught of nettles and vines. A chilly gust of wind kicked up an acrid black dust from the cobbles, and we were on the verge of fleeing down a long dark alley as an altogether-cheerier prospect, when I spotted a sign above the door of one of the neighborhood's few habitable structures. Shrugging off the sense of desolation that clung to our spirits, we ventured close enough to the building to read the sign and discover that the innkeeper had, in fact, steered us aright. SIMEON RUPP: BUILDER, ARCHITECT, UPHOLSTERER, UNDERTAKER, AND TOYMAKER the sign read, in brightly painted letters that cried out a woeful ignorance of the utter decrepitude of the street above which the sign hung.

"After you," Jean-Claude said, as we arrived at the front door, the smirk on his face indicating that he was no more eager than I to venture into the dimly lit shop on the other side. Not wishing to appear quite as reluctant to enter the shop as I actually felt, I lifted the latch with conviction and pushed the door open, setting into motion a little bell above the entrance whose piercing note announced our presence to the greater part of London. Hearing no response to our heralded entry, we suspected that the shop might be as deserted as the rest of the neighborhood and prepared, somewhat gratefully I must add, to leave the shop of Simeon Rupp for another day. As our eyes grew accustomed to the unseasonable twilight of the place, however, the shadows around us began to materialize into physical shapes, one of which was vaguely recognizable as a human being. Just at the moment when a face became decipherable, the spectral presence spoke, startling the both of us very nearly out of our skins. "Good morning, gentlemen," the voice oozed into an air already heavy with pine tar, lacquer, and another disquietingly unrecognizable scent. "And how may I be of assistance?" As he emerged from the shadows into the weak light filtering through the grimy front window, we could see that his appearance was a fitting match for his unctuous voice and manner, since oils of a variety of types clearly formed an essential part of his daily toilet. His hair clung to his head in a glossy raven black sheen, and the mustachios curling out beyond the corners of his mouth resembled human hair less than they did twin lamp wicks saturated with warm animal fat. I cast a rather desperate glance at Jean-Claude, imploring him to speak for the both of us, for I felt certain that simply opening my mouth under the circumstances would cause me to retch.

"Good day," he complied, although somewhat reluctantly, for he, too, appeared quite unsettled by the overpowering atmosphere that hung about the place. "We have come to make inquiry into the procedure for arranging a funeral."

"Oh, and who, may I be so bold, has cast off this mortal coil?" the man asked, with what I considered inappropriately excessive eagerness. "We offer such an extensive array of services that a thorough knowledge of the deceased individual's personal tastes—before he or she passed on, of course—is most helpful in arranging a fitting 'memorial.'" His perfumed words appeared to hang in the air before his face, and Jean-Claude clearly struggled to maintain control over his rebellious stomach.

"No one has died yet," he finally managed to say, producing a rather shocking display of mirth in our shopkeeper.

"I'm terribly sorry," he tittered into three gloved fingers held before his mouth. "It's just that so very many people have died, you know. They die every day."

"The person on whose behalf we are inquiring has not yet died," Jean-Claude clarified, his growing annoyance with the oily little man getting the upper hand over his fit of nausea. Would that I could get the upper hand over mine, I thought.

"Very well," the man replied, shutting off his laughter as instantly as one snuffs out a candle. "Who is the poor soul standing upon the doorstep of immortality?"

Jean-Claude silently pursed his lips for a moment, either out of mental concentration or an attempt to keep this morning's breakfast down. "It is my friend's dear mother," he finally said, to which unlooked-for revelation I reacted with rather obvious displeasure. A single withering glance, which said more clearly than words that I had already had, and willingly, forfeited, my chance to create the fiction under which we were to conduct our interview, forced me figuratively to step aside and leave him proceed. "The poor lady suffers greatly from dropsy, and will likely not survive the week." The man turned his attention to me, as if in invitation to join the deliberation, but misinterpreting my silence as a heart too full for words, he continued addressing Jean-Claude.

"You are very wise to initiate plans before the dreaded day arrives," he said, punctuating the stressed vowels with slight spasmic motions of his head. "Thus can the bereavement process be savored to its fullest extent." He ceased speaking for a moment, apparently deep in thought, then sighed, filling the air about our heads with his perfumed breath.

"Yes, well," Jean-Claude broke the fragrant, uneasy silence. "She cannot last much longer. And my friend wishes her to have a proper burial." I could see him groping about for a means of turning the discussion into a more productive channel.

"A proper and a *safe* burial," I offered, suppressing my queasiness in realization that the quickest way out of here was to simply play along. "I cannot endure the thought that the dear thing might wind up falling prey to nocturnal creatures such as the fiends who recently stole that lady's body from All Soul's churchyard. It's simply beyond comprehension that human beings in a Christian country should resort to such as that." Jean-Claude cast me a look of congratulations on my sudden ingenuity, which I gladly accepted, then continued the role with a veritable scowl of indignation.

"You are a wise man, my friend," the little man said, in a tone of growing excitement. "I tried to persuade the family to take advantage of the many precautions we have available to us now, but they consulted their purses rather than their hearts in the matter and paid a heavy price for their parsimony. Had they but heeded my advice, the poor lady's beautiful corpse would at this moment be quietly mingling with the earth and the mold of the churchyard rather than stretched out upon some anatomist's table for all the world to see. They should all be hanged, resurrectionists and medical men alike, such a grave threat are they to the sanctity of Christian death." He grew speechless with another unaccountable fit of silent mirth. "Do please forgive me," he pleaded from behind his fingers, "but I said the word 'grave,' you see. 'A grave threat,' I said. Completely unintentional, but quite fitting, don't you think?" And then just as suddenly, he lowered his hand, and his face resumed its former look of funerary earnestness.

"Indeed," Jean-Claude said, at a complete loss for words.

"Quite," I said shortly, and returned the conversation to the topic at hand, anxious to complete our interview and flee the strange little man's presence as quickly as possible. "An absolute outrage, that incident! To think that one should shuffle off this mortal coil, journeying onward to await the resurrection, only to return at the Judgment Day to find one's body—the temple of the soul—hanging on display in some school of anatomy." Jean-Claude looked on with outright admiration at my deft execution of the role for which he had cast me.

"I can see you are a man of deep spiritual sensibilities," our host responded. "Please let me extend my hand. I don't believe I have properly introduced myself. The name is Rupp. Simeon Rupp."

I took the proffered hand, which felt like glove all the way to the bone, so very soft and shapeless was it. "Paul Timson," I said, remembering the name of a childhood friend. "And this is my cousin William Jones." Jean-Claude shot me a barely perceptible scowl, clearly displeased with sheer "commonness" of the name I had selected for him. I stifled a satisfied smile and continued the discussion. "So pleased to meet you. When it became all too clear that this was to be Mother's final struggle with the illness that has plagued her lo these many years, I inquired about for someone with whom to make arrangements, and your name came up more than once."

"I am extremely honored to offer my services," he said with a sharp clicking of his heels and a slight bow.

"As might be expected, my primary object

initially was to find an establishment that would mark my mother's passage from this world with grace and dignity. But then, the shocking desecration of that poor woman's grave occurred and, well . . . I suddenly realized there were other 'considerations' in the matter, perhaps of even more immediate import."

"In addition to your profound spirituality, sir, you are also clearly a man of great wisdom," he replied. "For there are indeed many 'considerations,' as you say, that one must make when committing a loved one to the earth, if one wishes the loved one to remain there. At the risk of offending your delicate sensibilities, I must tell you that, as shocking as was the theft of Abigail Darcy's body from the graveyard, the theft was by no means an isolated occurrence." I opened my mouth and lifted my eyebrows, assuming a horrified expression. "Oh, no," he continued. "Would that it were an aberration. Call it rather, the rule, than the exception. Why, every night, in churchyards throughout London—throughout all of England—bodies are rudely and ignominiously 'snatched' from their graves and sold to anatomy schools, where they are subjected to unimaginable acts of desecration."

"Oh, is there nothing that can be done?" I pleaded, stifling a sob. "To think that poor Mother, in her final rest, should be subjected to . . . Oh!" I feigned utter speechlessness.

"There, there, sir," he comforted, patting me on the arm with his cotton hand. "I fully sympathize with your indignation." He held my eyes with his rheumy gaze for a moment of uncomfortable, earnest silence. Then, his face suddenly brightened. "That is why I am pleased to reassure you that there is very much that can be done to maintain the sanctity and security of your dear departed."

"Oh, do please tell," I said, with a look of the greatest relief spreading across my face.

"Well, to look to the coffin itself, we offer models that are completely enclosed in a cast-iron 'brace,' holding the lid in place far more securely than the customary handful of fourpenny nails. Of course, even iron straps cannot hold off a determined body snatcher with a crowbar, provided that man has great strength and sufficient time. And while there is nothing we can do to rob the man of his strength, we can take away some of his time. Encasing the primary coffin within a second, and perhaps even a third coffin, will keep the fiend occupied until the sun comes up, and he must flee the graveyard empty-handed."

"Amazing," I said, my show of surprise but half-feigned.

"But, alas, even with three coffins, one cannot be completely assured of the sanctity and security of the grave. That is why we offer yet another safeguard—somewhat costly, yes, but completely impervious to even the most determined body snatcher. We call it the 'mortsafe.' It is an iron cage secured deeply into the ground around the entire grave, keeping out anyone who might attempt to disturb its contents, until such time—from a week to a fortnight—as the body is no longer 'suitable' for medical study. Then the safe is removed, and the loved one is left to rest in peace, while the grass grows overhead." Jean-Claude and I remained silent for a moment, awaiting an "amen" or some other such benedictory remark, but it quickly became clear the man had said his piece, and was awaiting our—hopefully lucrative—response. Not wishing to commit myself just now regarding plans for my mother's burial—considering she was in the very flush of good health, and most likely at that very moment potting tulip bulbs in her greenhouse in Kent—I decided to veer the discussion away from Mother and back to Abigail Darcy, the reason for our being here in the first place.

"Am I to understand that the Darcy woman's family did not avail themselves of all of these safeguards?" I asked, incredulously. Rupp cast me a sideways glance, clearly reluctant for the discussion to drift into matters that had no immediate pecuniary significance, but then his face assumed an expression of pinched indignation—as if in recollection of a recent bitterness—and he relented.

"*All* of these safeguards?" he said, his perfumed speech now laced with acid. "That man availed himself of *none* of my safeguards."

"That man?" asked Jean-Claude.

"Yes. The lady's brother, Peter Worthington." He huffed as if to remove the taste of the name from his mouth. "That man purchased a simple elm coffin, and let his sister lie there in the churchyard free for the taking. To be sure, he saved a few pounds in immediate expenses, but he paid for those pounds. Oh yes, he paid dearly. His *dear* sister, tossed so carelessly into a few feet of loose soil, suffers a fate reserved by law for only the most desperate of criminals. She is sold to an anatomy school, to be paraded around before the lecherous eyes of a dozen or more 'medical' men. And beyond this initial display of the poor woman's body, the mind quite literally reels at the prospects for her further degradation." He remained silent for a moment, while his mind "reeled," I suppose, then continued.

"But his sister was not the only one to suffer, no. She, at least, was insensible of the indignities to which her body was subjected. But those she left behind are not thus blessed with insensibility. The body is stolen, yes—a not-uncommon fate, but at this theft, there is a witness present to broadcast the crime to the world. Now all of London knows what a miser that Peter Worthington is. And it's his dead sister's money he's holding on to, for he never made any of it. I don't wonder that he refuses to go out in public now. He hasn't been seen since that *Gazette* piece, you know."

"I had not heard," Jean-Claude interjected.

"Oh yes, it's true. And it's not one bit more ignominy than he deserves, I assure you."

"And was Mr. Worthington aware of the many security measures available for the protection of . . . the departed?" Jean-Claude asked, attempting to keep Simeon Rupp on a subject that promised to prove fruitful. "Did you tell him all the things you told us just now?"

"Did I tell him?" Rupp snarled, with growing indignation. "What didn't I tell him? Here's a fellow whose lovely, young sister has just died. 'Do you know what happens in graveyards, nowadays?' I asked. 'Why, nobody's safe,' I said. 'And a beautiful girl like your sister,' I say. 'You couldn't live with yourself if one of those fiends gets to her before the worms do.'" Jean-Claude and I exchanged a quick glance of surprise at the figure of speech, but he appeared not to notice. "But did he heed my advice? Did he take measures—any measures—to protect her? No! Peter Worthington saved his money, but he lost his sister *and* his reputation. And now he must live with the consequences."

"That is only just!" I agreed heartily, once again trying to keep him from drifting away from the subject at hand. "A man who would be so very careless of his sister's well-being . . . well, there is no punishment too great for such callousness. But there is one thing I don't understand. If Mr. Worthington did not purchase any of your services, how was the lady buried?"

"At minimal expense, I assure you," he snapped. "I arrived at the house shortly after the lady's death, as is my regular practice, to place myself at the family's disposal. The housekeeper greeted me at the door and led me to the room where the lady lay—so very beautiful, and so young. I began to take her measurements—for the coffin, you know—when Peter Worthington stormed into the room and demanded to know what the devil I was doing there. I nearly fainted across the woman's body, so greatly did he startle me. I composed myself and explained who I was, thinking that once he knew, we could have a civil discussion about arrangements for the funeral and burial. But do you know he nearly threw me bodily out of the house! I have never been so rudely dealt with."

"So who buried her, if you didn't?" I asked.

"Oh, I buried her. After shouting at me for a few moments, he stormed out of the room and disappeared into some other part of the house. Once he was out of the way, the housekeeper reentered the room, apologizing for his behavior, and asking could I please return to the house the following day with a coffin and a hearse to carry the lady to the church. 'What about the flowers and draperies?' I asked her. 'What about the horses and the mourning carriages? What about the mourners, and the food and drink to serve them all?' In short, what about a proper funeral?"

"What did she say, this housekeeper?" Jean-Claude asked.

"Well, she looked at the floor, and sighed. Poor thing, she knew how inexcusable her master's behavior was, but what could she do? Once more, she asked about the coffin and transportation to the church."

"And you returned to the house the next day, yes?" A slight furrow on Jean-Claude's forehead betrayed the cogitations going on behind it.

"Oh yes, I returned. And with an elm coffin, the cheapest money can buy. Worthington had made his wishes all too clear. 'Get her under the ground with as little expenditure and personal inconvenience as possible,' was his wish. And I complied. I didn't even charge for preparing the body for burial—another of my customary duties— for when I arrived with the coffin, I found the lady already cleaned and dressed in some sort of silk nightgown—an unusual shroud indeed. It was the housekeeper who had thus 'prepared' her. All that was left for me to do was bring the coffin into the house, and, along with the house-keeper, to arrange the body inside it, for viewing. Of course, for all the people Worthington let into the house to view her, the lady might just as well have been naked." He paused here for an uncom-fortably long moment, until Jean-Claude inter-rupted his reverie.

"And you carried her in a hearse to the church, yes?"

"The following morning. Once again, I found very little to do. The coffin had already been nailed shut, if you can believe it." We glanced at each other, finding it all too easy to believe it. "I drove the hearse myself, while two mutes on horseback— whom I provided free of charge, simply for propri-ety's sake—rode alongside. The lady's two servants followed the 'procession' in a simple carriage."

"What about Worthington?" I asked.

"Oh, his lordship had some 'business' in town, and slipped into the church just before the ser-vice got under way. Simply disgraceful." Rupp shook his head with pronounced disapproval, clearly reliving the inappropriately unceremoni-ous ceremony in his mind.

"Did you get an opportunity to speak with him at the funeral," I pursued. "To settle the account?"

"His man brought 'round the money a bit later," he replied shortly, as if suddenly remembering that he was, in fact, standing here in his shop, and not in the All Souls churchyard. "But that is all in the past." Just as quickly as it had fled, his unctuous manner returned, only now with the added moisture of a few droplets of perspiration glistening from his pale forehead. "Please do forgive me for drifting off like that, about other business. It was your dear mother of whom we were speaking. Making the arrangements to help her die a good death, as she no doubt lived a good life."

This sudden return to the topic of my mother's death caught me off guard, and my face clearly showed it, for Jean-Claude quickly intervened. "You can see how it is with my friend. He forgets the painful truth for moments at a time, then suddenly it all comes rushing back to him. That is how I was when my dear mother passed, some months ago."

"So sorry to hear it," he said regretfully. "And you have only just completed your mourning, I imagine." He passed a critical eye over Jean-Claude's gray suit.

"Only just," he replied, and quickly moved on. "But look how distraught my friend has become, talking about a subject that pains him so. I am afraid we shall have to postpone the arrangements until he has had time to compose himself."

"It is not wise to put these things off," Rupp cautioned, raising a gloved index finger. "Death could be waiting right outside that door . . ." Jean-Claude and I both caught ourselves stealing an involuntary glance in that direction, just to see. ". . . even for those of us in the very prime of life. But for those who find themselves under an imminent sentence of death, it is most important to be fully prepared. All part of dying a good death, you know," he repeated his earlier sentiment.

"We shall return, later this afternoon perhaps," Jean-Claude said, hurrying me toward the door. ". . . after he has had some brandy and takes a bit of rest."

"Well if you must." He sighed. "Good day, gentlemen."

CHAPTER 15

As bleak as Dinmont Street was, at that or any other time of day, it was a veritable breath of fresh air after our visit to the establishment of Simeon Rupp. Nonetheless, it was not a place we wished to remain a moment longer than absolutely necessary, so we immediately set our feet upon a course that would take us somewhere—anywhere, else. We hastened past the deserted shops and houses, and ducked down three blind alleys before finally finding one that actually led somewhere, and not a moment too soon, found ourselves once again in the grimy, noisy, and wonderfully crowded streets of Southwark. "Could I interest you in a coffin?" Jean-Claude asked, in a perfect imitation of Rupp. "Or perhaps a coffin or two in which to place your coffin?"

We enjoyed a good laugh for a few moments, then I grew half-serious and reproached him. "I say, Jean-Claude. It's really not good form to speak

of Mother that way. One can't help being somewhat superstitious about such things. I should
never forgive myself—or you—if anything should
happen to her."

"Come, my friend. You are a scientist and know
full well there is no substance in such beliefs.
They are the mere fancy of the foolish. And you
noticed, I hope," he added, "that I did not neglect
to include my own mother in the fiction."

"But your mother really is dead," I protested.
"When you were about ten years old, wasn't it?"

"*Précisément*," he responded, with irritating certainty. "The woman to whom I referred was a
pure fiction, created strictly for the occasion. It is
the objective detachment of the true scientist."

"Oh, really, Jean-Claude. *Must* you be so
damned scientific all the time?"

"But of course." He stopped in his tracks and
stared at me as if I had just asked him why he
didn't suddenly sprout wings and fly.

I simply ignored him and continued walking.
He soon fell in step once again. "One part of that
fiction," I said a moment later, "that I could very
easily tolerate in reality right now, was the part
about the brandy. I can't seem to get the scent of
that place out of my head."

"It was rather overpowering, was it not?" he
agreed. "One could not determine whether Rupp
carried the smell of his establishment, or vice
versa. But yes, it was quite unpleasant."

We spotted a sign in the street ahead announcing the Wandering Shepherd Tavern, and wasted

no time in making our way to the entrance. Once inside, we immediately saw that the place was in an advanced state of decrepitude. It served brandy, however, so the general décor faded into oblivion amidst the welcome rush of liqueur fumes into my nostrils, crowding out other less pleasant, less readily identifiable odors. After the first glass, I felt my equilibrium somewhat restored, and after the second, with the further assistance of a rather strong cigar, I was my old self once again.

"This Peter Worthington was certainly not one to stir fond feelings in the people with whom he came into contact," I reflected, absently watching the smoke from my cigar climb the updraft from the lamp on our table. "I suppose that's another way he resembles his double."

"Rather disagreeable people, the both of them," he agreed. "But of course one must consider the unusual circumstances surrounding each of the encounters of which we have heard, and the one we experienced ourselves."

"You're not defending the man, are you Jean-Claude?" I said incredulously. "Perhaps it's slipped your mind, but there's a very good chance that at least one of these 'gentlemen' is a cold-blooded murderer."

"I have forgotten nothing," he said matter-of-factly. "Two people are dead, one of whom was most definitely murdered and one of whom is suspected of having been murdered. In both of these deaths, one or the other Peter Worthington was in some way involved. But whether causally or no . . . this remains to be seen." He paused to take a pensive draw from his cigar. "This is what we must determine as the outcome of our search."

"Well, whether he killed his sister or no, the real Peter Worthington—Peter the first—certainly displayed a criminal disregard for her well-being after she died, and to offend everyone he met in the bargain. Based upon the experiences of both Dr. Edmonds and Mr. Rupp, one wouldn't be very much surprised to find that he simply tossed her onto the rubbish heap outside the kitchen door, if he thought it would save him a pound or two."

"I believe we would be very much mistaken," Jean-Claude reflected, "to accept Rupp's interpretation of the callous disregard Peter Worthington showed toward his sister's body. He purchased but a few of the 'amenities' offered by Rupp's establishment, it is true, but it is my feeling that something besides parsimony lay behind his strange behavior."

"Whatever caused him to behave that way, it clearly deprived Simeon Rupp of a sizeable amount of money. Did you see that look in his eyes when he told us about the 'elm coffin'?" I puffed my cigar, recalling the disturbing image to my mind's eye. "As meek as the little man appeared, at that moment one could easily have imagined him being capable of just about anything."

"Perhaps even murder?" Jean-Claude asked, raising an eyebrow in an expression of either skepticism or interest, it was difficult to say.

I considered the question for a moment, not

wishing to answer precipitately and thus expose myself to Jean-Claude's sarcasm, should that eyebrow prove cynical rather than sincere, but upon reflection I felt my intuition to be justified. "Yes, perhaps even murder, given the right opportunity, of course. And he certainly had access to the house, and to the people inside it." As I spoke, I grew ever more certain of the man's capacity for violence. "Think about it. Here's a man who spends most of his waking hours among the dead. Why, death is his very livelihood."

"When he is not making toys or upholstering furniture, of course," Jean-Claude interrupted, with an amused smirk that I completely ignored.

"So very familiar is the man with death and dying," I continued, "that he would almost necessarily come to regard life a bit more casually than other people do. And with so very many dead people in his daily experience, what does it matter if one of those people happened not to be dead until *after* the initial encounter, especially when that encounter proved to be as nettlesome as Rupp's meeting with Worthington."

"I hope you realize," Jean-Claude said smugly, "that you have just perfectly described the profession that you and I are preparing to enter. For does not anatomical study require subjects that can only be procured from among the dead? And does not much of the practicing physician's work involve close contact with the dying? I suppose, by your own logic, you would expect the two of us to become murderers, should we continue our pursuit of the medical profession?"

"No, I don't expect either you or me to become a murderer," I retorted defensively, but then found a welcome hole in Jean-Claude's "logic." "But I can't speak for *all* people in our profession. Dr. Edmonds, for example . . ."

"Ah, touché," he said approvingly. "Clearly some physicians are capable of harming as well as healing their fellow human beings. But I do not think this capacity for violence is a result of familiarity with the world of the dead, but rather of an excessive connection with the world of the living. *Regarde*, Dr. Edmonds journeys to Darcy House and finds Mme. Abigail dead. Compelled to determine what, or rather who, is responsible for her death, he demands that a close professional examination be made of the body. This demand being refused, by the very man whom the doctor suspects of having killed the lady, he commits himself to seeking justice for the lady's memory, even if it requires taking this man's life. It is thus out of extreme regard for the lady's living memory, rather than out of disregard for the man's life, that he kills. Assuming, of course, he is the killer." I opened my mouth to respond, but he held up his hand in a gesture that clearly indicated he had not yet exhausted the line of thought he was pursuing.

"And to consider the 'dealer in death,' Simeon Rupp. Were he as preoccupied with the world of the dead as you suggest he is, he would not feel so very deeply a monetary slight, such as that dealt him by Peter Worthington. For all his many 'eccentricities,' shall we call them, Monsieur Rupp is at heart a man of business. If it turns out that he was, in fact, capable of doing bodily harm to Worthington, it was a capacity born out of a regard for life rather than a disregard of it. Seeking to punish the man for the financial harm he perceives himself to have suffered, he robs Worthington of his single most valuable possession—life. So it is an appreciation of the value of life, rather than a disregard for it, that Rupp exhibited in his act of murder. Assuming, once again, that he is the killer."

"I don't know," I said, trying to digest Jean-Claude's "economic" theory of life and death. Finally, I settled for indigestion, and moved on to an aspect of Simeon Rupp that concerned me even more than his potential capacity for violence. "Whether Rupp places a higher value on life or death, in the abstract sense, he certainly seemed rather inappropriately preoccupied with the dead body of Abigail Darcy."

"Ah, you noticed that, as well," Jean-Claude replied, pursing his lips significantly.

"One would have to have been blind not to," I said. "Did you see that expression on his face when he described her 'youth and beauty'? And that talk of her being 'buried naked.' It was all very disturbing, is all I can say."

"Most disturbing, indeed," he agreed. "But probably not as uncommon as you and I would like to believe, especially among people in Rupp's 'profession.' In this matter, your speculations on the effect of a prolonged familiarity with death and dying may not be far amiss. Instead of resulting in a casual disregard for life, however, the result could be a less than casual regard for death—or more accurately, for the dead. You noticed, did you not, how very agitated Rupp became when describing how the body had already been prepared for burial before his arrival at the house with the coffin? In thus finding a portion of his 'work' taken away from him, he was deprived, not only of a fee, but also of access to the 'beautiful and young' lady's corpse. If we correctly interpret the man's strange behavior, he would have every bit as much reason as Dr. Edmonds to return to the house and steal the body."

"Even if he had to kill someone to get to it," I concluded.

"Précisément."

I sighed deeply and drained the contents of my glass, now trying as hard to get rid of the images lingering in my mind as I was of the odors lingering in my nostrils. "For all the troubling questions our visit to Rupp raised," I said, willfully changing the topic of conversation, "his story lays to rest at least one bit of speculation. The imposter—Peter the second—couldn't have been that groundskeeper, as you've suggested all along."

"And why not?" he asked indignantly.

"Weren't you listening when he described the funeral 'procession,' if one can call it that. It was Rupp, two mutes, and the two servants, one of whom was the groundskeeper. Had the man assumed the identity of Peter Worthington, he couldn't very well have been traveling to the funeral as himself, could he? A man can't be in two places at the same time."

"And perhaps *you* were not listening when Rupp described the funeral procession," he countered. "Worthington did not travel in the procession."

"He was already at the church," I said, somewhat irritably. "Yes, I heard."

"Ah, you listened, but perhaps you did not hear. He did not say that Worthington was already at the church. He said Worthington came in just as the service was beginning. There is a small gap in the narrative—a space of time in which the groundskeeper could, with assistance, slip out of the carriage and make necessary preparations to assume the identity of Peter Worthington. He enters the church, just as the service is beginning, and, *voilà*! The transformation is complete."

I tried to imagine all of the slipping in and slipping out, and the hasty changes of clothing, that this theory would necessarily involve. "I don't know, Jean-Claude. That's an awful lot of trouble to go to."

"Ah, but think of the reward. For a few hours of maneuvering in and out of a very small gathering—making certain to be seen in public, but not by too many, and not from too close a distance—a lifetime of comfort and leisure. In short, the entire Darcy fortune. Sir Alfred dying without heirs, his estate passes to the widow. The widow dies, and the estate now passes to the nearest male relative, Peter Worthington. With

Monsieur Peter out of the way, the estate passes into the voracious maw of the court, never to be heard from again. Unless . . ."

"Unless," I concluded, "someone who bears a very close physical resemblance to Peter steps in to assume his role, I know, I know. And still, it all seems rather far-fetched."

"There is one image I wish to be etched into your memory," Jean-Claude said gravely, all irony now absent from his voice. "It is a dead man with a puncture wound at the base of his brain. In the wake of such a violent and desperate act, nothing can appear 'far-fetched.' In matters of life and death, ordinary rules of human behavior are thrown out the window. The one thing we can count on absolutely is that there is absolutely nothing that can be discounted."

I mused quietly for a moment, trying to parse Jean-Claude's conclusion, but our visit with Simeon Rupp—the memory of which lingered more like a persistent odor than a series of mental images—together with the brandy I had consumed, made my head ache far too sorely to attempt such a feat of logical dexterity. "So, what's our next 'move'?" I asked, abandoning the effort as not worth the cost.

"It seems to me we are desperately overdue for our promised return visit to Darcy Estate," he replied with mock earnestness. "According to Jimmy, Mlle. 'Madeline' Worthington arrived two days ago, and we have yet to pay our respects. I would also very much like to have a word or two with the master of the house."

"So, when do we leave?" I asked, with no attempt to hide the resignation in my voice. "Tomorrow morning?"

"The day is young yet, my friend," he replied with exasperating eagerness. "If we catch the next coach in time, we will be there by two o'clock."

"For some reason I thought that's what you were going to say," I moaned.

"You see, in my company your powers of deduction increase by the hour."

CHAPTER 16

The coach ride out to Darcy refreshed me very nearly to the point where I was able to think clearly once again. The early morning's promise of fair weather had blossomed into a beautiful afternoon, and it was with great effort that I reminded myself that we were out and about for the purpose of investigating a murder rather than to enjoy the temporary hiatus of the winter's gloom. My indolent mind was in the very act of drifting off to Margate, to relive an enjoyable afternoon I spent there some five years earlier, when an all-too-familiar voice shattered my reverie and dragged me back to London.

"And do you remember your role?" Jean-Claude asked.

"We're bloody body catchers, searching the countryside for stray corpses," I growled, as the sound of seagulls receded into the far corners of my mind.

"In a manner of speaking, yes," he agreed, either ignoring, or miraculously insensible of the acid in my voice. "I am Christophe Dubres, and you are James Hodge."

"Hodge?" I grumbled. "Where did you find that name?"

"Would you prefer 'Hogg'?" he replied curtly. "That was next on my alphabetical list."

"Hodge will have to do, then, I suppose." I stretched my arms out to my sides, and inhaled a deep draught of air, trying to complete the repairs on my senses that the nice weather had already begun. "And what do you expect of this housekeeper—Madeline? What kind of woman do you think she is?"

"Having been the servant for a gentlemen for some time," he speculated, "she will know the conventions, but as if by secondhand. Her manners will thus be but half-formed. We can likely expect civility, but without grace. Having so little intercourse with London society, however, this thin veneer of gentility would very likely be sufficient to maintain the illusion before the world indefinitely." He paused, and his face took on a sharp look of determination. "It would be sufficient, that is, were it not for the deductive powers of two very clever gentlemen of my acquaintance. These gentlemen shall unmask these poseurs and force a killer out into the harsh, unrelenting light of day." He ceased speaking, and stared off dramatically toward the horizon, for the world as if he expected applause, or at the very least a rousing "hear, hear." What he received instead was a deep basso belch that had been paining me ever since our journey began.

"So what are we supposed to say about the status of our investigation into the theft of their 'sister's' body," I asked, feeling considerably better. "I shouldn't imagine they'd care very much, seeing as how neither of them is actually related to the woman. They'd probably be just as content if she were to never turn up."

"It is true that they have little reason to care about the location of Mme. Darcy's body," he said. "But if our theory is correct, they have very much reason to care about the location of the body that was actually stolen from Mme. Darcy's coffin—in the graveyard that night. If that body—the body of Peter Worthington—turns up, the man now posing as Peter Worthington, and anyone who may be in his immediate company, will be required to answer some very difficult questions."

"And of course it is we who have the distinct privilege of asking these difficult questions," I said, anticipating the unpleasant scene that inevitably awaited us at Darcy House.

"In time, perhaps," Jean-Claude said, narrowing his eyes and looking up the road in the direction of Darcy, not yet visible. "But we must not get ahead of ourselves. Today, we are simply stopping by to report upon the progress of our search for Mrs. Darcy's body."

"Oh? And precisely what 'progress' are we to report, without getting ahead of ourselves, as you say?

"We can report to them," he answered smugly,

already beginning to assume his role as detective Christophe Dubres, ". . . a number of very promising, and very vague, possibilities. Primarily, we will emphasize the many locations we have so far been able to eliminate from consideration. In thus speaking much, without saying much of anything at all, we will 'draw out' our hosts, who, eager to conclude the interview and simply be rid of us, will speak carelessly, and perhaps say something that can be of use to us in achieving the actual object of our search."

"That ought to be easy for one of us, at least," I said, then clarified, ". . . the saying much without saying anything, I mean." So rapidly was Jean-Claude rushing forward into becoming "Christophe Dubres," however, that my barb fell far short of its target. Not wishing to waste my breath further, I chose to remain silent for remainder of the journey, which passed very quickly as I became absorbed in mental preparations for assuming my own role—the distinguished James Hodge. After a few minutes passed thus in reflective silence, we arrived at the Rose and Crown Inn, and began our ten-minute walk to Darcy.

CHAPTER 17

As we crunched our way up the gravel walk
to the front of the house, I looked about me at
the now-familiar scene—the lawn, the trees, the
house—so benign at our first encounter, but
grown sinister by all we had learned in the inter-
vening three days. At the very best, the two people
behind that dignified gray façade were playing a
complicit role in hiding the occurrence of a murder, and thus harboring a murderer. Just as likely,
however, one or even both of the occupants of the
house had actually taken part in a murder. With
these troubling thoughts rattling around in my
brain, the walkway gave out surprisingly soon,
and we found ourselves standing once again at the
formidable black door of Darcy House. Announcing our presence with the brass dragon's head, we
awaited the "master's" arrival, I with sweaty palms
and the hairs standing on the back of my neck,
and Jean-Claude with a mask of authoritative

assurance that betrayed no self-doubt whatsoever, assuming there was, in fact, any self-doubt there to be betrayed—an altogether-unlikely assumption, I told myself, given the man who was wearing the mask.

When the door opened, and we once again faced "Peter Worthington," the physical similarity between the man standing before us and the body lying under a few feet of soil in the "compost heap" back at St. Alban's took us both aback somewhat once again, but we managed to conceal our discomfiture more successfully on this occasion than on our initial encounter, partly because of the preparedness of expectation—we had, of course, seen the man before—but even more so because of a change in our host's manner. Gone was the irritable impatience that marked our first visit with the man, and in its place were a casual charm and a complete readiness to provide whatever assistance lay within his power.

"Good day, gentlemen," he greeted us warmly. "I've been expecting you. Won't you come in?" We followed him into the front hall, whose dark walls were lined with delicate Japanese watercolor paintings of restful rural scenes and contemplative domestic gardens. "You must be thirsty from your ride out—where did you say it was?"

"Southwark," I started to say, but Jean-Claude interrupted before I could so much as get out the first consonant. "Brixton," he said.

"We were preparing tea, so you're just in time to join us." Jean-Claude and I both hung upon the word "us," but feigned disinterest. As we followed our host down the hall, he announced over his shoulder, "There's someone here I'd very much like for you to meet. My sister Madeline has just arrived from the Continent." Pausing at the open parlor door, he extended his hand in a gesture of invitation, and we entered the room. "Maddy," he said, ". . . here are the gentlemen I was telling you about. Gentlemen, please allow me to present my sister, Madeline." From a large chair turned away from the door, and facing the garden window, a hand reached out and placed a book upon a small end table, and the owner of the hand slowly stood up and turned around to face us. For a moment, I found myself utterly bereft of the power of speech as I beheld the single most stunning creature I had ever to that day, and quite frankly have ever to this day, laid eyes on. Of medium height and delicate build, her physical dimensions were in no way notable. Animating this slight physical frame, however, was an almost electrical aura of presence that made her by far the most noticeable feature of the entire room.

"It is a pleasure to meet you, mademoiselle," Jean-Claude said, clearly not as overwhelmed as I by the woman's beauty.

"The pleasure is all mine," she said, strolling lightly across the carpet and extending her delicate white hand.

And then she turned her gaze full upon me— deep, dark eyes that seemed to sparkle fire from their black depths. Thank heaven for English manners, because it was only a lifetime of familiarity with the conventions of civil comportment that prevented me from stammering like a fool. I have no recollection whatsoever of the words that actually emanated from my mouth, but they must have been of sufficient good sense not to arouse notice, for the next thing I knew we were all being seated in plush chairs while Madeline served up four cups of tea.

"Peter told me of your prior visit," Madeline said in a musical, bell-like voice. "We both so appreciate your efforts to locate my dear sister. It's all been an enormous shock, as you might imagine. First poor Abby's death, and then . . ." At this last remark, tears filled the lady's eyes, and she could no longer continue.

"We realize it's all been very traumatic for you," I said, rescuing her from this rush of emotions. "And we shan't rest until we discover who is responsible for such an outrage."

While I was talking, I could sense Jean-Claude's gaze upon me, and the distinctive clearing of the throat that accompanied it confirmed my suspicion that it was not an approving gaze. "It is a most unpleasant business all the way around," he said, in a voice utterly devoid of the sympathetic tone one would expect as due course under the circumstances. "You were very close to your sister, yes?"

"You haven't the faintest idea," she responded, gently dabbing the corners of her eyes with a handkerchief. "For you see, we were more than just sisters. We were identical twins, and throughout our entire lives had the abiding impression

that we were in actuality but one soul divided between two physical bodies. It was this bond, in
fact, that brought me back to Darcy."

"How do you mean, mademoiselle?" Jean-
Claude asked dispassionately.

"Don't you find it just the least bit odd that I
managed to arrive here from France within days
after Abby's death?" she said, with the slightest
hint of amusement underlying her tears. "Why, I
imagine the messenger Peter sent to inform me
has not made it as far as Calais, and yet here I
sit."

"Yes, here you sit," Jean-Claude responded.
"How very strange." I glared at him, resolving to
speak next, in order to forestall any further show
of insensitivity on his part.

"Nearly three weeks ago," Madeline continued,
"Abby appeared to me in a dream. She smiled at
me sadly, saying she had come to bid me farewell.
'We shall be reunited in eternity,' she said, 'but
never more shall meet on this side of the grave.' I
put my affairs in order, and left for England the
very next morning."

"So you had a presentiment of her death," I said,
cutting off the remark that doubtless hung upon
Jean-Claude's lips. "I have heard of such things."

"Oh, I know it must appear foolish to you gentlemen," she explained. "The rational mind has a
difficult time comprehending such 'irrational'
phenomena. But there are more things in heaven
and earth, as the saying goes—things that the rational mind simply cannot comprehend. It was
just such a bond that Abby and I shared.

"Are you gentlemen familiar with the writings of Emanuel Swedenborg?" she asked. We answered in the affirmative, and she continued. "He believed very strongly in such 'things,' and was visited on a number of occasions by beings from the spiritual realm—angels, demons, and souls departed from this life. In addition to showing him visions of both heaven and hell, these spirits also frequently informed him of matters here in the sublunary realm of earth. One evening, for instance, he was struck by the profound conviction that his house, three hundred miles away, was on fire. When he returned home, sometime later, he found the place burned to cinders. And that is but one example among many."

I could hear Jean-Claude shifting about uncomfortably in his chair and decided I must once again speak before he had a chance to. "So you believe your sister's spirit appeared to you to warn you of her imminent death."

"I don't 'believe,'" she replied with conviction. "I know. Abby and I routinely paid spiritual visits to one another, sometimes from room to room, when we lived in the same house, and sometimes, in later years, from one continent to another. But it was not at all an unusual occurrence. So very familiar were we both with such visitations, that when she appeared to me three weeks ago, I knew beyond the shadow of a doubt that I would never again see her alive." She paused, and sighed sadly. "I had no warning of the horrible fate that awaited her body after death, however. Of that, her spirit left me in the dark, perhaps because she herself had no knowledge of purely physical matters, in which spirit played no part."

"Ah, most unfortunate," Jean-Claude said dismissively, and then turned his attention to our host. "And as for you, Monsieur Worthington, are you a believer in such contact between two worlds—the spiritual world and the physical?" I cast an apologetic glance toward Madeline and shrugged my shoulders to indicate that Jean-Claude's opinions were his and his alone. She sent me a slight, though enormously welcome, smile in return, while Jean-Claude continued his logical dissection of Madeline's philosophy. "In my experience, every phenomenon—even the seemingly most inexplicable—has an entirely rational explanation."

"Temperamentally," "Peter" said reflectively, "I'm inclined to agree with you, for I, too, am a rationalist at heart. But having said that, I must also confess to having seen things over the years that completely defy rational explanation. Some of these occurrences have been laughably trivial, such as Abby finding Madeline's lost cameo locket, simply by having a dream that it was hanging on a pear-tree branch in the garden. Other occurrences have been of greater import—Maddy waking up with a piercing pain in her breast the very night that our poor father died in his sleep of a heart attack, for example. Any such incident alone could easily be written off as mere coincidence, but a lifetime of such phenomena is hard to ignore."

While Peter was speaking, Jean-Claude's mouth

drew up into an increasingly tight knot, and his eyes blinked with noticeable rapidity. When Peter concluded, Jean-Claude likewise remained silent, his "rational" mind groping about in the dark for something sturdy upon which to hold. With the silence growing unbearably oppressive to three out of the four of us, I interceded, attempting to divert the discussion onto a less controversial subject

"We believe we are making genuine progress in our search for . . ." I paused, looking for wording that would not offend Madeline, and finally gave up. ". . . in our search," I concluded. "And while we cannot claim to have brought the matter to a successful close, we have been able to eliminate a number of possible avenues as unproductive." I shifted about uncomfortably in my own seat, as I realized I was unwittingly doing just what Jean-Claude had planned—speaking a great deal without saying anything at all. Mercifully, our hosts seemed not to notice my oratorical meanderings, being preoccupied with sending significant glances back and forth in apparent prelude to an announcement that they had clearly planned beforehand.

"Maddy and I have given this matter a great deal of consideration over the past couple of days," Peter began, slowly and deliberately. "It is our belief, based both upon practical, rational consideration, and upon Maddy's own spiritual 'insight,' that it would be best for all concerned if we simply discontinue the search for poor Abby's remains."

Jean-Claude inhaled audibly, clearly preparing to protest, but Peter silenced him with an upraised hand. "Practically—rationally—one must consider the likely condition of the body. 'Distasteful' does not even touch the feelings that would be evoked by such an encounter, and quite frankly, we would both prefer to remember Abby as she was in life. To find her now," he continued pensively, letting his gaze drift down toward the floor, "after what she's no doubt been through at the hands of a student or students of surgery . . . well, it just seems that perhaps we should all simply let nature take its course, from this point on."

Then, suddenly lifting his eyes from the floor and looking directly into Jean-Claude's face, he said, with some heat, "And to tell you the truth, I believe this is what Abby herself would want, could she express her wishes. If you had been granted the privilege of knowing her in life, Mr. Dubres, you would have been struck, as was virtually everyone who met her, by her extreme intellectual enlightenment. That is what most captivated her late husband, Alfred. It wasn't mere physical charm that persuaded a seventy-five-year-old man to abandon a lifetime of confirmed bachelorhood and embrace the 'yoke' of marriage. And goodness knows, it wasn't charm that drew Abby to him. They were 'intellectual soul mates,' as she herself described their unique relationship, and their time together was probably the most intellectually stimulating of each of their lives. One intellectual 'hobby' the two of them were particularly fond of was the study of science.

In addition to his unrivaled knowledge of history and the arts, Alfred was quite a distinguished amateur scientist. He was many times recommended for membership in the Royal Society, but actively discouraged the nomination, fearing it would shift his mental energies away from his historical researches.

"Through his guidance," Peter continued, a bit less heatedly, "Abby had attained quite an impressive knowledge of the fundamental principles of science, as well as embracing an altogether-'scientific' outlook on life. In keeping with this outlook, I genuinely believe that Abby would not be entirely opposed to having her body used in the advancement of medical research." He held up his hands once again, to silence the protest that Jean-Claude was on the verge of lodging. "I know it must seem 'unconventional' to you gentlemen. But then again, Abby and Alfred were anything but conventional. I suppose you know how Alfred's remains were, shall we say, 'disposed of'?"

"Cremated, was it not?" Jean-Claude replied curtly.

"Yes. And all for the advance of science. Now given Abby's like-mindedness with her late husband, it seems only logical that she would share his opinion regarding the proper 'usages' of one's body after death, even if that body happened to be her own."

"But she never told you this herself, I assume," said Jean-Claude.

"No," Peter replied matter-of-factly. "But then again why should she? The woman was barely thirty years old. She would have no reason even to consider such things, let alone speak of them. No, my conclusion is pure surmise, but it's entirely consistent with patterns I observed in my sister's behavior over an entire lifetime, so I shouldn't think I'm too far off the mark."

"If I may be so bold," I ventured, having grown a little uncomfortable with the "drift" of Peter's discussion, "there are other 'considerations' besides the physical in matters such as these."

"Do you mean the soul, and all that church talk of Judgment Day and the Resurrection?" Peter asked incredulously. "The soul needing a body to come back to, and all that?"

"Actually, I was thinking more in terms of fundamental human dignity," I said, remembering stories I had heard of some medical students' entirely 'unscientific' usage of a female cadaver who happened into their possession. ". . . but now you mention it, the 'soul' is a concern that many people have in matters of death and burial. It's the whole rationale behind not allowing executed murderers to be buried."

"Regarding my sister's soul," Madeline said abruptly, interrupting Peter before he could give vent to the rebuttal he had no doubt formulated, ". . . let me assure you that Abby's spirit is entirely at peace. She has appeared to me in dreams on two separate occasions since my arrival at Darcy, and human words simply cannot describe the profound contentment and lustrous radiance emanating from her spiritual presence. She is in a far better place than we, Mr. Hodge, and has no concern whatsoever regarding the ultimate disposal of her physical body."

"Well . . ." I began, not sure exactly how to respond, but Jean-Claude interrupted me before I had the chance to try."

"How very convenient for you," he said, with exaggerated formality, ". . . that you can accept with such great equanimity the disappearance of your sister's body. And as it was primarily on the family's behalf that we were charged with locating the corpse, your expressed wishes in the matter are paramount. In short, we will discontinue our investigation at once."

Peter and Madeline looked back and forth at one another, as if trying to "read" Jean-Claude's pronouncement for irony or hidden meaning. Finally, satisfying themselves that he was, more or less, sincere, they visibly relaxed. "Would you care for some more tea?" Madeline asked.

"That would be nice," I said, relaxing somewhat myself in the wake of this sudden evaporation of nervous tension. But just as Madeline was filling my cup, Jean-Claude gave utterance to one of his infernal "afterthoughts."

"Even with the matter of the missing body now effectively 'laid to rest,'" he began, ". . . there is one thing that troubles me."

"Oh?" said Peter, on his guard once again.

"In cases where someone as young and altogether healthy as your sister Abigail dies suddenly, it is customary for a close medical examination, or even an autopsy to be performed. Was such an examination performed in this case?"

Peter sent Madeline a slight, almost imperceptible glance, and then answered, "There was no need for an autopsy, but, yes, a thorough medical examination was performed."

"She was, then, taken to a hospital, yes?" Jean-Claude asked.

"No," Peter replied, carefully. "The examination was performed right here. By a physician from Sloane's Hospital.

"Ah, very good." Jean-Claude nodded in apparent satisfaction. "The newspaper reported the cause of death as 'cataleptic seizure,' which is, of course, as good as saying 'unknown causes.' And what did the physician from Sloane's conclude?"

"It was an apoplexy," he answered, "causing severe bleeding in the brain. He assured me that, from the moment she first fell senseless to the floor, there was nothing that could have been done to save the poor thing. It's something of a family predisposition, I'm afraid. Our mother died in the very same manner, although she was considerably older, so it wasn't as great a shock."

Throughout this last verbal exchange, I became aware of a noise in an adjacent room, as of someone moving chairs across a floor. Jean-Claude was so preoccupied with the discussion that he appeared not to notice the sound at first, but I grew quite uneasy as it continued for some seconds, then was replaced by a clattering, as of dishes being put away. According to Jean-Claude's assessment of the situation, the man and woman sitting before us were supposed to be the only people on the premises, but there in the next room was quite unmistakably another person, or else an extremely large rat.

The clattering finally caught Jean-Claude's attention as well, and when it was succeeded by the sound of footsteps, approaching the parlor where we sat, we exchanged glances very similar to the ones we exchanged when we thought we had seen a ghost upon our first visit to Darcy. Not knowing what to expect might soon materialize in the doorway, we simply held our breaths and watched, with unnaturally large eyes, I'm quite certain.

"Are you quite done with your dishes, now sir, ma'am?" said a small woman of rather advanced age, but obviously quite spry for all that, who entered the parlor carrying an empty tray.

"Only just, Mildred," Madeline replied to the woman. "All but Mr. Hodge, that is. I'll bring his cup in later."

"Very well, ma'am," the woman said, quickly and efficiently gathering up the tea dishes, *my* cup included. Observing this blatant disregard of her request, Madeline smiled at me and shook her head in amused vexation. Jean-Claude and I sat silently in a state of our own vexation, until the woman glided out of the room, and Madeline identified the unexpected third party.

"Poor old Mrs. Bow," she said affectionately. "Very nearly blind as a bat, but as faithful as the day is long."

"Mrs. Bow?" Jean-Claude asked hesitantly, sensing the first gust of wind that threatened the house of cards that was his theory regarding this "case."

"Oh yes. The housekeeper here at Darcy." I watched Jean-Claude's face fall, along with his house of cards. "She served Alfred for decades, and continued on after he and Abby married. Talking to her these past two days, it's clear that she had grown to love my sister almost as much as if she were her own daughter. She's really quite distraught over Abby's death but hides her feelings so as not to be a burden to Peter and me."

All the while Madeline was speaking, I paid scant attention to what she was saying, so very preoccupied was I with other, more important matters regarding her person. In short, the miraculous appearance of "dear old Mrs. Bow" had in an instant cleared Madeline of any involvement in either the disappearance of her sister's body or the death of the real Peter Worthington. Whoever the man sitting across the room from her might actually have been, Madeline, at least, was exactly who she claimed to be. My heart now literally soared with the memory of all the attentions she had paid to me during our visit—attentions that I had forced myself to disregard when I believed her to be what Jean-Claude believed her to be—a greedy, opportunistic domestic servant posing as the sister of a deceased woman in order to take advantage of the dead woman's inherited wealth. What a tangled web, indeed. And what an enormous relief to discover that the majority of the tangles were of Jean-Claude's creation—the product of an overly active, albeit logical, imagination.

Seeming to sense that the dynamics of the situation had somehow, inexplicably changed, and that the "sting" of Jean-Claude's rhetoric had lost a good deal of its venom, both Peter and Madeline visibly and instantly relaxed, and the remainder of our visit was purely "social" in nature. Peter reminisced over the past few months he had spent with "Abby," and Madeline, who had not seen her sister "in the flesh" for the past several years, told stories of their childhood together—the adventures and misadventures experienced by two intelligent and curious identical twins. So very identical were the sisters, in fact, that their own parents had a difficult time distinguishing one from the other, a source of confusion that provided the girls all manner of opportunities for domestic subterfuge. Shortly before the time arrived for us to leave, the conversation turned to Madeline's restless life on the Continent, and how very happy she was to be back in England. "It seems as if an entire lifetime has passed since I last visited London," she said, with just the hint of a wistful tone in her voice. "I want to go plunge into the life of the great city while I'm here, but I shouldn't even know where to begin. Peter here has no spirit of adventure. The only thing that ever takes him into London is 'business,' the poor dear." She patted Peter fondly on the forearm.

"I have some business tomorrow morning, in fact," he said.

"And I shall come along," she added, "if only to experience the bustle of the crowd as we pass through the streets."

I suddenly saw a rare and wonderful opportunity materialize right before my eyes, as it were, and I determined to grab hold of it by the proverbial forelock.

"At the risk of appearing forward," I ventured, "I should be most delighted to show you around town while your brother is engaged."

"Oh that would be splendid," she responded, clapping her hands together and smiling in a most delightful way. "What do you say, Peter? Do you think you can conduct your business by yourself?"

"I should think so, Maddy," he answered, with a wry grin. "Although I can't imagine anything that would be more stimulating to a young woman fresh in from the Continent than an afternoon in the smoke-filled law offices of Hessey and Smith. Nonetheless, I shall deposit you upon the front steps of Saint Paul's Cathedral at noon, and you may wander where you will."

"Very well," I said, muting my admittedly extreme enthusiasm as much as I was capable. "I shall see you at noon."

With the departure of our coach from the inn a mere thirty minutes hence, we bid our hosts farewell and headed for the road. When the front door of Darcy House closed behind us, I couldn't resist the temptation to fling a good-humored barb in Jean-Claude's direction, so very delighted was I in the unexpected turn of events. "Well that didn't come off exactly as we had planned it, eh, Jean-Claude," I said, tapping him lightly on the shoulder, to which remark, the only reply I received was a scowling silence, which remained fully in place throughout the duration of our trip back into town. And to be completely honest, I must admit that I rather welcomed this uncharacteristic lapse in oratorical fluidity, so very preoccupied was I with thoughts of my own.

CHAPTER 18

"Why can't you simply admit it, Jean-Claude? You were wrong. *We* were wrong. And what of it?" After dinner and a bottle of port, which we were just in the process of finishing, Jean-Claude had relinquished his silence, but not his dark mood.

"About some things—some small details—perhaps we have been in error." Jean-Claude paced the floor, punctuating his thoughts with thrusts of his wineglass, thus threatening our rug with every accented syllable. "In the main, however, I refuse to believe we are so far off the mark as you suggest."

"Oh, come now. You can't tell me that you still think Madeline had anything to do with all of this. Face it, your entire theory was based upon the premise that the two servants—the housekeeper and the gardener—assumed the roles of Peter and Madeline Worthington, when Peter turned up dead. And today we saw living proof that the housekeeper, at least, is still very much 'in character,' which completely clears Madeline of suspicion. And as for Peter . . . well, he acts so very 'normal' and unaffected, that it's difficult to imagine him being anyone other than who he claims to be. He's certainly no gardener, or else he's the most polished gardener in all England."

"But Peter Worthington is dead," he protested, setting his glass upon the table with such force that it very nearly shattered.

"A gentleman is dead," I said in a calm, and hopefully calming, voice. "That is true. But there's no real proof that the dead man was Peter Worthington. That was just a hunch based on the physical similarity between the two men."

"It was no 'hunch,'" he argued. "It was instinct—instinct guided by reason. And my instinct is rarely in error."

"About most things, true," I reassured. "But this is a murder we're talking about here, not some scientific experiment. Someone irrational enough to take another person's life thinks differently from other people. Not being guided by reason, his behavior most likely can't be understood by reason, either—not even yours."

"And what do you suggest?" he asked, with only a hint of sarcasm in his voice, which was a distinct improvement. As I opened my mouth to reply, the expression on his face indicated that he was almost actually interested in what I might have to say. Unfortunately, I suddenly found myself with very little to say.

"I don't really know that I could 'suggest' anything," I said hesitantly, not wishing to relinquish
this rare intellectual advantage but not seeing any
ready means for holding on to it. "I just don't think
the answers we're searching for have anything
to do with Darcy and the Worthingtons. Has it
occurred to you that the gentleman's murder, and
the theft of Abigail's body, might very possibly
have taken place somewhere other than Darcy?"
Suddenly a thought—an astonishingly simple
thought—occurred to me. "What if Jimmy took
us to the wrong grave that night, and the body he
sold us has no connection whatsoever with Abigail Darcy, or the theft of her body?" The more I
considered the possibility, the more I liked it. "It's
quite simple, actually. Just imagine you're a lad
of fourteen, with no home to speak of, making a
desperate living as a resurrectionist. One night,
in a pitch-black graveyard, you exhume a body
and deliver it to a couple of medical students, who
promptly accuse you of murder. Knowing full well
that you're innocent of the charges, but realizing
that your word would mean very little next to the
word of these two gentlemen, should they take
you before a judge, you resort to the only means
you can think of to prove your innocence. You
take the gentlemen back to the cemetery, which
you search with the light of a dim lantern until
you find a freshly dug grave. So eager are you to
demonstrate your innocence that you set to work
immediately, without first completely verifying
that this is, in fact, the grave you visited earlier in
the evening. The coffin is unearthed, and to your

great relief, as well as that of the two gentlemen, it is empty. But the empty coffin at your feet is not the same one from which you took the gentleman's body. It is empty, true, but then again, so are probably half of the graves in London, so very common is the resurrection practice. This grave, robbed sometime before or after you snatched the gentleman's body, is actually the grave of Abigail Darcy, a fact that becomes public knowledge when you are quite suddenly and unceremoniously chased from the graveyard, leaving the coffin exposed for all the world to see. When the gentlemen read the account of the theft in the next day's paper, discovering the identity of the former occupant of the coffin they helped to unearth, two coffins merge into one, and the gentlemen set out in the direction of Darcy on a path that turns out to be nothing more than a red herring." I folded my arms in triumph and awaited Jean-Claude's congratulations. Instead of congratulations, however, what I received from him was a long, quizzical stare.

"And this is your 'simple solution'?" he asked, finally breaking the awkward silence. "Two empty coffins in one evening—an enormous coincidence, yes?"

"No more coincidental than finding a murdered gentleman in a lady's coffin," I said, falling back into my customary posture of defensiveness.

"Touché," he said, halfheartedly, an expression of deep pensiveness creeping into his face. "And yet, there are so many signs that point toward Darcy." He stood transfixed in silent thought for a full minute, as if chasing a mental hare through an intricate maze.

"Well," I said, trying to pull him out of his reverie, ". . . what do you suggest that our next 'move' be?"

He blinked rapidly a few times, and looked at me as if he had forgotten I was there. "Why, you are meeting Madeline and Peter at Saint Paul's, of course," he said matter-of- factly. "And as for me, I shall take the opportunity of their absence from Darcy to pay a brief visit to dear Mrs. Bow. Although 'blind as a bat,' there is a great deal she could say to one who knows the right questions to ask."

I felt suddenly overcome with a wave of apprehension. "Don't go antagonizing those people, Jean-Claude," I warned, although considering the intended recipient of my warning, "pleaded" would perhaps be a more accurate term.

"Do not worry, my friend. I shall be the very embodiment of discretion." And then he added, with a meaningful smirk. "I am a Frenchman, *mon ami*. Far be it from me to ever willfully obstruct the pathway of l'amour."

CHAPTER 19

The following day dawned far more beautifully than I had reason to expect, given the lateness of the season. The sun beamed down upon my grateful face as I strolled in the direction of Saint Paul's. Having breakfasted lightly, and read the morning paper, word for word, I still found myself with some three hours of time on my hands, so I decided to go ahead and make my way toward the appointed location, "killing" time at some bookstalls I knew along the way. In this manner, the morning wore slowly on, until finally the hour of noon arrived, and with it, the Worthingtons' carriage. I spied them just as Peter was helping Madeline down onto the street. Catching sight of her thus unaware of being observed, I was quite overcome by her unaffected grace and beauty. And when her feet were firmly planted upon the ground, and she looked up and saw me approaching, she flashed a smile that rivaled the morning sun for sheer luminescence.

"Good day, Mr. Hodge," she said brightly, extending her delicate hand.

"Good day," I replied, taking her hand. "And I must insist on 'James.'" I winced slightly at the pseudonym.

"Very well, then, James"—she laughed—"and it shall be 'Maddy' for you."

"As you wish," I replied with exaggerated formality, and then joined her in laughter.

After speaking briefly with Peter, to make plans for meeting later in the evening, "Maddy" and I strolled off into the bright sunshine without a care for where our footsteps might lead us.

"I hope you don't think me unduly forward in accepting your invitation to show me 'round," she said, once Peter had disappeared into general traffic of the street. "But having lived on the Continent for so many years, I don't place a great deal of stock in some of the formalities of English social custom." Then she added, much to my great pleasure, "And besides, you're so very 'nice' that one gets the impression she has known you for practically an entire lifetime."

"I can assure you that my only reaction to your accepting the invitation was sheer unmitigated delight," I protested. "And as for English formality, you'll no doubt find that some of those customs have 'relaxed' a bit since you were last here . . . When was it?"

"Let me see, now," she thought aloud. "Five years? No, six. Six years." Smiling reflectively, and shaking her head, she continued, "Can it really have been that long? When I first crossed the Channel, my intention was to take a six-month tour. But when I arrived in Paris, I quickly realized that six months would hardly do justice to that grand city, let alone the entire Continent. And by the time I got to Venice, I tossed out all thoughts of keeping to a schedule. I believe it was in Florence, over two years after I first left England, that I suddenly realized I was no longer a visitor to the Continent but a resident. One enchanted city gave way to another, two years turned into three, then three to four, and in the wink of an eye, six years have come and gone.

"So you see, Mr. Hodge . . . James." She caught herself just before I spoke up to protest. "I have lived quite an unconventional life. Some might even call it positively scandalous. But I can honestly say I wouldn't have had it any other way." She grew silent for a moment, looking up at the buildings surrounding us on either side, and then turned her attention fully upon me. "And what about you, James? What sort of life have you lived? Have you traveled much?"

I believe I actually blushed when I considered how extraordinarily conventional my life had been, when compared to hers. Quickly, and somewhat apologetically, I reviewed the details—childhood in Kent, university study in Oxford, and so on. I was on the very verge of mentioning medical study, when I remembered the confounded fiction Jean-Claude had created for us in which we were "detectives," and sketched in the

vaguest possible lines of my "career," wishing all
the while I could simply abandon the façade and
simply be Edward Montague. Of course, I then reflected, were it not for this fiction, and the murder that precipitated it, I would never have had
the opportunity of meeting Madeline, so I resigned myself to it for the time being.

Passing a delightful little café with which I was
well acquainted, we stopped in for a bit of lunch,
where we continued talking about Maddy's "unconventional" life in Europe. "So what it is about
Italy that so attracts you?" I asked, in regard to
her having spent four of her six years abroad in
that country.

"Two things, really," she replied thoughtfully.
"The vast antiquity, for one. The spirits of the Roman Empire, and of the Middle Ages, are very active throughout Italy. One cannot walk a hundred
yards without feeling the palpable presence of the
remote past. Venice is particularly rife with spiritual activity. The whole city is positively magical.
Have you had the pleasure of seeing it?"

I reflected over my own six-month "Grand Tour,"
following the completion of my studies at university, and felt as though, compared to her experience, I could hardly be said to have truly "seen"
any place, even though I had visited many. Venice,
however, was one I had not even visited.

"Oh you must spend some time there," she
said, growing animated. "To glide upon the water in a gondola, passing from the majestic Grand
Canal into a labyrinth of dark romantic passage-
ways is simply an indescribable experience."

"Yes, I shall have to go there someday," I said regretfully. "But you mentioned two reasons you're so fond of Italy. What was the other?"

"The people," she replied without hesitation. "They're so very passionate, and altogether alive. Unlike so many of the dark-visaged specters you encounter in other places." She glanced out the window at the throngs passing busily down the street, and sighed. "The Italians know the proper way to live."

When our food arrived, we talked intermittently, between mouthfuls, about everything, and about nothing at all. After lunch, we casually made our way toward Pall Mall, to visit the newly opened National Gallery. Passing a bookseller, Maddy asked if we could drop in to buy some stationery, so she could send word of her whereabouts to friends on the Continent, whom she had not had time to bid farewell upon her hasty departure. While inattentively perusing some loose volumes laid out upon a table, I suddenly noticed that tears had welled up in Maddy's eyes as she flipped though the pages of a magazine. "What's the matter?" I asked, afraid I had perhaps unwittingly said something to upset her.

"Oh, it's nothing, really," she replied, dabbing the corners of her eyes with a handkerchief. "Just this." She held out a copy of the *British Historical Quarterly*. "Here's an article by Alfred Darcy—a translation. I believe it's one he dictated to poor Abby."

"There, there," I said, taking the magazine from her hand and placing it back on the stand. "I

know this has all been a terrible shock to you—
your sister's sudden death, and the theft . . ." I re-
frained from explicitly mentioning the object of
the theft, not wishing to upset her further.

"Oh, I'm all right," she said, breathing deeply
and straightening her back, in a willful act of
self-composure. "Let's keep walking. I can purchase the stationery later."

Once back out on the street, she regained her
good cheer but grew nostalgic over thoughts of her
departed sister. "Abby and I were identical in so
very many ways, but quite different in others. We
both had a strong sense of adventure, as you've no
doubt gathered by now. But while my adventur-
ousness was of a physical, geographic nature, leading me to leave the easy familiarity of England to
explore an unknown continent, Abby's was of an
intellectual variety, never taking her physically
outside of England, but making her perpetually
restless to explore new worlds of ideas, for all her
geographical insularity. Did you know she was
fluent in four languages?"

"No," I replied. "That's quite remarkable."

"Remarkable, yes, but merely one of the 'adventures' of her great intellect." Suddenly, she stopped
walking and looked directly into my face. "Do you
believe," she asked, intensely, "that women are
as innately capable as men in matters of the
mind?"

"Why yes," I answered, somewhat reflexively,
without having given the matter a great deal of
thought. And then I reflected upon the strength
of character of the woman standing before me,

and of the scholarly work in which her sister had engaged, side by side, with her late husband, and I added, with complete sincerity and conviction, "Yes, I do believe women as capable as men. In some cases even more capable."

Clearly sensing the dialectic drift of my thinking, Maddy rewarded me with one of her brilliant smiles, then continued, both walking and speaking. "Well, had you known Abby, you would have found your belief to be fully justified. It was the sheer stature of her intellect that 'won over' Alfred Darcy, an eminent scholar who recognized greatness when he saw it. His death was unfortunate, certainly, but he at least had a full career's worth of work to leave behind him. Abby was cut off before she barely scratched the surface of her potential. She lost her life, but the world lost a great source of enlightenment. All her life, ever since we were children, Abby dreamed of greatness—greatness that, for a woman, would have been condemned as heresy in many households. But our dear father, perhaps because he found himself with two very headstrong daughters on his hands, or perhaps simply because he was very, very wise, encouraged us to dream without limitation. I dreamed of seeing the world, and Abby dreamed of changing it. I have, to an extent, realized my dream, but Abby, alas, was cut down in the pursuit of hers."

"How do you mean 'cut down'?" I asked, recalling Dr. Edmonds's suspicions regarding Abigail's death. "Do you think her studies had something to do with her death?"

"No," she answered pensively, as if considering the possibility. "I shouldn't think so. But then again, she 'thought' so very intensely . . . I wonder if one can overtax the brain to such an extent that it literally ruptures, as Abby's did. Ah, well, whatever caused her brain to burst, it ended a very fruitful life before harvest season."

We walked in reflective silence for a few moments, then I ventured onto a new, hopefully less painful subject. "So do you think you'll remain in England now—to live? Or will you return to Europe?"

She looked at me so intently, and searchingly, that I was forced to turn my eyes away, out of sheer vulnerability. "I have sojourned there for so very long now, that I can think of few alternatives. But then again, my life these many years has been such a vagabond existence, that I have come to realize there is really no place on earth that I can call 'home.'" She paused thoughtfully, and, I sensed, significantly. "It would be quite nice to put down 'roots' somewhere," she concluded.

Our conversation trailed off in midthought, when we found ourselves at the entrance to the National Gallery. As we stood upon the steps, preparing to go inside, Maddy laughed, suddenly and brightly, like the sun bursting out from behind a dark cloud on a windy late-autumn day. I smiled in return, and we left off "serious" subjects for another time, turning our attention instead to "art" as an altogether-more-comfortable topic of conversation.

Since its grand opening the previous year, I had

visited the National Gallery on two separate occasions, but was quickly driven away by the intolerable tightness resulting from hundreds of people crowding all at once into a long narrow hallway. Today, I was pleased to see, attendance was a good deal less abundant than on my previous visits, so that one could actually see the paintings without having to climb upon someone else's shoulders. Being accustomed to the wider, more open spaces of the major European galleries, however, Maddy soon felt oppressed by the closeness of the place and wished to cut our visit short.

Ambling down the street once again, we very intentionally restricted our conversation to light subjects—the Uffizi Gallery in Florence, the omnipresent cats of Rome, the smell of Venice's canals in the summer—feeling that we had perhaps ventured into deep waters a bit too rapidly. We were such kindred spirits, and felt so entirely comfortable in each other's presence, that talking freely and candidly seemed the most natural thing in the world. Still, whatever our futures might hold in store for us, we sensed that it was best to permit it to mature in its own good time, so we simply reined the whole thing in just a bit.

In the afternoon, we had tea in St. James's Park, then, whimsically pursuing the address listed on a sign posted there, attended an electrical demonstration in the parlor of a well-known authoress. The highlight of the demonstration was the bestowal, by the hostess herself, of "electric kisses" upon the cheeks of any gentlemen present who cared for a "shock." I, for one, gratefully declined.

After the demonstration concluded, it was time for us to make our way back to St. Paul's, where we were to meet Peter. Throughout our walk back up the river toward the church, I struggled to fight off the melancholy that threatened to settle upon my spirits like a dark, wet fog. As delightful a day as we had passed together, I couldn't imagine when, or under what circumstances, I should be able to see Maddy again. Having effectively withdrawn from any further involvement in the search for their sister's body, Peter and Maddy had no "official" need for our continued service as "detectives," and seeing as how this ruse was the sole basis for our communication with the Worthingtons, the cessation of this role effectively closed off that avenue of contact. Suddenly, the thought of a moment made my heart soar. The termination of our detective services closed off contact between the Worthingtons and James Hodge. But what about Edward Montague? He, or rather, I, was not bound by the ridiculous role Jean-Claude had created for me, in order to chase down a "wild goose." It was I, Edward Montague, not James Hodge, who had spent a delightful afternoon with Maddy. It was I, not James Hodge, to whom she had revealed her fondest memories of the past and strongly hinted at her dreams for the future. And it was I whom she felt she had known an entire lifetime. "Why not simply tell her the truth?" I asked myself. Why not drop the façade and reveal the true identity of the man she already truly knows?

Then just as quickly as my heart had soared, it dropped once again. And what if I were to admit to her that I am not who I said I was? I asked my-self. Was it not my "disarming sincerity" that most distinguished me from other Englishmen she knew. Was not my "spirit," in this sense, "more Italian than English"? To reveal but a hint of dis-semblance would strike at the very heart of that which she most valued in me.

So very perplexed was I as to how best to pro-ceed in the future, that I let the present slip by unawares, and in what seemed the mere blink of an eye, St. Paul's Cathedral, with Peter Worthing-ton standing upon the front steps, materialized before me. Mercifully, fate, or rather Peter, granted me a three-hour reprieve in which to give the thorny question further consideration. A spectac-ular nautical show, *The Pilot: or A Tale of the Sea*, was playing at the Adelphi, and Peter suggested we go and see it. I readily agreed. So very dis-tracted was I, however, with the issue of what I should tell Maddy regarding my identity, if I ever wished to see her again, that I saw precious little of the play, and, I fear, rather sorely neglected my companions. Fortunately, they were so captivated by the spectacle that they appeared not to notice my inattention, and when the hour of our parting once again drew near, we all remained on good terms, so I decided for the moment simply to let the matter rest until I should have more time, and solitude, in which to think it through.

As I helped her up into the carriage and bid her good evening, Maddy left me with a parting smile that utterly vanquished my doubts and fears of the past few hours. Whatever solution I managed to come up with regarding the distant future and the issue of my confounded identity, I felt certain that the immediate future, at least, would take care of itself.

CHAPTER 20

While I was gallivanting around London with Maddy Worthington, Jean-Claude traveled out to Darcy to take advantage of its master's and mistress's absence and "have a word" with the housekeeper, Mrs. Bow. As certain as I was of the Worthingtons' ignorance of, and innocence in, the bad business surrounding the gentleman's murder, Jean-Claude stubbornly persisted in his belief that they were somehow involved. Recalling Simeon Rupp's vitriolic observation that the Darcy housekeeper had prepared Abigail's body for burial before he arrived, and thus robbed him of a fee he considered to be his right, Jean-Claude had concluded that the lady might very well have information that would prove useful to us in our ongoing investigation. Knowing my friend far too well to think I could dissuade him from this purpose, once he had made up his mind, I merely cautioned him that it might be a very good idea, while he interviewed the housekeeper, not to make unsubstantiated accusations against the lady's employers. At just about the same moment that Maddy and I were having lunch in the café, Jean-Claude dismounted from a coach at the Rose and Crown and set out on foot for Darcy House.

An initial knock at the front door producing no result, he feared Mrs. Bow might have gone out, perhaps even with the Worthingtons. A second, louder knock, however, invoked the faint sound of footsteps across a slate floor, followed by the appearance of Mrs. Bow in the open doorway.

"Good day, Madame," he greeted her.

"Mr. Peter and Miss Madeline are out, sir," she unceremoniously replied. "Gone for the day, I believe."

"But that cannot be," he protested. "I was supposed to meet them here at one o'clock, to discuss a matter of great urgency. Are you quite sure it is for the entire day they plan to be gone?"

"Quite sure," she repeated. "They told me not to bother with dinner because they'd be dining in town."

"I suppose they have forgotten. Very well, then. I shall be on my way." He turned upon the walkway toward the road he had just a moment before traversed, and sighed. "Do you think, Madame, that you could be so kind as to provide me with a refreshment of some kind before I begin my journey back to London?"

"Well I suppose," she agreed, reluctantly. "Come

take a seat in the foyer, if you must sit down. I'll fetch you something to drink."

"Thank you very much, Madame. You are quite kind." He followed her through the door and sat on a bench along the wall. While Mrs. Bow was in the kitchen, he allowed his gaze to wander casually down the hall, pausing briefly at each of the Japanese watercolors. At the rear of the hall, he saw a door that appeared to lead onto a porch, perhaps in the rear garden. Not wishing to disobey, and hence antagonize, his hostess, he resisted the strong urge to creep quietly down the hall and have a look outside, which was a fortunate decision, since Mrs. Bow reappeared just at the very moment he would have had his hand on the doorknob.

"Here's a bit of tea," she said matter-of-factly, placing a serving tray upon the bench at his side.

"Ah, so very swift," he said, relieved at having thus decided not to leave his seat. Then, pouring himself a cup, and, with an exaggerated show of thirst, taking a few grateful sips, he sighed contentedly. "Delicious, Madame. I shall be restored to full health by the time I get to the bottom of my cup."

Somewhat mollified by the compliment, Mrs. Bow tempered her defensive tone slightly, and even went so far as to offer Jean-Claude "a tea biscuit or two," which he refused, not wishing to put her to any further trouble than he had already caused.

"It's no trouble, really," she protested, warming to his excessive demonstration of politeness. "I have so much time on my hands, these days, that it's rather a pleasure to have something to do."

"You are very kind," he said, draining his cup, and setting it gently on the tray beside him. "But surely you are too modest about the work you do, Madame" he ventured. "A big house like this, and only you to take care of it, and its inhabitants? I should imagine the work would keep you very busy indeed."

"Would that it did, sir." She sighed, shaking her head. "Would that it did. But there's practically no cleaning to do, since most of the rooms are closed off now. And as for cooking, well Mrs. Darcy sees to much of that." She caught the mistake as it crossed her lips, and as she corrected herself, a wistful, bemused expression drifted into her face. "Mrs. Darcy *saw* to much of that." She sat in complete silence for a moment, and when she began speaking again, it was almost as if it were only to herself. "It's so hard to believe they're gone, Alfred and the missus. And her so young, too. I'd have never thought it possible."

"You have endured a great deal these past few months, yes," Jean-Claude said, trying to direct her reverie into a useful course. "How long had you worked for Mr. Darcy before his death?"

"Right on thirty years," she replied. "Ever since he came back here to reopen the house."

"Reopen?" Jean-Claude asked.

"Yes. After his father died, he set out to travel the world and gather together his collection." Mrs.

Bow waved her hand vaguely around her head, indicating, Jean-Claude supposed, the contents of the house. "Since he had no brothers or sisters to look after it, he shut the place up tight before he left, and for the better part of fifteen years, not a living soul darkened the door. Except, of course for the occasional raccoon or squirrel, you know.

"When he was finally satisfied that he'd seen just about as much of the world as he cared to, he came back here to the house and started setting things in order. And it wasn't an easy job, either. It took him more than two years just to get the place livable again. Well, actually it was him and a whole team of builders—masons, and carpenters, and such. Finally, the place looked just the way he wanted it to—something like a museum, as you can see now—and he declared it finished. That's when I came along. Back then, though, it wasn't just me and George . . ."

"George?" Jean-Claude asked.

"George Jenkins, the groundskeeper. Or George's father, rather. The one that's here now is old George's son. Back then, though, we had over a dozen people on the staff. And we stayed busy, too. Because he dearly loved to entertain—did Mr. Alfred. He was all the time having those friends of his—the Athens Club, they were called—out here. Sometimes they'd stay for days at a time, too."

"And as he grew older, he decided he did not need such a large staff?" Jean-Claude guessed, trying to keep her within sight, at least, of the beaten path.

"Oh, no. Age had nothing to do with it at all," she said incredulously. "He kept a full staff until the lady came to work here."

"The lady?"

"Mrs. Darcy. Although she wasn't Mrs. Darcy then. It was Miss Worthington when she first arrived, to help out Mr. Alfred with all his papers and books, and the like. But as I was saying, before that we had a much larger staff. A 'real' staff, since you can't exactly call me and George a staff, properly speaking. Back in those days, there were always two or three of us in the kitchen, a handful of workers on the grounds—Mr. Darcy did love his gardens—and three or four more ladies just to keep the place tidy. And for a while there— I can't say exactly how long, because it's been a few years back—there was this Japanese fellow that Mr. Alfred brought here, to make him special Japanese dishes, you know. He didn't last too long, though."

"And what became of this Japanese chef?" Jean-Claude asked, his curiosity suddenly piqued. "He was not the victim of violence, I hope?"

"Why no, nothing like that." Mrs. Bow chuckled, and seeking out Jean-Claude's face in the dim light, stared with great amusement at a spot just above his head. "Why should you say such a thing? Nothing happened to Kye—that's what we all called him, since we couldn't pronounce his real name. He just got to missing his family and went back to Japan. Mr. Alfred didn't much seem to mind, either. The poor fellow just never did quite fit in. Of course it's no wonder, really, him not speaking a word of English, and all."

"So Mrs. Darcy dismissed the majority of the staff?" Jean-Claude asked, returning her to the subject at hand.

"She wasn't Mrs. Darcy back then, like I said. It was Abigail Worthington. And, no, she didn't dismiss the staff herself, at least not at first. Not until later, *after* she was Mrs. Darcy."

Jean-Claude felt his brow tightening from the effort required to follow Mrs. Bow's circuitous narrative and resigned himself to the headache he would no doubt have by the time she was finished. "Who did dismiss the staff, then?" he asked, with willful patience.

"Why, Mr. Alfred, of course. When she first came to work here, writing down all the things he would read to her—his eyesight wasn't so good by then, you know—she was always helping out with other household duties, when he didn't need her. She worked just as hard as any of the rest of us, and didn't mind getting her hands dirty, either. Yes, she was quite helpful." She trailed off, and sat in complete silence for a moment, as if she had entirely forgotten Jean-Claude's presence.

"She was quite helpful, and . . ." he offered.

"She was quite helpful, but in the end, it cost a lot of people their employment. She was so helpful that Mr. Alfred didn't see the need of keeping a full staff when he had one person who was willing do so much, you know. By the time they got married—Mr. Alfred and Miss Abigail—it was just six of us. And that's the way it stayed until he died, and her brother, Mr. Peter, came to stay. Then she dismissed everybody but George and me—young George that is. Old George retired some years back. He's living at his brother's dairy farm in Jersey, now. Good old fellow. I do miss him."

"And Mr. Darcy's death," Jean-Claude prodded. "Was it sudden?"

"I can't exactly say as it was," she replied thoughtfully. "But then again I can't entirely say that it wasn't, either. He'd certainly slowed down a good bit in his later years, and he was always such an active, busy man, was Mr. Alfred. After he married Miss Abigail, he didn't go into town nearly as much as he used to, and he didn't have his gentlemen friends out here, either. And they used to come out once a month or so. But I suppose that's to be expected, when a man's newly wed, and all, even if that man is over seventy years old. But he did slow down, there's no denying that." She sighed and drifted into a silent reverie.

"And at the time of his death . . ." Jean-Claude assisted.

"He'd slowed down, of course, but just before he died he wasn't any different than he had been for the past several months. Slow, like I said, but no slower than before. And then one morning I came into the study and found him sleeping on the couch, with a book lying open on his chest. Course, he wasn't actually sleeping, as it turns out. I went about my business for the rest of the morning, and when I came back to the parlor, and found him exactly like I left him before, I knew then something wasn't right."

"What did you do?"

"Well, I called him. 'Mr. Alfred,' I said. And then a bit louder, 'Mr. Alfred.' Then I gave him a little shake, and when he didn't wake up then I fetched the missus. And that was that. He was dead."

"How did Mrs. Darcy respond when she found him that way?"

"It was me who found him, like I already said," she corrected. "But when I showed him to Mrs. Abigail, she immediately sent George—young George, that is—to fetch a doctor from town, one of Alfred's gentleman friends, you know. But by the time they got back here, there was nothing to be done, seeing as how he was already dead."

"Do you recall the physician's name?" Jean-Claude asked, considering a possibility.

"Do I remember? Why, hadn't I been serving the man tea and dinners for upwards of thirty years?" She shook her head in disbelief over the absurd question. "Do I remember?" She chuckled.

"And what was the doctor's name?"

"The doctor? Oh, yes. The name was Stuyvesant—Martin Stuyvesant. He was one of Mr. Alfred's acquaintances from Holland, from the time he used to live there. He certainly was sorry to see Mr. Alfred that way—dead, you know. A heart attack, he said it was. Died in his sleep—peaceful-like—so it was really a blessing. He did live such a full life."

"And how did Mrs. Darcy handle the unexpected loss of her husband?" Jean-Claude asked.

"She was very brave—didn't go on and on like some new widows. But then again, it wasn't like he was twenty years old, you know. She knew when they got married that he'd go before she did." Mrs. Bow frowned slightly and shook her head. "But it wasn't by as much as one would have imagined, was it now?"

"And so after Mr. Darcy's death, Mrs. Darcy dismissed the remaining servants?"

"That's right. All except for George and me, of course. And then Mr. Worthington came to visit—you know, to help Mrs. Abigail sort things out. He's still here, as you well know, and it's a good thing, too. Otherwise, when she died, nobody would have known how to contact her next of kin. She was very private—was Mrs. Darcy. None of us knew about her brother until he arrived on the doorstep. And as it turns out, there's a sister, too. Nice lady, although I've never quite warmed up to Mr. Worthington. He's rather . . . how do you say . . . temperamental. He's a temperamental man, much given to temper. He was a pleasant as a peach around Mrs. Abigail, but not around anybody else. I just keep my distance most of the time and don't bother him.

"It's a funny thing, though," she continued, ". . . but since the other sister arrived—Miss Madeline—he's a lot more tolerable than he used to be. Sometimes he can even be quite friendly, in fact. Maybe since his sister died, he appreciates people more. It happens, you know. My father never seemed to notice I was alive until my older sister died—nine years old, she was. But then I became his 'little dumpling,' and he didn't like to let me out of his sight. Nearly broke his poor heart when I left home and took my first job as a domestic." She sighed and brushed away a tear that had materialized in the corner of her eye. "Maybe that's how it is with Mr. Peter. He had to lose somebody close to realize how much the people in his life mean to him."

"Speaking of Mr. Worthington," Jean-Claude prompted, ". . . it must have been an enormous shock to him when his sister died."

"You can't imagine," she replied emphatically. "He was fit to be tied, but not in the way you might think. People feel sorrow in different ways, you know. With some, it's weeping and wailing and keeping the shutters drawn—all of that. With others, it's just a lot of continual sighing and drooping around the house. Mr. Worthington, though—he was just angry, plain and simple."

"With whom was he angry?"

"Who wasn't he angry with? Me and George, of course. We didn't go near him, unless we absolutely had to. And then there was that doctor, and the undertaker . . . I thought he might come to blows with those two gentlemen. Of course, neither of them was too happy, either, so it was about even, all things considered. I sure was glad when they were out of the house, though." She nodded her head, as if in recollection of her "gladness," and continued.

"But of all the people he was angry with—Mr. Peter, I mean—I think he was most angry with Mrs. Abigail herself. It happens, you know. After my aunt died, my mum wouldn't let anybody speak her name for the longest time. She was angry that her sister had up and died, you see. And that may be how it was with Mr. Peter. She died— Mrs. Abigail—so sudden, leaving him behind like that, when they'd just gotten to know each other again. After all those years apart, you know. Maybe he just couldn't forgive her for it."

"In what manner did he display this anger?" Jean-Claude asked.

"He acted like he wished to have nothing further to do with her." She pursed her mouth, and shook her head at the recollection. "In such a situation, one would expect a nice funeral. And it wasn't like they lacked for money, of course. He could have buried her as grandly as any woman was ever buried—excepting royalty, and such, of course. But he seemed to want nothing so much as to just get her out of his sight.

"When he first found her that way—lying on the floor unconscious, he sent right away for the doctor. When this doctor came—he was another friend of Mr. Alfred's, a Dr. Edmonds—and found her already dead, Mr. Peter had a fit and started shouting at the doctor. I was in the kitchen— keeping my distance, you know—so I couldn't tell what he was saying, but it was none too nice,

I promise. Finally, the doctor does some shouting of his own—and why wouldn't he, being used so—and storms out of the house. Then, just when things start to calm down a bit, the undertaker turns up, and the whole thing starts all over again."

"This undertaker," Jean-Claude mused aloud. "How much time passed before he 'turned up'?"

"That struck me as queer, too," she replied. ". . . for it wasn't much more than an hour. But as it turns out, it was George."

"George?" Jean-Claude asked, puzzled.

"Yes. After the undertaker left—in a huff, just like the doctor—I asked George, 'George,' I say. 'Don't you think it's odd for this undertaker to turn up so, before the doctor's barely had time to examine poor Mrs. Darcy?' But then he told me that, when Mr. Peter called him in—you know, into the parlor—to tell him to run fetch the doctor, he took one look at Mrs. Abigail and knew right away she was dead. He's a practical thing, is George, and thought he might as well kill two birds with one stone, as it were."

"He stopped in at the undertaker's, while he was in town 'fetching' the doctor?" Jean-Claude mused silently over the "practicality" of this young man. Country people . . . he thought, shaking his head.

"That's right. And of course, as it turns out, George hadn't made a mistake. She was dead, all right, the poor thing."

"What did they quarrel about, Mr. Worthington and this undertaker?" Jean-Claude asked.

"The arrangements," she replied matter-of-factly, "for the funeral, you know. The undertaker, a Mr. Simon, came out here all ready to plan a proper ceremony. And like I say, it wasn't as if Mr. Worthington couldn't afford it, either. Do you remember the funeral for that Lord Pickering . . . the one that fell off his horse on a foxhunt? Well, Mr. Simon's the one that planned it. What a grand affair it was!" Mrs. Bow sighed at the memory. "Did you have the pleasure of seeing it? The procession to the church went all over London, so you couldn't very well have missed it, could you?"

"I am afraid I was, regrettably, not in town for the spectacle," he replied, then added quickly, hoping to forestall a full detailed description of the festivities, "but you say that Mr. Worthington was not inclined to avail himself of the undertaker's 'services'?"

"He bought a coffin, all right, and paid to have it carried to the church, but that was all. Mr. Simon considered it quite a disgrace, and I was inclined to agree with him. Although, like I said, it may have all been just his way of grieving—getting angry that way. So I suppose one should forgive it." She pursed her lips, and stared at the wall for a moment, clearly carrying on an internal debate of some sort. "But to be so hard-hearted as to let that poor woman—his own dear departed sister—travel to her grave, without a family member to accompany her on her final journey?" A ticking of her tongue, and a pronounced shaking of her head, indicated her feelings more clearly than any words could.

"So Mr. Worthington was not present for the procession?" Jean-Claude asked.

"No, he wasn't. Like I say, after that quarrel with Mr. Simon, he fairly well washed his hands of the whole thing. That's why it fell on me to make sure the missus was buried properly. When Mr. Simon left, I right away sent George to fetch my two nieces, Emily and Jane, to help with the preparations. 'She might not have a proper coffin,' I said to myself, '. . . but she shall be properly prepared before she goes into it.'"

"So you and your nieces, Emily and Jane, took this duty upon yourselves?"

"That's right. She, Mrs. Abigail, was always very fastidious, you know, so there wasn't a lot of cleaning involved. It was mostly just dressing her." She paused reflectively for a moment. "I can't imagine what Mr. Peter would have put her in—assuming he'd had anything to do with it, of course. But I knew exactly what to do." A long silence ensued.

"And that was . . . ?" Jean-Claude prompted.

"What?" she asked, appearing puzzled.

"You say you knew what to do," he said, trying not to grind his teeth together. "What was it that you did? How did you 'prepare' Mrs. Darcy?"

"Why, we put her in the same clothes she was married in, of course. That Japanese dress he gave her. I put Emily in charge of the hair, though, since my vision's not so good anymore, in case you haven't noticed." The faintest hint of a disapproving expression crept into her face. "Looking back on it, though, I should have let Jane do it. Emily's always had a small streak of vanity in her, you see, and that beautiful gown really caught her eye. But it was the combs I had to watch her for."

"Combs?" Jean-Claude blinked hard a couple of times, trying to decide whether to steer Mrs. Bow back on course or allow her to continue her digression on clothing. Before he could open his mouth to speak, however, she made the decision for him.

"They were beautiful combs, you see, and quite valuable, I would imagine. Carved out of tortoise-shell, they were. Twice I caught my Emily trying to slip them in the pocket of her apron." She frowned, and shook her head sternly. "The second time, I took them away from her and put them in the missus's hair myself. They might not have been completely straight, but at least they were in there."

Jean-Claude took advantage of another brief, thoughtful pause to bring her back to more salient issues. "After you 'prepared' her, you placed the body in the coffin, yes?"

"Not yet," she answered impatiently, unable to conceive how so polished a gentleman should not have a firmer grasp of all the facts surrounding such a signal event as the death of her mistress. "Mr. Simon didn't bring the coffin until the next day, around noon. When she was ready, we laid her out in there"—gesturing toward the parlor—"on the very couch where Mr. Alfred died. And there she stayed until the next day. Since Mr. Peter apparently didn't want to be bothered, Jane, George, and I took turns watching that first night."

"Watching?" Jean-Claude puzzled.

"The missus's body, of course. We sat up with her, as is customary and proper. I took the first watch, Jane stayed for a couple of hours in the middle of the night—she kept dozing off, you see—and George came in until dawn. When Mr. Simon arrived with the coffin, George and I placed her inside, just so, and set it up between two chairs. We didn't have a chance to pay proper final respects to Mr. Alfred, him being burned up like that, the way he requested, so we really wanted to do things right with her."

"The next night," Jean-Claude asked, seeing a welcome opening, "did you take turns 'watching' the coffin once again? You must have been very tired, after the previous evening's vigil."

"There was no need," she mused. "Mr. Peter insisted on sitting up with her that night. Wouldn't let us go near her. I asked him if he needed anything—you know, before I went to bed—but he just waved me off with his hand. Yes," she said, nodding decisively, "there's a man with some mixed feelings indeed."

"How did he act in the morning?" Jean-Claude probed.

"I didn't see him in the morning," she replied, in a tone of wonder at Jean-Claude not already knowing this for himself. "He was already gone, and I didn't see him again until later, at the church. By the time I woke up, Mr. Simon's people had already come in and nailed up the coffin. They must be early risers, those people."

"And they immediately placed the coffin on the hearse?" he asked, with mounting interest.

"No. They had left after securing the coffin and didn't come back to retrieve it until a little later in the morning. And it was such a lovely procession to the church, even if a little 'sparse,' like I said before." Suddenly, her wrinkled features twisted into a scowl. "And to think that poor dead woman was not even allowed to rest in peace for a solid day! Why the gall of those . . . those . . ." Words that would do justice to the crime simply would not come, so she settled instead for an emphatic, "Oh!"

"How did you first learn of the theft?"

She thought for a moment, letting her anger settle into a simmering indignation, and replied, "It was George. After the funeral, he stayed in town with some men of his acquaintance—dining at an inn, you know—and they got to playing cribbage. Well, before you know it, the sun's coming up, and the rooster's crowing. They've been playing all night, as it turns out! George has always fancied a game of cards and just lost all track of time.

"Well, he and his acquaintances step out to find a bite of breakfast, and passing by the church, they see a commotion. He told me no one even had to tell him what happened, because he already had a feeling. It's such a common thing nowadays, you know. But he stepped into the churchyard anyway, just to learn the details, and the fellow that had been set upon told him all about it. Even showed him the knot on his head, where the robbers had tried to knock him senseless with a footstone. Then he flew back here as fast as Millie—that's the horse—could carry him, and gave us the shocking news." The outrage on her face gave way to an expression of eager surprise, as if suddenly remembering something she hadn't realized she already knew. "But that's what you two gentlemen have come for, isn't it? To try and track down the missus?"

Somewhat taken aback at having the tables of interrogation thus instantly turned, he stammered helplessly for a moment before regaining his composure, and his role as Christophe Dubres. "Yes, Madame. That is, indeed the reason for our interest in the Darcy household. We wish to 'track down' Mrs. Darcy." And then he added, with a benedictory tone in his voice, "And you have been of the utmost assistance to us in our search."

Mrs. Bow's indignation evaporated instantly in the warm glow of flattery, and she absent-mindedly brushed a stray, gray hair up off of her face. "I'm pleased to provide any assistance that's within my humble powers, I'm sure," she said modestly, then added, "Anything to help find the missus."

"We will not rest until we have dragged into the daylight any person or persons who may have been involved in this terrible crime." He stood and bowed formally, uncertain whether or not his hostess actually saw the gesture. "I shall personally keep you informed of our progress in the search. Good day, Madame."

"Well if you really must go," she said, and reluctantly showed him to the door.

Jean-Claude's first reaction on being outside of the house was a sense of great relief. It was far easier, he realized, to maintain his fictitious role as Christophe Dubres when he had his "assistant" James Hodge to play his foil. Such individual interviews as he had just concluded with Mrs. Bow placed far too great a burden on an actor's memory, requiring one to be writer, director, and lead player, all at once. That evening, when we returned to the apartment at the conclusion of our long, busy day, he made the surprising and unprecedented confession that maybe, just maybe, he would have been better off had he had the benefit of my assistance, and I have never forgotten the confession, nor have I let him forget it.

As he strolled down the walkway to the road, however, and had the chance to "catch his breath," his relief was soon replaced by the realization of a new opportunity. Here he was, after all, at Darcy, upon whose grounds perhaps lay the very key that would unlock the secret of a man's murder, and perhaps reveal the whereabouts of a lady's stolen body. And the gentleman and lady of the house were out for the entire day. While the cat is away, the mouse might as well play, he thought, with a self-deprecatory smirk at the juvenile analogy.

Formulating a plan, but not altering his brisk footsteps, in case anyone might be watching, he strode purposefully down the walk and turned onto the road, continuing to walk until a tall hedge lay between him and the house. Then, looking all around him for signs of human presence, he mentally reviewed Jimmy's account of the covert visit he had paid to the house three days ago and searched for topographical landmarks that matched the lad's description of the place. Convinced that the hedge behind which he stood was the very hedge that had concealed Jimmy in his approach to the house, Jean-Claude assured himself that he was quite alone and ventured off the road and into the patch of trees surrounding the estate.

As he picked his way through a labyrinth of thornbushes and brambles—Jimmy hadn't mentioned these—Jean-Claude reflected upon precisely what it was he was looking for here. After formulating what he considered to be a fairly plausible theory of the events leading up to his and Edward's coming into possession of a murdered man, whose body had been surreptitiously placed into the coffin of a young widow, whose own remains had yet to be accounted for, every new detail he had learned had undermined one or more of the pillars upon which that theory rested. Every surmise had been replaced with a doubt until all that remained for certain was an enormous question mark. One aspect of his original theory that had remained constant throughout the past few days' discoveries and deliberations was the suspicious and inconsistent behavior of "Peter Worthington," which left Jean-Claude more convinced than ever that the man was quite simply not who he said he was. And close upon the heels of this conclusion logically followed the strong probability of dissemblance on the part of Madeline Worthington, it being highly unlikely that an intelligent woman would not notice the substitution of a strange man for her brother, even if she hadn't seen that brother for a number of years. Since all that remained of his original theory were questions regarding the actual identities of these two "Worthingtons," it stood to reason that anything he could learn about the pair would likely take him toward, rather than away from, the truth. So instead of searching for anything in particular on the grounds of Darcy, he decided simply to look about the place with open eyes and an open mind.

After considerable effort, and no slight damage to his suit and shoes, Jean-Claude found himself peering through the bamboo screen bordering the rear garden. There, as Jimmy had described, he saw the statuary, the two ponds, the "church," which, as he had suspected, was actually a small pagoda, a tea pavilion—the "shed" from Jimmy's account, and the overgrown stone path leading from the garden to the rear entrance of the house. Surveying the area from his bamboo cover, he saw no indication of any human presence on the estate except for himself and Mrs. Bow. Peter and Madeline, he knew absolutely, were in town for the entire day, and the groundskeeper "George" was nowhere to be seen—more likely than not on one of his regular jaunts into London, for, based upon Mrs. Bow's description of the man, he kept that horse "Millie" rather uncommonly busy. And so long as he took care not to make an excessive amount of noise, he knew he would be completely invisible to the aging housekeeper, provided he did not stroll directly before her and touch her on the arm.

His undetected passage through the garden thus virtually assured, he nonetheless took the extra precaution of skirting the enclosure through the underbrush and bamboo that surrounded it, keeping a screen of greenery between himself and the house for as long as was absolutely possible. As he made his way through the edge of the woods, he came upon a small narrow clearing leading deeper into the shade of the trees. It was clearly a path, and, in the interest of keeping open eyes and an open mind, he permitted himself to be diverted from his immediate plan of exploring the rear, and if possible, the back rooms of the house, and entered the path, just to see where it would lead. Initially, it appeared to lead nowhere, narrowing quickly to a nearly impassable thicket. Just as Jean-Claude was on the verge of turning back toward the house, however, he noticed a patch of white on the other side of the thicket, which, upon closer investigation, proved to be a small cottage—a servants' quarters, it appeared to be, but uninhabited for quite some time based upon the structure's obviously advanced state of disrepair.

Making his way up what at one time must have been a front walk, but now was nothing more than a few randomly scattered stones peeking up through the tangled grasses that surrounded the place, he noticed that the shutters were tightly closed—apparently nailed shut—but the front door stood slightly ajar. Absolutely certain he was alone, but feeling an instinctive hesitation at entering a civilized dwelling place unbidden, he

lingered on the doorstep for a long moment, looking and listening for any sign of life about the
house. Neither hearing nor seeing anything to
contradict his initial impression of utter desolation, he overcame his baseless reluctance and
pushed the door open. Not surprisingly, the rusted
hinges squealed with such great gusto that he
imagined his uninvited—and hence entirely
illegal—trespass onto this forlorn patch of past
civilization to have been broadcast throughout the
surrounding countryside and all the way into
London, whence the police were undoubtedly already on their way to apprehend him. A moment's
tense reflection, however, quickly assured him
that the echoing report that sounded in his ears,
sounded in *his* ears alone and that his presence
here was known to no human being on earth save
himself. He laughed aloud at his timidity and proceeded into the cottage.

At first, the close dimness of the one-room
dwelling prevented him from making out anything but gray shadows upon a black background,
but as his eyes adjusted to the feeble lighting, the
shadows began to resolve themselves into indis-
tinct shapes that clearly had an interesting, if
ambiguous, tale to tell. The interior of the cottage
was Spartan to say the least, the only furniture
in the place being a cot, a desk, and a chair. The
cot, however, rather than being rotted out with
dampness and disuse, as one would expect of such
a dank, uninhabited enclosure, was surprisingly
sound, and covered in bed clothing that was not
only free of visible decay but actually appeared

quite fresh and clean, as if it had recently been changed. The desktop revealed nothing of interest—dark-stained wood covered in a patternless landscape of scratches and dents—but the chair in front of it told a different story, in that it actually had a story to tell. Carefully draped across the top rung of its ladder back was a man's suit of clothes, obviously quite expensive, based upon the cut and fabric. Lifting the suit from the chair and holding it out at arm's length in front of his face, he examined it closely and frowned slightly at not seeing exactly what he expected to see. But then, recalling his own self-injunction to keep his mind as well as his eyes open, he looked at it once again, trying to read whatever message it might have to tell him. "Curious," he said aloud, narrowing his eyes in concentration. "Most curious."

After he had gleaned all of the information this out-of-the-way cottage had to offer, Jean-Claude made his way back up the tangled path until he was within sight of the house once again. Pausing on the edge of the thicket until he assured himself that there was no one around—Mrs. Bow included—who might see him making his way across the open garden toward the back of the house, he set out rapidly but unevenly across the unkempt grass until he reached the "tea pavilion," where he hid himself from open view in order to take another reassuring survey of the premises. Much to his relief, still no creature stirred. So centrally located was the pavilion, however, that even though he felt secure enough from possible discovery, he maintained this position for several minutes while taking a more leisurely inventory of the garden and its contents. Behind him was a long, narrow pond spanned by a graceful little footbridge. Immediately to his right lay a somewhat larger oval pond, with the stone lantern rising up from its glassy reflective surface. It was in this pond, he assumed, where swam the 'normous goldfish that had made such an impression upon Jimmy. Leading away from the pavilion and stretching toward the back of the house, were the nearly completely concealed flagstones that formed what once must have been a tidy little pathway connecting the house and the small structure in which he now crouched. Visually following the path to the house, his gaze hung upon the rear entrance immediately opposite him. The door, apparently leading into the winter garden of which Jimmy had spoken, stood halfway open. When he had seized opportunity by the forelock and ducked behind the hedge leading up toward the house, he had no intention whatsoever of actually reentering the building he had exited only moments before—the full extent of his plan was to have a look around the exterior grounds only, and he had already overstepped that by breaking into the little cottage in the woods. But here he found himself faced with an open doorway to a part of the house that, based upon Jimmy's report, would give him access to virtually the entire residence, without serious risk of discovery, provided he took care not to make any noises that might alert Mrs. Bow to his uninvited presence.

Taking one last precautionary look around the garden, he left the sanctuary of the pavilion and walked as rapidly as his feet would carry him across the stones leading to the house.

Thus completely out in the open, Jean-Claude found the pathway to be far longer than it had appeared from his former concealed location. Throughout the entire torturous journey, he could not escape the feeling that someone was watching him. Several times, he slowed his gait and considered rushing back to the pavilion, or better yet, all the way to the woods, where he could regain the "cover" of the hedge, make his way to the road, and flee the property altogether. At each of these moments, however, he deliberately reassured himself that he was, indeed, all alone in the garden, and simply kept walking. On the final such occasion, when he felt the pavilion strongly beckoning him from behind, he looked ahead of him and noticed, to his infinite relief, that the open door, and the safety of the house, were but mere yards away. He breathed a deep sigh of relief, chuckled silently at his near loss of nerve, and lifted his foot to take the first step of the eight or ten more it would take him to gain the door. When his foot descended this time, however, the sole did not meet with the familiar uneven solidity of the flagstone pathway. The stone was there, yes, but between the stone and the sole of his shoe lay some disturbingly unfamiliar object. Round and firm was the object, but altogether more pliable than the stone upon which it lay. In a span of time that seemed to drag on for an hour or more, but probably occupied no more than a full second of real time, Jean-Claude forced his head to face downward, toward his feet, and saw, cruelly pressed between the sole of his shoe and the surface of the flagstone, a furry, gray tail. And the cat to which it belonged lay sleeping not three inches from his foot. Every nerve in his entire body shrieked in sympathy with the bloodcurdling yowl of the rudely disturbed feline, whose cry sounded an unmistakable alarum announcing his trespassing presence to any sentient mortal being within a square mile.

And then, in an instant, even before his offending foot had had time to respond to his brain's exhortation to move, it occurred to him that, as loudly as his nerves were crying out inside his head, his nerves were the only things crying out. The cat whose tail lay pinned beneath his foot remained silent, and completely still. Releasing the tail from beneath his sole, he looked down at the sleek gray animal lying motionless in the grass, curled up in a posture of contented relaxation, its eyes gazing lazily toward the woods. Not a mark was visible anywhere on the body that would indicate violence or injury, and yet there it lay, clearly lifeless. He prodded the feline body with his toe, wincing instinctively in anticipation of protest from the animal, but only continued silence ensued—a silence that was rendered all the more incongruous by the bodily suppleness and flexibility with which his exploring toe met. Kneeling down, he placed a gentle hand upon the cat's side, which gave slightly and softly under the pressure of his hand, and even felt distinguish-ably warmer than the chilly air around it, and yet not a single breath stirred within its body. "Curi-ous," he found himself saying once again, and then immediately snapped his mouth shut as he remembered where he was and that he was not supposed to be there.

Looking toward the half-open door immedi-ately before him, he considered his original in-tention of entering the house and having a good look around the place. But he reconsidered. His encounter with the cat had thoroughly under-mined his nerve, reminding him of how very in-appropriate, not to mention illegal, had been his actions of the last half hour. He remembered Ed-ward's injunction that he not "go antagonizing those people," and it occurred to him how su-premely antagonistic his lurking surveillance of the Darcy House would appear should Mrs. Bow suddenly step out the back door, to empty the dishwater, for instance—or more embarrassing yet, should Peter and Madeline make a prema-ture return to the estate and find him creeping about the winter garden. With these imagined prospects playing out all too vividly in his mind, Jean-Claude concluded that he had seen quite enough for one day and resolved to return whence he had come, immediately.

Standing up from his crouched position, he stretched his legs and back in preparation for the long, circuitous walk back to the road. Then, tak-ing a reluctant parting glance at the half-open door, he turned to make his way toward the pavilion, but was halted in his tracks when he found himself standing face-to-face with a burly middle-aged man whose deeply weathered face wore an unmistakable expression of suspicious disapproval. "May I help you?" the man asked, folding his hairy arms across his chest, and raising a bushy eyebrow into an attitude of pronounced skepticism. Jean-Claude's mind reeled, both from the sheer surprise of the unexpected encounter, and from the sudden necessity of constructing a plausible explanation for his inexplicable presence on the estate.

"I have come to see Mr. and Miss Worthington," he lamely attempted, then added, to no greater avail, "They are expecting me."

"They're out," the man replied, brusquely and unceremoniously.

"Yes, I knew they might be," Jean-Claude offered, trying his best to sound casual. "I thought I would show myself around the gardens while I awaited their arrival."

"They're out for the entire *day*," the man insisted, pointedly.

"Ah, indeed?" So very off-balance had the man caught him, that Jean-Claude struggled vainly to right himself. Words that might serve to redeem the situation fled his every desperate grasp. "Perhaps I shall try again tomorrow."

The man stared at him in stony silence for an interminably long moment, clearly calculating how best to proceed with the intruder he had apprehended. Thoughts of jail, or worse, assaulted Jean-Claude's imagination, further interfering with his search for words that might purchase his release from this intolerable situation. Finally, the man appeared to resolve some indeterminate question with which he grappled, and a slight relaxation of his posture indicated the decision lay in his Jean-Claude's favor. "I expect them back late this evening," he said, a shade less aggressively than before. "Who shall I tell them stopped by to call?"

"I am Monsieur Dubres," he replied, grateful for the reprieve, but still unsettled enough to temporarily forget his assumed first name. "If you will be so kind, please extend my regrets that I was unable to see them today." Every word that emerged from his mouth heightened the sheer ridiculousness of his situation. He longed for nothing more than simply to flee the man's stony gaze and regain the comfort and anonymity of the open road.

"I shall tell them, sir," the man responded, with slightly exaggerated formality. "Good day."

"Good day," Jean-Claude said, and then, somewhat recovering his sense of purpose, added, "I believe I did not get your name."

"George, sir," he replied. "George Jenkins."

"Very well. Good day then, Mr. Jenkins." Thus freed from the exigencies of the moment, and eager to be on his way, Jean-Claude strode purposively up the path toward the pavilion, until he was halted in midstride by the man's voice, now bearing a distinct undertone of amusement. "Excuse me, sir," he said, ". . . but wouldn't you prefer to leave by the *front* of the house?"

Jean-Claude turned upon his heels and permitted himself to be led around the house to the front walk, down which, for the second time in just under an hour, he proceeded toward the road.

CHAPTER 21

"But how could you, Jean-Claude?" I fumed. After bidding farewell to Madeline and Peter, I wandered the streets in no particular direction for the better part of an hour, mentally retracing the day's events in search of some indication of how best to proceed. I felt as though I had known Madeline for years—so very comfortable were we together—and she gave every appearance of feeling the same way. And yet, in spite of impressions to the contrary, we had only just met a little over twenty-four hours earlier. There was no need to be overly hasty about all of this. I was not going anywhere in the foreseeable future—my medical studies restricting me to London for at least another year—and neither was she. Had not Madeline expressed her profound weariness over the "vagabond existence" she had been living? Did she not pronounce herself "absolutely contented" for the first time since she had left England, so many years ago? Clearly we had time to let our sentiments for one another ripen gradually, and in due time.

Such were my luxuriously unsettled reflections as I walked the streets of London. When I returned to the apartment, however, sometime after midnight, all of my inchoate, meandering speculations suddenly resolved themselves into a single desperately urgent question: "Will Maddy ever want to see me again?" Jean-Claude's careless midday stroll through the Darcy gardens could not help but get back to Peter and Maddy, announcing in no uncertain terms, that not only were we still in pursuit of Abigail Darcy's body—against the expressed wishes of the woman's brother and sister—but we suspected them of being somehow involved in her disappearance, and perhaps even of worse. I could see my slowly blossoming relationship with Madeline being snuffed out in an instant, like a daffodil in a late frost. And it was all Jean-Claude's fault. "How could you?" I repeated.

In reply to my protestations, all I received from Jean-Claude was an uneasy silence, though whether born of guilt, as would be entirely appropriate, or of some other indeterminate impulse, lay beyond my powers of comprehension. For once, I had no interest whatsoever in what he might think about what I was saying, so long as he heard it. "Did I not tell you to be careful? Of course, when I said that, I thought I was only cautioning you not to ask Mrs. Bow any indiscreet questions. I never imagined I should have to warn you against out-and-out trespassing. The gall!" I paced the floor for a few silent moments, giving Jean-Claude a chance to offer some defense for his indefensible behavior but knowing that nothing he might say would mitigate the offense.

"And even if my relationship with Maddy weren't at stake here—although that's a rather difficult hypothesis, since it is, after all, my paramount concern in the matter—but for argument's sake, let's say the relationship is not a consideration. Has it occurred to you that that man . . . George . . . was perfectly within his rights to shoot you where you stood, roaming around private property that way? Of course, even though you escaped the immediate situation unharmed, we can't be certain that the Worthingtons won't pursue prosecution, once the man informs them of your intrusion onto their property. And since I, 'James Hodge' am your 'partner,' the police could very well haul me off when they come to get you. Why, before all this is over, we may very well wind up on the dissection table ourselves, after our public hangings." During the latter part of my diatribe, Jean-Claude shifted his attention from the bare wall in which he had apparently been engrossed to the spot, directly across the room, where I stood. When I had fairly well exhausted one vein of righteous indignation, and was silently searching for another one to begin mining, Jean-Claude took advantage of the pause to interject a word or two in his own defense.

"Your anger is completely understandable," he said quietly, and with uncustomary humility. "It was very foolish of me to be seen in the garden at Darcy." He paused, apparently contemplating what he would say next. "And yet," he continued, ". . . my solitary foray onto the grounds of Darcy Estate provided me with critical information that I could not have attained otherwise."

"And precisely what is this 'critical information'?" I demanded, in utter disbelief that he was still thus preoccupied with the world of the dead, when the world of the living presented so many perils of its own at the moment. Either in response to my lack of interest in his "findings," or out of uncertainty over what these findings might actually mean, he remained silent and gazed absently out the window into the darkness. As angry as I was, I couldn't help feeling just the slightest bit sorry for him as he stood there in silence, clearly still shaken by the day's unsettling events, and uncertain what to do with the "information" he had purchased at such a dear cost to his own dignity, not to mention his nerves. It has ever been one of my failings that I find it virtually impossible to remain unequivocally angry for than a few minutes at a time.

"Look, Jean-Claude," I finally said. "I don't know how all of this will affect Maddy and me." Then I shook my head, and laughed under my breath as I caught myself once again putting the proverbial cart before the horse. "I don't even know if there *is* a 'Maddy and me.' What's done is done, either way, and we'll just have to wait and see how it all turns out." I gave full expression to the yawn that had been building inside me for the past few minutes. "For now, though, I'm off for bed before I drop where I stand. Good night, Jean-Claude."

"*Bon soir,*" he replied. I left him still staring out the window.

CHAPTER 22

The following morning being the last day of our forced hiatus from medical studies, I slept unusually late, and upon arising found Jean-Claude already on his third cup of tea and reading the morning's paper. "Ah, and so Lazarus arises from the tomb at last," he said with a smirk.

"Good morning, Jean-Claude," I said, scratching the scalp under my unruly hair and far too sleepy to bear any ill will from the previous day's adventures and misadventures. "What's the news?"

He folded up the newspaper and placed it on the table before him. "In here, absolutely nothing." And then, lifting an envelope from beside where the paper now lay, he added, "But in here, something of great potential interest—to you, or to me. Or perhaps even to the both of us." He held the envelope out toward me. "But most definitely of interest."

I took the proffered envelope, and, with some effort, focused my sleep-filled eyes upon its face, where appeared, in a graceful feminine script, two unfamiliar names. The reflection of a moment instantly brought me to my senses, however, and the names that suddenly swam into view were none other than Christophe Dubres and James Hodge. "When did this arrive, and by what courier?" I asked eagerly, now awake with the realization that only two people on earth knew us by those pseudonyms, and only one of those two had a delicate enough hand to have written the names at which I stared.

"About an hour ago," Jean-Claude responded, in a quizzical tone, as if trying to gauge my reaction. "It was delivered by a youth—the nephew of George the groundskeeper, I believe he said."

So very eager as I was to read the contents of the missive, that my fumbling hands initially refused to carry out the simple command my brain was sending them. I expected Jean-Claude to offer some sarcastic observation about my all-too-apparent discomfiture, but he merely continued to hold me in that enigmatic quizzical stare. Finally, the recalcitrant paper released its captive contents, and I found myself staring at a brief note written by the same delicate hand that had committed our pseudonyms to the envelope. "Gentlemen," it began, and I cannot deny experiencing a pang of disappointment at the plural salutation. "My brother and I request the pleasure of your company at Darcy House this afternoon for tea and conversation. We have a matter of some importance to discuss with you. If you will please be so kind as to send your reply with Bill, we will expect your arrival at around four o'clock. Sincerely, Madeline Worthington." My spirits surged at the unexpected opportunity of seeing Madeline again so soon, but flagged somewhat from the chilly formality of the invitation. The postscript, however, lifted them once again. "P.S." it read. "Thank you for a lovely time, James. Your company yesterday was most agreeable."

Reluctantly lifting my eyes from the note, I found Jean-Claude still holding me in that same probing gaze, and felt a wave of irritability wash over me. My irritation quickly gave way to another, more pressing, emotion as I considered Madeline's request for an immediate response to a note we had received over an hour ago. "We must reply to this, Jean-Claude," I said, in a growing state of something very akin to panic. "Where is the boy who delivered this note . . . Bill? We must send word with him."

"Do not concern yourself, my friend," Jean-Claude said calmly, and, I sensed, not a little patronizingly. "Since you were sleeping so soundly, I took the liberty of accepting the invitation. Young Bill was on his way back to Darcy with my . . . with our reply, scant moments after his arrival upon our doorstep." He paused for a moment, and I noticed his left eyebrow rise significantly. "There is one thing I do not understand, however," he mused, breaking the silence. "In our dealings with the Worthingtons, we are operating under assumed identities, yes? How then, did Bill know where to find Christophe and James?"

So very quickly was my mind racing with the "revelations" of the past few moments—the invitation, the request for a prompt reply, and the subsequent fear that we had missed the opportunity, then the discovery that "we" had, in fact, already replied—that I did not at first realize the implications of Jean-Claude's query and my own personal culpability in the matter. I felt the blood rise to my face with the sudden embarrassing perception of how my actions must appear from Jean-Claude's point of view. The simple truth is that I had grown so very close, to Madeline, so very quickly, during the time we spent together on the previous day, that I had quite voluntarily given her the location of our lodgings. In the clear light of a new day, however, I could easily see how this disclosure did rather compromise the secrecy of our true identities. But just as quickly, I recalled all the needless sidestepping and subterfuge into which I had been forced throughout my day with Madeline, all because of this fiction Jean-Claude had cooked up in his imagination, and a fair degree of resentment mingled with my embarrassment, tempering it considerably.

"I couldn't see the harm in it, Jean-Claude." Although trying to sound indignant, and generally "put-upon," I managed to sound merely defensive, in spite of my best efforts. "After all, they have no knowledge that two such people as Jean-Claude Legard and Edward Montague exist," I said, lowering my voice an octave. "And more's the pity, come to think of it, for how shall I ever explain this charade to Maddy, once all this murder business is behind us."

"Ah," Jean-Claude interjected, holding up an index finger in a gesture that I found infuriatingly didactic. "So you have not completely forgotten our unfortunate gentleman back at St. Alban's. I am so pleased to see that this murder 'business' has not slipped your mind. But 'business' though the murder may be, it is an extremely serious business, and we would do well to remember it."

"I don't need to be lectured to," I bristled. "I'm not the murderer. In plain matter of fact, I'm a simple medical student who would very much like to get on with his studies, and with his life, the sooner the better. All of this police work—and that is exactly what it is we are doing, not medicine—is standing directly, and obtrusively, within the path before me."

"Then it seems to me," Jean-Claude replied calmly, and even with a hint of empathetic understanding in his voice, ". . . that the best way to proceed forward, is to put the impediment behind you. And the only means of putting the impediment behind you is to resolve two simple questions of identity. To wit, who is the dead man buried in the compost heap at St. Alban's and who is the person responsible for his being there?"

"But that could take forever," I complained. "Why, you and I might die of old age before we ever get to the bottom of this."

"Do not worry about dying of old age, *mon ami*," he said mysteriously. "We are far closer to the 'bottom' than you know. But first, we have an appointment to keep, do we not? And looking at you now, I would estimate that you have several hours worth of repair to do upon your appearance before you will be presentable to polite society."

I grumbled an irritable, though involuntarily placable, protest against the insult, and poured myself a cup of tea.

CHAPTER 23

The day passed remarkably quickly. As Jean-Claude only half-jestingly predicted, getting myself "presentable" was no easy task, for my hair gave one the unmistakable impression of its owner having slept with his head near an open window during a cyclone. Additionally, it was over an hour before I even had the opportunity to survey the damage I had to repair, for the cup of tea I poured myself had whetted my appetite for some toast and jam, which took me so long to prepare that my tea grew cold in the meantime, so I wound up putting another pot on to boil. As the hour of departure approached, however, I grew more energetic in my preparations, and three o'clock found us, as planned, on a coach bound for Darcy.

When we arrived at the Rose and Crown, Jean-Claude sent me on to Darcy House ahead of him, citing some business he had to conduct before joining me there. As I strolled, with unaccountable lethargy, up the now-familiar front walk, I took in my surroundings, and reflected on how very much had changed since our first uninvited journey nearly a week ago. Could it have only been a week? It felt more like a hundred years, or a lifetime.

The brass dragon once again announced my presence, and almost instantly, the door swung open, startling me out of my meandering reverie. I cannot deny that it was with considerable disappointment that I found myself face-to-face with Peter Worthington rather than his sister, and based upon the look on his face, he was no more pleased to see me than I was to see him. "Good day," I said, somewhat stiffly, to which Peter responded with a barely audible grunt and an exaggerated glance over my shoulder. "I am here at the request of your sister," I added, thinking perhaps she had not informed him of her invitation.

"Yes, but the invitation was for you *and* Christophe," he said, altogether unceremoniously. "Our business involves the both of you."

"Christophe had a bit of business of his own to conduct," I explained. ". . . but will be joining us directly."

Peter looked over my shoulder once again, then relaxed, becoming more like the man with whom I had spent a portion of the previous day. "Won't you come in, then?" he said, stepping aside and waving me into the house. "Maddy's in the kitchen preparing tea. Mrs. Bow's old mother is down with an ague, poor dear, and will require some assistance for a few days." I followed him into the parlor, where he bid me make myself at home while he went to fetch Maddy. Left thus alone, I allowed my eyes to roam freely around the room, taking in the exotic collection of prints, statuary, and armor. Like a museum, indeed, I thought. But then again, no more sinister than a museum, either, despite Jean-Claude's wild speculations to the contrary.

Delighted feminine laughter rang out from the rear of the house, followed by the sound of quick, small footsteps, as Maddy raced down the hall. "Why James," she exclaimed, clapping her hands together in apparent delight. "How very good to see you. It seems like it's been ages." I instantly caught her infectious giddiness, and soon found myself laughing heartily with her at absolutely nothing. "How I have missed you," she said, when our laughter subsided sufficiently for her to catch her breath. "I honestly could not endure going an entire day without seeing you."

"The feeling is entirely mutual," I said, recalling all too clearly the restless night I had spent, wondering if I would ever see her again. "But was it absolutely necessary that I bring Christophe along?" I pretended to scold. "I would so prefer to have you all to myself."

"And I, too, would prefer to be alone," she protested. "But Peter insisted that the both of you come, since he has a rather momentous revelation to make that involves Christophe just as much as it involves you." She hesitated and looked toward the parlor door. "But where is the good Mr. Dubres? Perhaps he decided that he is simply too important to associate with the likes of us."

"Oh, no. Nothing of the sort," I assured her, wincing internally as I thought of Jean-Claude's rather remarkable sense of self-importance. "He had a bit of correspondence to complete while he was at the inn, in order to take advantage of the mail coach on its outward journey. I expect him here any moment."

An immediate knock on the front door made me appear a veritable prophet, sending Madeline into renewed paroxysms of laughter. She was still laughing when she returned from the hallway, leading a somewhat startled-looking Jean-Claude by the arm. "You'll have to forgive us, Mr. Dubres," she said, taking a deep breath to compose herself. "But James and I have been having the jolliest time. We simply cannot contain our hilarity." A slight, formal bow being the only reply she was able to wrest from Jean-Claude, she sighed resignedly, wiped the tears of laughter from the corners of her eyes, and excused herself to finish preparations for tea. "I have some savory biscuits in the oven," she said on her way out the door.

"Why don't you take a seat, Jean-Claude?" I asked, when we were alone. "And do cheer up, would you? From the expression on your face, one might conclude that you had just lost your last piece of candy."

"An extremely amusing simile, my friend," he said humorlessly. "I shall have to remember it the next time I am called upon to play the jester." While Jean-Claude most unequivocally ignored my former exhortation, he at least consented to sit down, so that he appeared more like a human being than a pillar of salt, for all his stiffness. "Did our hosts reveal anything of interest before my arrival?" he asked, sitting bolt upright in a plush chair, his hands folded primly upon his lap.

"Not a word," I replied. "I only just arrived a couple of moments before you did. I say, you must really have been hoofing it."

His eyes drifted around the room, fitfully lighting upon first one thing, then another, for all the world like a troublesome fly. "My business did not occupy me as long as I expected." Whether or not he had any intention of expanding upon this vague remark, I shall never know, because Peter appeared in the doorway at just that moment, with Madeline closely in tow, carrying a silver tray of tea and biscuits.

"So happy to see you gentlemen have made yourselves comfortable," Peter said warmly, now playing to perfection the role of gracious host, in stark contrast to his initial "greeting" upon my arrival. "Did James tell you about the splendid play we attended last evening—*The Pilot*? Most enjoyable. You really must see it before it closes, although based upon the number of people who crowded into that stuffy theatre, I should imagine it will be playing for some time to come." While Peter recounted the merits of the performance, noting in particular the "extraordinary fidelity to nature" achieved onstage through the use of the theatre's sophisticated machinery, Madeline handed around teacups and saucers.

"You really must tell me what you think of these," she commanded, placing two saffron-colored wafers upon each of our plates. "It's the first opportunity I've had to try this receipt, given me by a baker I knew in Florence."

"I believe your invitation mentioned something about an announcement, no?" Jean-Claude said, casting aside all social niceties and tossing a proverbial wet blanket over the proceedings. Madeline would have none of it, however.

"No you don't," she admonished, wagging a finger in his direction. "It's pleasure before business around here. And it is, indeed, a pleasure to have gotten to know you gentlemen."

"The pleasure is all ours," I protested, trying to make up for Jean-Claude's stuffiness. "And may I take this opportunity to say how very thoroughly I enjoyed our day in town? The art gallery was a bit close, I'm afraid, but otherwise, I had a wonderful time."

Madeline looked at me with eyes that seemed to peer into the very depths of my soul. Her facial expression was serious at first, but almost immediately melted into one of those radiant smiles that seemed to be far more in keeping with her temperament than a façade of high gravity, such as Jean-Claude made a custom of wearing. "I shall never forget it," she concurred, in a hushed, melodic voice, and instantaneously turned her full attention upon Jean-Claude.

"I must insist, Mr. Dubres, that you tell me at once what you think of the biscuits I worked so hard preparing for you. They apparently don't disagree with you too terribly, since you've already 'polished' yours off. Mr. Hodge, I'm afraid, is rather lagging behind."

I raised my hand to protest, but, having a mouthful of tea, was temporarily bound to silence. Fortunately, Jean-Claude remembered his manners sufficiently to avoid an awkward, and, I must add, impolite silence, following our hostess's obvious request for a compliment. "They are quite agreeable, Madame," he unbent himself long enough to say. And then, apparently warming somewhat to the Worthingtons' abundant hospitality, he added, "There is a rather unusual seasoning, that I have been trying to identify."

Madeline cast a quick, almost imperceptible glance toward Peter, and replied, "You are quite the connoisseur to have noticed, Mr. Dubres. The receipt calls for freshly grated ginger—just the faintest hint of it—to contrast with the other, more savory, ingredients. I am impressed." And then she looked at the biscuit remaining on my plate, and shook her head. "I'm afraid we can't say the same about our Mr. Hodge here, can we?"

"He does not have the adventurous palate, I am afraid," Jean-Claude explained. "If the menu features anything much more exotic than kidney pie—baagh—he had better have access to plenty of beer, or he simply cannot get it down." While Jean-Claude thus critiqued, or rather criticized, my taste in foods, I nonetheless managed to finish off my second biscuit.

"I'm entirely in agreement with Jean-Claude's

opinion," I said, then felt compelled to clarify. ". . . regarding the biscuits, that is. I'm afraid I must take exception to his assessment of my skills as a gourmand. The biscuits, however, are most exquisite indeed. And I, too, had been trying to place the seasoning—ginger, you say? It is quite subtle, but leaves behind it, not so much a taste as a feeling." I ran my tongue over my lips, and pondered. "Yes, a feeling. It sets one's lips to tingling." Madeline glanced at Peter once again, and a strange, inscrutable expression drifted onto her face. Almost as if in response to a predetermined signal, Peter stood up and began pacing the floor, obviously preparing to speak.

"Now that the 'pleasure' portion of our little convocation has concluded," he said, with a tone in his voice that matched the expression upon Madeline's face, "it is time to get on with the business for which you were invited out here this afternoon. You will recall, gentlemen, that Maddy's note made reference to an announcement we wished to make this afternoon, and I would assume that you are, at the very least, mildly curious as to the contents of that announcement."

I opened my mouth to respond, but instead of words, only an indecipherable gurgle emerged. With some effort, I turned my head toward Jean-Claude to silently communicate my baffling condition, but found him rather desperately occupied in loosening his shirt collar. He, too, appeared to be making vain attempts at speech. In response to our obvious show of distress, our host continued speaking, while our hostess simply stared at us, her inscrutable expression having given way to one of cruel amusement, such as cat wears when it has a mouse helplessly pinned in a corner.

"The news we have to share involves our imminent, and necessary, departure from England," Peter said, and sighed dramatically. "As much as we would like remain here and assist you gentlemen in your search for the missing body of Abigail Darcy—our dear departed 'sister'—I am afraid that circumstances absolutely require our immediate presence abroad." While Peter droned on thus nonsensically, my head fell back helplessly upon the cushion at my back, its motionlessness disturbingly consistent with that of the rest of my body. Through my peripheral vision, I could see Jean-Claude was in a state virtually identical to my own. We both stared blankly before us, as stock-still as statues—or corpses.

"Our guests appear to have decided they have nothing further to say to us, Peter," Madeline said glibly, without taking her eyes off of us. "I do hope we haven't offended them in any way."

"Well if they've been offended by anything," Peter joined in, "I'm willing to wager that the offense won't last long."

"And I'm inclined to agree with you, 'Peter,'" she replied, with a faint though unmistakable alteration of her dialectal accent. "We'd better talk quickly, then, so they won't miss anything."

Peter returned to his seat beside Madeline. "My sentiments exactly," he said. Madeline searched our faces with mock earnestness. "Are you quite comfortable?" she asked. "Is there anything I can get you? More tea perhaps? Maybe another biscuit or two?" Peter broke into uncontrollable laughter, but Madeline maintained her sardonic mask of mild amusement. "I suppose not," she added. "The biscuits didn't seem to agree with either of you, I'm afraid. As for myself, I could do with another drop or two of tea, Peter." She held her cup and saucer out to her side, still not taking her eyes from our faces. "Would you be so kind?" Peter retrieved the teapot from the table and filled her cup. She sipped her tea with great relish and took a deep contented breath before beginning to speak.

"It's really quite a pity, you know," she said, with the slightest hint of true sincerity, ". . . because you're not at all bad company—James, I mean." She looked me directly in the eye. "Christophe's another matter entirely. The world will be a far prettier place without him, I'm certain." She paused briefly. "Pleasant company or poor, however, it's six of one, half a dozen of the other, because the world will simply have to learn to get along without the both of you, very soon.

"Oh there's no need to try to speak," she said matter-of-factly, in response to a slight movement of Jean-Claude's head. "You'll never speak again. You'll never do anything again, in fact, except of course rot in the ground. It was the biscuits, you see . . . yours, not ours, of course, although perhaps you failed to notice we were not eating from a common tray. Far too risky. Why, if one of your biscuits had so much as touched the side of one of ours, we might be in as bad a state as you by now.

"What did you ask, Mr. Dubres?" she asked, leaning toward Jean-Claude in a pretense of trying to make out what he was, most definitely, not saying. "What was the special ingredient in those biscuits? You're absolutely dying to know, I can see, so I shan't keep you in suspense—you really haven't the time for it. The biscuits—yours, at least—contained an extract of a deadly poison found in the organs of a tropical fish called the puffer. In Japan, they actually eat the thing—fugu, they call it—cut into thin slices with just the slightest hint of poison remaining . . . to get that tingling sensation you described, shortly before total paralysis set in. Not surprisingly, dozens of people die in Japan every year as a result of eating this rare 'delicacy,' for it only takes a pinhead's worth of the poison to kill a man. Of course," she said with a chuckle, "there was enough poison in each of those biscuits you ate to kill a small army. A funny thing about the poison, though," she added, growing slightly more serious, ". . . is the way it affects people. It doesn't always kill a person at once, you see, even though someone who has consumed the poison—such as each of you—gives every appearance of being dead. Not even an expert on such matters—a physician, say, or an undertaker— can tell the difference between actual death and advanced fugu paralysis. Which is why, in Japan, victims of fugu poisoning are not buried for three days, or at least until decomposition begins, in order to avoid putting them underground alive. Those unfortunate enough to suffer every symptom of poisoning except for death, retain full consciousness until such time as they actually die. Imagine," she said, with an involuntary shudder, "being buried alive, fully conscious, but with no way of letting anyone know what a terrible mistake they're making by committing you to the earth." She paused, and looked at us with a mixed expression of curiosity and pity.

"Perhaps you gentlemen won't have to just imagine what that's like," she continued, "—being buried alive. Chances are, though, you'll be long since dead by the time Peter dumps you into the pit that he prepared for you, out there in the woods—you ought to know the spot, Mr. Dubres." She turned her head, although not her eyes, toward her brother. "I do hope you didn't blister your hands, poor dear, not being accustomed to such physical labor."

Being thus acknowledged as a part of the conversation, Peter spoke up. "I say, don't you think we ought to just get along with this? George might return at any moment, and how would we explain these fellows to him?"

"George?" she replied, laughing incredulously. "I sent George on a week's leave. He's still so torn up over Abby's death that I thought he could use a little time away. But even if he were to walk in right now, I doubt we'd get much of a protest from him. These gentlemen here somehow managed to get on George's bad side in their brief exposure to him. No, Peter, we've nothing to worry about, and I want to make sure our guests are completely informed of the circumstances surrounding their timely demise.

"Excuse me?" she asked, cocking an ear toward my face. "Why is it necessary for us to kill you? Well, it's a long story, actually, but as you don't seem to be in a particular hurry to be on your way, I suppose you have time to hear it. The story begins with a couple of overly curious gentlemen making a journey to Darcy House to bother a total stranger, still freshly grieving from the combined shock of the death of his beloved sister and the subsequent theft of her body from the graveyard where she was intended to have her final rest. 'Why should these gentlemen be so very interested in a matter that seemingly concerns them not in the least?' the brother asks himself. And lest you think for a moment that the cock-and-bull story you made up—about your being detectives on an 'official investigation'—deceived anyone for so much as a moment, you might as well disabuse yourself of that notion at once. To find a body stolen from a graveyard, one need look no farther than the nearest anatomy school. No," she said, narrowing her eyes in contemplation, ". . . they were not acting at the behest of any official inquiry. And they were not searching for my sister's stolen body . . ." With this last accusation, she glared directly into Jean-Claude's blank eyes, ". . . because my sister's body was not stolen." She stood up and walked to the window, staring silently out to the garden for a moment. Then she turned and faced us once again.

"At first, you seemed harmless enough—bothersome, yes, but not an apparent threat. We willingly played along with your game at first, thinking you'd eventually grow bored and run along back to wherever it was you came from. And to hasten that moment, we even went so far as to tell you outright that we wished to discontinue the 'search.' But did you pay attention? Of course not. You persisted in your bullheaded desire for 'information,' until it became necessary for us to glean some information of our own. Poor James," she said, walking over to me and patting my cheek with her hand. "Surely you didn't actually think I was so silly a girl as to be smitten by your charms in our very first encounter? Ah, well. You're to be pitied, really. And to be quite honest, I have nothing whatsoever against you personally. The day we spent together was not at all objectionable, and it brought nothing to light that made me think of you as anything worse than a mere nuisance. When we parted last evening, I had every intention of simply letting you sigh over me for a while, wondering why I didn't answer your letters, then harmlessly move on to the next woman who caught your fancy."

Suddenly, her eyes grew cold, and she leveled her gaze at Jean-Claude. "But while I was in town with James, *you* came sniffing around out here, and suddenly the whole thing made perfect sense—why you were so bloody interested in finding Abigail's body in the first place, and why your 'search' kept bringing you out here to Darcy, the very last place her missing body would be, had it actually been stolen. Oh, yes. My servants are quite loyal, and forthcoming to a fault. Not the slightest thing happens around here but either Mrs. Bow or George feels compelled to inform me about it. Mrs. Bow told me of your lengthy visit with her, and of all your 'odd' questions. That alone, however, would only serve to make you appear 'odd,' which is how I already viewed you. But when I spoke with George," she said, pursing her lips and nodding significantly, "your oddness suddenly became unacceptably dangerous."

She walked to the window once again and peered into the garden. "You're actually quite lucky he didn't shoot you on the spot, you know, trespassing that way. George is a very direct person, not much given to idle chatter—I imagine you noticed that about him during your brief encounter in the garden. No, George infinitely prefers action to words, and I'm quite certain he would have shot you dead on the spot had he not recognized you." She crossed the room and regained her seat directly in front of Jean-Claude. "Oh, yes, he recognized you at once. He's got quite a memory for faces, and he knew exactly where he'd seen you before. It was at the medical school, where you two gentlemen are—or perhaps for strict accuracy I should say 'were'—studying to be physicians. I'm quite surprised you didn't recognize him, as well, seeing as how you two passed within feet of each other just a few days ago. It was when he toured the hospital with that 'peasants delegation' Ben Edmonds invited inside. George was largely responsible for all of that, you know. He took the sudden death of 'Mistress Darcy' quite hard, the poor thing, and when he learned of the theft of her body, at the hands of a couple of gentlemen, no less, he vowed to make the persons responsible pay in full for their reprehensible actions. The identity of the guilty parties was no mystery to anyone, of course—George included—and after spending a few drunken hours in the tavern, enlisting the aid of any of his cronies sober enough to listen to him, it's a wonder he didn't go out and burn down half of London. As it turns out, though, when the sun came up next morning, he was too drunk to walk, much less start a riot, so he returned to Darcy and waited until the following day to go back into town to stir up trouble. He must have made a fairly compelling case for himself, too, from what I heard of the mob that took to the streets next evening, and they were out for blood, too. You gentlemen had quite a narrow escape, and if it weren't for Dr. Edmonds taking George and a few of the others into the school—showing them just enough to get them back outside to assure the angry mob that none of their own dear departed were lying in pieces about the place—you might not be sitting here right now." She paused and smiled slightly at the unintentional irony. "After his visit with the 'doctors,' George dispersed the crowd, drank all night with some remnants of the mob, and came back to Darcy to sulk until he felt like working again. He'd only just stepped out into the garden for the first time when he ran into you. Must have been quite a surprise for the poor fellow, leaving you behind there at the hospital, only to have you turn up here at Darcy, and in his own garden, no less. He remembered you all too well, and none too fondly, I might add, but instead of shooting you, as he was inclined to do, he quite properly came to me with word of your trespass and let me decide how best to proceed." She looked back and forth between us, and chuckled. "I suppose it's crystal clear by now how I decided to handle the matter."

A slight crease suddenly appeared on her forehead as a thought occurred to her. "Now I don't want you gentlemen to imagine that I'm taking this rather drastic measure"—she paused, and waved her hand vaguely in our direction—"simply because you're students of medicine. I'm not like those simple peasants running about in front of the hospital, waving pitchforks over their heads and threatening to tear down the place, just because the men inside happen to learn their trade by cutting up dead bodies fresh from the parish cemetery. It was no personal offense with your profession itself that forced me to take this course of action. It was that your profession—or rather my discovery of your pursuit of it—explained all too clearly your seemingly inexplicable interest in a simple body-snatching incident—likely but one of many such incidents occurring throughout England on that very night. It had to have been something about this particular incident—or about this particular body—that first drew you out here to Darcy, and my discovery of your association with the hospital told me what that 'something' was." She bent over close to our faces, and said in a low conspiratorial voice, "You were the ones who took the body from Abigail's coffin, and it was not the body of a woman, was it? It was a man, and a murdered man, at that! Puncture wound to the back of the neck, was it not?"

She sat back in her chair, with a self-satisfied smile spreading across her face. "You discovered the body," she continued, "and quite correctly surmised a connection between that body and us 'Worthingtons' out here at Darcy. In point of fact, there's a better-than-average chance that you were on your way to actually 'proving' something or another, not that you could have persuaded anyone to listen to your proof. But then I discovered your discovery, by the means I have just described, and now you shall not have the opportunity of proving anything to anyone." A look of concern crept into her eyes, and she impulsively placed a hand upon each of our chests, feeling for signs of life. "I'm afraid I shall be forced to abridge my fascinating story, gentlemen. I shouldn't wish you to die before I reach the denouement.

"To come directly to the point, then," she said, speaking more rapidly, although still savoring every word, ". . . the body you removed from Abigail Darcy's coffin was a gentleman of my former acquaintance, and it was I who put him there. Or, to be more precise, it was I who killed the man, and Peter who actually placed the body in the coffin. Now if you could speak at this point, I'm sure you would undoubtedly ask the logical sequitur to the questions of who the dead man was, and who killed him, now that the dead man and the murderer have both been identified, for even with these crucial questions thus successfully disposed of, one glaring mystery yet remains. What on earth ever became of Abigail Darcy's body? That was, after all, the reason you came out here in the first place, was it not? At least that's what you told Peter here, although we now know your curiosity ran much deeper than that."

"I say, Maddy," Peter said nervously, having temporarily suspended his pacing long enough to speak. "Is all this really necessary? I mean, how do we even know they can hear what you're saying?"

"Oh, they can hear me, all right," she snapped back sharply. "I know all too well that they can hear every word I'm saying, whether they wish to or not." With an effort, she reined in her temper, clearly not wishing to spoil the "moment," and addressed her brother in a more measured tone. "And as for the 'Maddy' business, there's really no need for that any more now, is there 'Peter'? For you see, gentlemen," she returned her attention to Jean-Claude and me, ". . . my name is not Madeline Worthington. And I am most definitely not the sister of Abigail Darcy, née Worthington. Nor am I the sister of this good gentleman standing beside me, here," she added, smiling slyly at Peter, ". . . am I, Robert."

She stood up and placed a single kiss upon the cheek of the man we had until that very moment known as "Peter," then continued her story. "My true name is Cathleen Smithson. I was born in

Ireland, County Cork, the only issue of a star-crossed marriage between a failed apothecary and a woman whose sole ambition in life was to someday appear upon the London stage. Not that there weren't theatrics enough in our household, with my father's drinking, and my mother's constant entreaties for him to move us all to England, or to Dublin, at least. As it turned out, he died—kicked in the head by a horse—before he had the chance to take us anywhere, and my mother seized the opportunity and had us on a ship to England with the next high tide. To her incalculable disappointment, however, she quickly discovered that London had a far greater need for domestic servants than for untrained actresses, and within a month's time, we had settled into the household where we were to remain for the next twelve years, until her death, and my flight abroad.

"I was five years old when we took up residence with the Hallams, and not sufficiently mature to appreciate our servile status among the family. As far as I knew, I was fully the social equal of the three Hallam children, and by practically living in Mr. Hallam's abundantly stocked library—where I often hid to escape my mother's frequent demands for my help with the household chores—I quickly established myself as their intellectual superior. The two girls resented me for it and kept at a proud distance from me, but the boy, Samuel—two years my elder—seemed fascinated with my ready grasp of learning, and often asked me for assistance with his own studies. He and I became virtually inseparable, in fact, which only served to further inflame the sisters' jealousy of me, and when it finally dawned on them one day that no one had ever taken the trouble to clarify for me my true position within the household, they wasted no time in disabusing me of my delusions of equality. For that day onward, I vowed to escape my servitude with the first opportunity that presented itself.

"That opportunity arrived in my eighteenth year, with the miraculous conjunction of two events: the death of my mother from extreme despondency—her dreams of acting having never, alas, materialized—and Samuel's 'coming of age,' along with the requisite 'Grand Tour' of the Continent that it entailed. With my poor mother thus 'off the stage,' as it were, I informed the Hallams that the time had come for me to seek employment elsewhere, and bid the family a bittersweet farewell. Rather than flying to yet another family of means who sought domestic help, however, I took the first coach to Dover, where I meet Samuel and embarked for Calais, and my own freedom.

"I roamed the Continent with Samuel for just over a year, playing the part of his young bride. Eventually, however, I began to find the role—and Samuel too, frankly—unendurably dull, and started to look about for some new means of escape. In Rome, while exploring the Coliseum, I noticed an extremely well-to-do middle-aged man staring at me in a most inappropriate manner. My Italian being fairly fluent, it took me very little time to learn that this gentleman was just what he appeared—a Roman nobleman of distinguished ancestry, and virtually unlimited means—and in exactly the amount of time it took me to pack my trunk, I left Samuel behind and set out for Naples, and then on to Greece, with Ippolito Bianchi.

"Five years passed in the blink of an eye, with Ippolito being succeeded by a Florentine jeweler, and the jeweler being followed by a Venetian banker, who was followed in turn by a German count, and then a Parisian wine merchant, and a whole series of highly interesting and extremely wealthy gentlemen, many of whose names I can no longer recall. Around two years ago—it was in Lyon, I shall never forget—I looked into a mirror, and suddenly realized that my better years were perhaps already behind me, or very nearly so, at least. As completely satisfying as had been my vagabond existence since leaving England, I realized that the time had come for me to seek a more permanent situation than I had thus far known. In an inexplicable fit of something closely akin to homesickness, I settled upon London as the place where I should seek such a situation.

"Taking up residence in a small apartment in Kensington, I set about devouring the daily papers to reacquaint myself with the goings-on of London society. I had not been in town a full month yet when I read a story about the eminent historian Sir Alfred Darcy, whose failing eyesight would soon force him to seek an amanuensis in order to complete a translation with which he had been struggling for the better part of ten years. Seeing such a gloriously clear pathway opening up before me, I decided to approach Sir Alfred and offer my services. On the rare chance that someone might remember that such a person as Cathleen Smithson ever existed, but even more so out of a desire to turn over a new leaf in my life, I abandoned forever the name of my birth, and became Abigail Worthington."

CHAPTER 24

"Of course, you know much of the story after this—how I went to work for Alfred, how we became inseparable companions, eventually deciding to formalize the relationship through marriage, and how we spent a lovely year together as husband and wife, until his unfortunate although not entirely unexpected death. One detail of which you weren't, perhaps, aware, however, was the actual cause of Alfred's death. Oh, I realize that no less competent a physician than Martin Stuyvesant declared the death completely natural—a heart attack was the official judgment—but there was nothing natural about it, I assure you, any more than your deaths will be natural. Of course, there's no need to make your deaths appear natural, since you'll soon be under the ground, and no one will be the wiser. You'll miss a few lectures at the medical school, and anyone who takes the time to notice will

simply assume you grew weary with the routine
and set out in search of adventure—the Mediter-
ranean is *so* enticing this time of year. With Alfred it was different, though, for practically the
entire civilized world was keeping close watch
over our marriage, so fascinated were they by our
May-December 'romance.' The great irony of Alfred's death is that I initially had no intention of
taking measures to hasten it. The old man couldn't
have lasted forever, I knew, and until such time
as he saw fit to depart this life, leaving me behind
to enjoy his fortune, I was content to enjoy my
comfortable life here at Darcy and just wait for
nature to take its course.

"Not long after our marriage, however, I made
the extremely unpleasant discovery that the great
majority of that fortune I was waiting so patiently
for had gone into the vast collection of dusty artifacts you see all around you. Now, I have no personal bias against antiquity—I married Alfred,
after all—and was perfectly content to live in the
British Museum, if need be, provided I could live
there comfortably. But so very much of his wealth
had he spent on his precious collection that he
barely had two pence to rub together, much less
the guineas required to provide me the sort of life
to which I had become entitled the day I married
the old man. As intolerable as I found this existence, however, I nonetheless resolved continued
patience, knowing that, whenever he did finally
see fit to cast off this mortal coil, I could simply
sell his precious collection to the highest bidder,
and live happily, and lavishly, ever after.

"But then he began making plans to leave his entire collection to the British Museum, and I realized I could no longer wait upon nature to take its course. It became imperative that I hasten Alfred on to immortality if I was to have any hope of enjoying the remainder of my own mortal existence here on earth. And quite fittingly, it was Alfred himself who provided me with the means of dispatching him in a manner that would not raise too many grizzled eyebrows among those cronies of his at the Atheneum Club.

"One part of Alfred's plan for turning Darcy into an Oriental paradise involved importing some of the indigenous cuisine of the Far East. A Dutch merchant he knew, procured for him, illegally I would imagine, an authentic Japanese chef, who spoke not a word of English, and was absolutely miserable from the moment he first set foot in Darcy until the day he boarded a trading vessel bound for Japan. In the meantime, he attempted, unsuccessfully, to prepare the native Japanese delicacies for which Alfred had enslaved the poor man. One of these delicacies, as you have no doubt already guessed, was fugu. Alfred was mad for fugu, you see, having first tried it during a brief visit to the Orient in his younger days, and went to great lengths to try to provide himself with a supply here. He turned his library into a constant-temperature winter garden, and built a salt pond in the center of it, which he kept stocked with those hideous puffer fish. Have you ever seen one? They're positively dreadful.

"Well, Alfred's Japanese chef was no more successful in preparing fugu than he was with any of the other dishes he attempted, so rather than having himself accidentally poisoned, Alfred sent the poor man back to Japan, and kept the 'puffer pond' strictly as a conversation piece, regaling his acquaintances with tales of the deadly delicacy. He even had a small vial containing a highly concentrated extract of the poison—a 'gift' to him from a German scholar—with which he thrilled guests by explaining the properties of the poison and describing the unusual manner of death it induces in its hapless victims. When Alfred started that mad talk of giving away his priceless collection, and depriving me of my rightful inheritance, I knew exactly what I had to do, and exactly how to do it. One evening, I prepared him a special bowl of egg drop soup, and the following day I gave my blessing to his fellow Atheneans in their plans to cremate him.

"With Alfred thus out of my way, I set about trying to find a dealer in rare antiquities with whose assistance I might translate the collection I had just inherited into something a little more practical, with which I might embark upon the life of independent means for which I had been born. I was greatly assisted in this process by the renewal of an old acquaintance. About the time I began 'working' for Alfred, my dear Samuel Hallam grew weary of roaming the Continent and returned to England. He had only just returned when Alfred donated some pieces to the British Museum, and paraded me around in those ridiculous clothes as a living part of the exhibit. Having absolutely nothing better to do with his time, Samuel was in the museum that same day, sulkily dragging himself from one hall to another. When I spied him, wandering off toward the Elgin Marbles, Alfred was busy delivering one of his interminable lectures to the public, so I approached Sam and reintroduced myself. Poor thing, he nearly fainted—hadn't been able to get me off of his mind. Being rather desperately in need of some companionship at the time myself, I told him of my situation out at Darcy and invited him to pay me a covert visit at the abandoned servants' cottage in the woods. Thus we renewed our old relations, and I amused myself with his regular visits for the next several months.

"When Alfred died, however, it suddenly occurred to me that Samuel might be able to provide me something other than mere amusement. English society being so damnably narrow-minded in its opinions regarding a new widow's behavior, I knew I should have a difficult time moving about London society in search of an antiquities dealer. But if someone else were to do the searching on the young widow's behalf—the woman's brother, for example—there would be far fewer objections to overcome. And thus was born Peter Worthington, my dear older brother.

"Samuel was all for the deception from the beginning. It would make him a legitimate member of the household, you see, and eliminate the necessity of his sneaking around the woods about the estate—a practice he found rather thrilling at first but eventually grew tired of. Before I could present him to the world as Peter Worthington, however, I had to assure myself that he wouldn't be recognized as Samuel Hallam. I needn't have worried, as it turns out, because since his return from the continent, poor old Sam had spent the great majority of this time reading Lord Byron, and trying his own hand at writing poetry. He hadn't even bothered to notify his family that he was back in England and had no plans to do so until his money ran out. And living with me at Darcy would allow him to put off that day indefinitely.

"With all fears of Sam's recognition thus out of the way, Peter Worthington made his London debut one week after my husband's death. It was a meeting with Alfred's attorney—a simple matter of clarifying a point of estate law—and 'Peter' handled himself beautifully. Sam really took to the role, I must admit. It seemed to give him a new confidence he had never before known, and within a month's time, he had become quite the man of business, maneuvering about the antiques trade like an old hand. Many of the dealers he contacted were only interested in individual pieces, but he absolutely refused to trade with these 'men of small vision,' holding out instead for someone willing to take the entire collection at once and able to pay what we asked.

"Around two months ago, Sam made contact with an agent representing an extremely wealthy Viennese baron who'd been following Alfred's career for decades, hoping for an opportunity someday to make a bid for my husband's—or rather my—unrivaled collection of artifacts. Sam presented his opportunity, and the baron seized it without a moment's hesitation. Hired men were to arrive here from Vienna within the month to begin gathering the pieces for transportation to the Continent, at which time the baron, accompanying his men to assure their honesty, would make an unimaginably large deposit on my behalf in the Bank of London. My plans for an independent life of ease were thus within my grasp.

"Alas, the unlucky conjunction of two separate developments threatened to destroy those plans outright. First off, Sam, flush with his newfound success as an antiques mogul, began to presume upon his importance as a fixture in my life. As tiresome as I had found his diffidence during our year together on the Continent, it was vastly preferable to the titanic self-assurance he began to display as the date of the trade approached. I frankly don't see how I could have tolerated it for very much longer, even if the second development had not occurred when it did. But, the fates do not make a habit of inquiring into our wishes before throwing opportunities, or obstacles, in our way, and just as the door was closing upon my time with Samuel, another opened up most unexpectedly with the arrival of Robert here." She reached out her hand and gave an affectionate squeeze to the elbow of the man we had met five days ago under the name of Peter Worthington. "Robert Hunt. The man's a shameless mountebank, but I'm terribly fond of him.

"He quite literally showed up on my doorstep one afternoon while Sam was in town on business. Upon returning from an extended visit to Scotland, where he was undoubtedly engaged in cheating someone out of something, he was reading some old newspapers in a tavern and came upon the story of Alfred's death. The fact that the wealthy old man left behind him a widow—and a young one, at that—caught Robert's attention, and the sun didn't go down before he hopped a coach out here to Darcy, where he shamelessly presented himself as a distant relative of my husband, offering his condolences, and whatever assistance might lie within his power to render. Having a good deal of experience in dissembling myself, I saw through his ruse immediately but found him so absolutely charming that I simply played along. That initial encounter ending inconclusively, we scheduled another meeting three days hence—the date of Sam's next appointment in town. One thing led to another, and within a week's time, I found myself once again making routine visits to the servants' cottage in the woods.

"As you might well imagine, this happy new turn of events made Sam's company absolutely intolerable for me. I could no longer bear the sight of the man, so when arrangements for our exchange with the baron were finalized, I informed him that his presence here at Darcy was no longer required, or welcome. The time had come for my 'dear brother' Peter Worthington to take a long trip abroad. Well, from the stunned expression on his face when he learned the news, one would have thought he'd been hit in the forehead with a hammer. It was the same expression he wore that day in Rome, when I told him I was leaving with Ippolito, only with a few more creases around the eyes. Completely pathetic. I honestly thought he might burst into tears. Whatever pity I may have felt for him before turned into utter contempt during those few minutes, and I longed to be rid of the sight of him at once. Not wishing to appear overly insensitive, however, I gave him three days to pack up those few possessions he had accumulated over the past few months and be on his way. His family would be more than happy to welcome their prodigal son back into the fold, I told him.

"To celebrate Samuel's departure, I arranged for an extended visit from Robert three days hence. What I did not arrange for, because I could not foresee, was Sam's unwillingness to relinquish the hold he felt he had upon me. As the third day approached, he grew increasingly restive and eventually resolved that if he could not possess me, neither would anyone else.

"I had made the fatal mistake, you see, of strongly hinting at my involvement in Alfred's death. We were sitting in the winter garden one afternoon, enjoying the tropical warmth, when he became curious about the puffer fish in the pond beside which we were seated. Having heard Alfred lecture so many times on the uniqueness of these hideous creatures—how they swell up like balloons when they sense danger, how they can close their eyes, unlike other fish, how they seem to cry when they are killed—and describe the hidden danger lurking just beneath their mottled gray skin, I instinctively launched into a lengthy exposition on the puffer, not omitting to relate the chilling tales of death served up on platters of their delicate white flesh. Having something of a theatrical bent—a gift from my poor mother I suppose—I became a bit carried away with my narrative, and drew a rather indiscreet connection between the poisonous fish and my husband's death. Sam simply laughed it off, refusing ever to take exception with anything I said, and began relating his own story about a fishing expedition he took off the coast of Greece. He gave every appearance of having forgotten all about the incident, but on the day before he was to make his final departure from Darcy, it became obvious that he had remembered all too well.

"It was a broiled hen Mrs. Bow had prepared for lunch. Sam actually carried the tray into the dining room—he often did that, preferring for Mrs. Bow to remain in the kitchen so we could be alone. The first few bites I took had an odd, fishy taste, but old Mrs. Bow's eyesight often led her to take the wrong ingredient from the cupboard, so I didn't pay the matter a great deal of attention. When my lips started to tingle, however—you both know the feeling—and I began to feel a creeping coldness throughout my limbs, I knew at once what was happening. Within moments, I was lying helpless on the floor, essentially dead in every part of my body except for my mind. Dear, sweet Samuel knelt beside me to feel for a heartbeat and listen for breathing. Clearly convinced that I was, as I appeared, dead, he gazed into my blank face for a few moments, sighing pathetically, then cried out desperately for Mrs. Bow to come at once. Mrs. Bow in turn cried out for George, whom Sam sent immediately into London to fetch a doctor. The physician, Dr. Edmonds, an old family friend, pronounced me dead, accused Sam of being somehow responsible—'Yes, yes!' I tried vainly to scream—and stormed out, vowing to make him pay for my murder. Close upon the heels of Edmonds was the undertaker—a strange and disturbing character—who also exchanged harsh words with Sam and left in a huff.

"The next twenty-four hours, during which I had to endure the indignity of being stripped, bathed, and dressed by Mrs. Bow's meddlesome nieces, dragged by with excruciating slowness. During that first night, while I was lying there upon the couch, with Mrs. Bow sitting faithfully by my side, I literally believed that time had stopped altogether. It hadn't, of course, and when finally the sun came up, Sam began making preparations for my funeral. Whether from a desire to get me underground as quickly as possible, or simply out of a deplorable lack of imagination, Sam bought me the cheapest coffin available and arranged for me to be buried in the first churchyard that came into his mind, All Souls clearly being at the top of the short, alphabetical list of churches with which he was acquainted. Because of the prominence of my married name, the church readily consented to having my mortal remains grace their hallowed premises, and by nightfall, I was less than a day away from becoming one of those living burial victims with whose stories my husband used to horrify his guests.

"Most likely to ensure that Dr. Edmonds didn't break into the house and whisk me off to the hospital for a quick autopsy, Samuel insisted on sitting up with my body that final night. Being in no position to protest, I had to endure his loathsome presence at my side throughout the evening and halfway though the night. Sometime around midnight, he fell fast asleep—in the very chair you're reclining in now, Mr. Dubres—and began snoring in a most annoying fashion. My mounting irritation was further aggravated by a sharp pain I began to feel at the nape of my neck. Having plenty of time for reflection, I searched for a likely cause of this pain, and correctly settled upon the long hairpin of my kanzashi, an ornamental Japanese headpiece—part of the 'costume' Mrs. Bow saw fit to dress me in, imagining that I simply adored the outfit because it's what I married Alfred in. As I lay there, thus considering the source of my pain, an astonishingly obvious fact occurred to me. Never mind *why* I was feeling pain, the miracle was *that* I was feeling pain, after going for more than a full day with no physical sensation whatsoever. Mentally exploring the different regions of my body, I realized that I had an itch on my foot, a painful cramp in my leg, and a nauseous feeling in my stomach. In short, I was *feeling* everywhere, and a quick experiment with my fingers and toes informed me that mobility had accompanied my renewed powers of sensation.

"Over the course of the next hour, my body slowly came back to life, tingling and prickling like frostbitten feet warming by the fire. Finally, gathering together all of the strength that had returned to my body, I sat bolt upright in the coffin. Had Samuel awakened at that moment, he quite likely would have died of shock. He was clearly not destined to die of shock, however, for he remained as deeply asleep as he had been for the past two hours, sitting there with his hands folded in his lap and his head hanging stupidly upon his chest. The fool was actually drooling on the front of his shirt.

"A quick check of the lower half of my body gave me the confidence to raise my legs from the floor of the coffin and ease my body over the side, one heavy limb at a time. After a few minutes I found myself standing—unsteadily, yes, but standing—directly in front of Sam, staring down onto the back of his neck. At that moment, I wanted nothing in this world so badly as to crush his loathsome skull and scatter his brains across the carpet at his feet. I looked around the room for a suitably heavy object, but realized my arms were still too weak to lift anything that would answer to my purpose. And then I remembered the pain in the back of my neck. The hairpin—kogai, they call it in Japanese, which translates roughly into 'sword,' quite an apt metaphor, if you've ever seen one. Without a moment's hesitation, I lifted my hand to the back of my head, pulled the kogai out of my hair, and drove it straight down into the base of Samuel's skull. He exhaled loudly, once, and died, without so much as moving a muscle. I pulled the pin out of his neck, slid it through a fold of my kimono to wipe of the blood, and placed it back in my hair.

"As I stood there, staring down at Sam's still-seated body, wondering what to do next, I became aware of a presence in the parlor doorway. It was Robert, who had rounded the corner just in time to see me plunge the pin into Sam's skull, and the expression on his face was an indescribable mix of shock, relief, and pure horror. He had arrived at the servants' cottage earlier in the evening, as scheduled, but when I failed to meet him there as we had planned, he waited until dark and approached the house to see if he could learn what had kept me. Finding everyone apparently asleep, he entered the garden door, and crept down the hallway to the parlor, where he could see a light burning. Peering around the doorjamb, he encountered the scene I have just described. For the first time since I met him, Robert was, quite understandably, speechless.

"When I began trying to explain to him what had occurred over the past thirty-six hours, my jaws felt like the hinges of a rusty gate, greatly in need of oil. Robert was in no condition to interrupt me, however, so with slow, painful effort, I told him of Sam's treachery, and of the subsequent events that had precipitated the violent act he had just witnessed. And lest he think ill of me for the extreme measure to which I had just been driven, I reminded him that, when he rounded the corner into the parlor, he just as easily could have found me lying dead in my cheap coffin and Sam sleeping as soundly as an innocent babe at my side, were it not for a simple, fatal mistake on Sam's part. Instead of feeding me the fugu powder—the concentrated extract of the poison— which would have left me in the same 'condition' in which it left Alfred, and in which it's going to leave the two of you, Sam went fishing in the puffer pond, and gave me a bit of fresh fugu liver along with my broiled hen that fateful afternoon. I had not mentioned the extract in my story, you see, as it seemed somehow less 'romantic' than the thought of a deadly living menace swimming beneath our very feet. A bit of poetic license, I suppose, but it saved my life, for as deadly as those creatures are in the open ocean, once one domesticates them, as Alfred did, they lose a good deal of their potency. So while Sam's treachery left me as good as dead, it was a death from which I was able to recover.

"Sam's death, on the other hand, was quite obviously irremediable, and once Robert had somewhat regained his manhood, I pressed him with the rather urgent need to dispose of the body. Unlike today, there were actually other people in the house that night who might wander in here and force us into a most embarrassing attempt at explanation. Not being quite myself yet, I was for simply dragging the body out into the woods and burying it under a few feet of soil. It was Robert who thought up the brilliantly simple expedient of placing Sam's body in my coffin and letting the undertaker haul away the evidence of my 'crime.'

Nailing the lid shut was a bit trying, admittedly, but with the inventive use of a sofa cushion and a paperweight, we managed not to rouse anyone.

"With Sam thus taken care of, Robert and I repaired to the servants' cottage to try to decide how in heaven's name to proceed next. As understandably relieved as I was simply to be alive, after my harrowing ordeal of the past two days, my relief was soon tempered by a realization of the extreme awkwardness of my current position. Abigail Darcy, heir to her husband's priceless Oriental collection, which in a few days time was to become a cash fortune of unimaginable proportions, was effectively dead to the world, and 'Peter Worthington,' Abigail's sole heir to this fortune, was simply dead. As things stood at that dark moment, the fortune that I had worked so hard to acquire, and which was to secure me a life of wealthy independence, would now inevitably revert to the almighty courts, where it would evaporate like fog on a summer morning, leaving no trace behind. I had my life, yes, but I had lost, at one fell swoop, everything that made life worth living. For the first, and only, time in my life, I began to wonder if I wouldn't, perhaps, be better off dead.

"But, my irregular life having taught me resilience among many other things, I soon shook off these dark thoughts, and began to search about me for some remedy to the predicament in which I found myself. When my eyes—those both literal and metaphorical—lighted upon Robert, the tiniest seed of a solution began to germinate in my mind. I had never before noticed, but Robert bore a striking physical resemblance to Sam— looking back upon the succession of men in my life, I now realize it's a type to which I have been rather routinely attracted. But so similar was Robert's physical appearance to that of Sam that he could, without effort, pass as Sam's brother. With a little effort, however, along with some assistance from me, I thought it might just be possible for him to pass as Sam himself, at least long enough to inherit his dead sister's Oriental collection, complete the trade with the Viennese baron, then disappear forever, before anyone caught so much as a whiff of anything amiss. Sam's dealings with the baron's agents having been somewhat extensive, I realized from the start that Robert would need to keep a prudent distance from these men, but figured that a distraction of some kind would answer that purpose nicely. And what more powerful distraction than the charms of a beautiful, worldly woman—say, a sister of the deceased Abigail Darcy, for example? Three days later, Madeline Worthington arrived in London, in response to a number of disquieting dreams she had experienced recently, regarding her dear sister's well-being.

"'And did it work?' you're no doubt asking yourselves. 'Were they actually able to get away with their diabolical deception?' Considering the circumstance in which you find yourselves right now, I'm sure you'd have to lay better than even odds on our success. And had you the luxury of another forty-eight hours of life in which to wait, and watch, you'd find that your bet was a sound one, for the baron is scheduled to arrive with his men at Darcy first thing tomorrow morning, to begin packing up and hauling away Alfred Darcy's unparalleled collection of rare Oriental artifacts. The baron himself will place a large sum of money directly into our hands upon his departure, and deposit an even larger sum under our names in a somewhat obscure Parisian bank with which I once conducted some business, in my younger days. After having given life in England another try, I've concluded that the Continent is far more suited to my temperament, and Robert here agrees with me. We'll ship out as soon as the money is in our hands, and Madeline and Peter Worthington will disappear into the European sunset, never to be heard from again. Robert Hunt and Cathleen Smithson, on the other hand, will live happily, and comfortably, ever after."

She looked out the window into the darkness, then turned back to face us. "Please forgive me for going on and on like that, gentlemen. I tend to get carried away sometimes—my theatrical bent, you know." She narrowed her eyes at us, reflectively, then addressed Robert. "Go and check the gentlemen for me, Robert, there's a good lad. I fear my lengthy narrative may very well have bored them to death." Robert walked over and placed the back of his hand in front of our noses, feeling for breath. Then, holding the palm of a hand upon each of our two chests, he pursed his lips and shook his head, clearly very much annoyed. "They're still alive, Cathleen," he said, irritably. "Whatever shall we do?"

"There's no need to whine about it, Robert," she huffed. "It's not manly. We shall just have to wait them out. It can't be much longer, as much powder as I put in those biscuits." She paused and tapped the tip of her index finger upon her cheek, obviously considering something. "And what if we don't wait them out? Just look at them. They shan't be any more difficult to move like this than they will be once they finally decide to give up the ghost. Perhaps we should just go ahead and bury them now, so they'll have some quiet time underground to consider all the bother they've caused us."

"And perhaps you shall *not* bury us now, Madame," said Jean-Claude sharply, sitting bolt upright in his chair, with an expression of triumphant annoyance on his face. "I, for one, am not nearly ready for the grave yet. And what about you, *mon ami?*" he asked, turning toward me. "Do you believe that you have some good years of life remaining ahead of you?"

"As a matter of fact, I believe I do," I replied, sitting upright, then wincing at a sharp pain in my lower back. "For now, though, I have a few kinks to work out of my body. I've been in a damnably awkward position. It was all I could do just to remain still."

"And yet, you did not move a muscle," he said,

in a congratulatory tone. "Your performance was absolutely splendid. You have become quite the actor since we first came out here, a week ago."

Throughout our mutual exchange of congratulations, Cathleen and Robert stood utterly transfixed to their spots, wearing such blank expressions on their faces that one might very easily conclude that they had just consumed a large dose of the poison that had been intended for us. "Surely you did not really believe we would be so foolish as to eat anything prepared by your hand," Jean-Claude addressed Cathleen, raising an incredulous eyebrow. "And speaking of food . . ." He turned his attention once more to me. ". . . you must take great care in handling those biscuits you slipped into your coat pocket, my friend. As our hostess kindly informed us, there is enough poison in each of them to—how was it?—'kill a small army.' And we are one small army I would prefer not to see killed."

While Jean-Claude spoke, Cathleen—resilient as ever—began to take small, discreet steps toward a corner desk, upon whose surface a pair of scissors glinted in the firelight, and Robert, responding to a silent command from Cathleen's eyes, reached toward the fireplace for a poker. "Come now, Madame," Jean-Claude said, with that familiar, supercilious clucking of his tongue. ". . . further violence will avail you nothing."

"If it will avail me of getting rid you two meddlesome creatures," she veritably hissed, "I shall consider it worth whatever effort it costs me." Then suddenly, clutching the scissors in her hand, she lunged for Jean-Claude. Simultaneously, Robert came toward me with the poker raised above his head. Before either weapon reached its intended target, however, both Cathleen and Robert stopped dead in their tracks, and stared dumbly at the doorway behind our chairs.

"I am guessing, Madame," Jean-Claude said calmly, "that you have discovered we did not venture out here alone this afternoon. I hope you do not very much mind the imposition, but we invited a few acquaintances to accompany us on our journey." Looking behind me, I saw with great relief the sight that had produced such consternation in both of our "hosts." Standing just inside the doorway were five officers of the law, and our young friend Jimmy, who had escorted the gentlemen quietly through the house to a covert location from which, he knew from personal experience, one could hear every word that was uttered in the parlor.

"I believe . . ." Jean-Claude began, but before he could finish, I interrupted him, unable to resist the simile that had just sprung into my mind.

"I believe, sir and Madame, that this is checkmate," I said, with enormous satisfaction.

"Touché," Jean-Claude agreed.

EPILOGUE

"Care for a game of chess, Jean-Claude?" I asked, next afternoon in the apartment.

"As a matter of fact," he replied, "I would most decidedly *not* care for a game of chess. For the first time in my life, I find my poor brain to be quite weary from games of ratiocination. Why do we not play something a little less complex—a nice game of draughts, perhaps."

"Suit yourself," I said, walking to the bookcase to retrieve the pieces. "I'm delighted simply to be in a position to play any game at all today, never mind what." I scattered the disks upon the board, and we sorted black from brown. "And it's all thanks to you, I must admit. As difficult as it was for me to swallow your unlikely theory of that woman's malign intentions toward us, it certainly was a great deal easier on the digestion than those biscuits would have been, had I not listened. It's no exaggeration to say that I owe my very life to you."

"You flatter me, *mon ami*, but it was all quite simple really." Jean-Claude arranged his pieces on the board, and made the first move. "I was contemplating the possibility of something of that sort ever since Jimmy mentioned the strange fish that could blow himself up like a balloon. Most peculiar, did you not think?"

"Yes," I replied, moving my first piece, ". . . but I never gave it a great deal of thought afterward. The lad does have a tendency toward hyperbole."

"Indeed, but in this case, the seeming exaggeration matched exactly the features of a preserved specimen I once saw in the Museum of Natural History in Paris. I was only a child when I saw it, but it made a very distinct impression upon my youthful imagination, especially when the director of the exhibit explained to me that the creature contained a deadly poison. I thus filed it away in my memory under the general category of 'dangerous creatures of the ocean'—along with stingrays, electric eels, and other such exotic species. Even though I remembered the blowfish, however, I may very well not have foreseen the danger this creature would pose to our own persons, had I not read an article—written by Alfred Darcy himself—on the rare and perilous Japanese delicacy fugu. While you were sleeping off the effects of your brandy, the night before last, I was perusing Sir Alfred's landmark *Cyclopedia of Oriental History and Culture*, and read the 'fugu' entry in the chapter on 'Indigenous Cuisine.'

"Even having read about fugu, however," he continued, jumping four of my pieces with one move, ". . . I still might not have perceived any relation to our personal circumstances, had it not been for the mysteriously compliant cat whose tail I stepped upon in the Darcy garden. When I saw the cat—whose curiosity unfortunately, if rather tritely, did him in—I knew immediately what species of fish was swimming in that indoor pond and began to develop some nagging suspicions regarding Sir Alfred's death. The close conjunction of my encounter with the cat and the sudden appearance of George upon the garden path, established in my mind a connection, albeit a tenuous one, between these events and the murdered man who turned up on our dissecting table."

"Samuel Hallam, yes," I interrupted. "I suppose the poor fellow, or what's left of him at least, has been returned to his family and given a Christian burial by now."

"Undoubtedly," he replied, then continued, unfazed by my interruption. "I recognized him at once, of course—George, that is—and I assumed he remembered me as well and would report my intrusion to his master and mistress. If Mlle. 'Worthington' were not somehow involved with the murder, I knew, her discovery of my association with St. Alban's would lead her to suspect me of a fraud, but nothing more. Her most probable, and understandable, reaction in this case would be a complete cessation of communication with the two of us. She would never wish to see us again." I captured three of his pieces, evening the game. "But when she sent 'round an invitation to tea," he went on, ". . . the very next morning after I was caught trespassing on her property, I knew her motives could not be entirely hospitable." In a series of six jumps, he cleared the board of my pieces.

"Really, Jean-Claude," I protested, then collected my pieces to begin another game. We played silently for a moment, and the events of the past several days flitted in an out of my head like moths around a lantern. "I must hand it to you, Jean-Claude," I said, in a tone of the deepest sincerity. "Your powers of reasoning are most extraordinary. You saw your way clear through this labyrinth of deductive reasoning while I was wandering aimlessly down the primrose path after 'Madeline.'"

"Do not be so hard on yourself, my friend," he consoled me. "This pursuit of ours presented us with a number of crossroads and blind alleys, it is true. But in following your heart as you did, you took a straighter path toward the truth than I did in thus following reason. It was, after all, an *affaire du coeur* that precipitated Samuel Hallam's desperate attempt upon the life of Cathleen Smithson. And as for the lady's violent reaction to this attempt, it was merely the age-old story of an eye for an eye, and a tooth for a tooth. He tries to kill her, so she kills him in retaliation." He pursed his lips in concentration, surveying the board, then moved a single space. "Yes," he said, nodding. "The path we followed was a convoluted one at times. But the murder that first set us onto this path . . . It was but a simple case of revenge."

PREMIUM PLUS

WHAT IS A PREMIUM PLUS EDITION?

The "Premium" offers you a more readable type and larger page format. The "Plus" is our gift to you.

Log onto www.harpercollins.com/premiumplus, enter code TA0408, select one of our free newsletters, complete the entry form, print the resulting confirmation page and mail it to us with the original receipt from your purchase and you will receive a FREE HarperLuxe title from HarperCollins Publishers (approximate retail value: $15.95 or greater). You must enter this code online to receive your free copy. No mail-ins accepted without the confirmation page attached to your receipt.

This offer is valid for U.S. consumers only from 3/25/08 – 5/26/08. Please allow twelve weeks for delivery. (Shipping and handling are FREE, too.) See complete details at www.harpercollins.com/premiumplus.

Visit www.HarperLuxe.com for information on a more comfortable reading experience.

Visit www.AuthorTracker.com for exclusive information on your favorite HarperCollins authors.

Masterworks of historical suspense by critically acclaimed author

OWEN PARRY

FADED COAT OF BLUE
978-0-380-79739-4

A recent immigrant to America at the time of the Civil War, Abel Jones finds himself chosen as a confidential agent to General George McLellan.

SHADOWS OF GLORY
978-0-380-82087-0

In a snow-swept Northern town, Union officer Abel Jones struggles to solve the murders of Federal agents who were tortured to death.

CALL EACH RIVER JORDAN
978-0-06-000922-9

Union Major Abel Jones survives the battle of Shiloh only to face the riddle of a different kind of massacre . . . forty murdered slaves.

HONOR'S KINGDOM
978-0-06-051079-4

Major Abel Jones returns to London and Glasgow, the lands he once left in hope of a better life, on a mission essential to the Union cause.

BOLD SONS OF ERIN
978-0-06-051391-7

Major Abel Jones battles the multiple layers of deceit surrounding the murder of a general who lied about his own name.

REBELS OF BABYLON
978-0-06-051393-1

In 1863 New Orleans an uneasy truce between freed slaves and their former masters stretches to the breaking point.

Visit www.AuthorTracker.com for exclusive
information on your favorite HarperCollins authors.

Available wherever books are sold or please call 1-800-331-3761 to order.

OP 0108

Edge-of-your-seat thrillers from
New York Times bestselling author

JAMES ROLLINS

BLACK ORDER

978-0-06-076537-8/$7.99 US/$10.99 Can
Buried in the past, an ancient conspiracy now
rises to threaten all life.

MAP OF BONES

978-0-06-076524-8/$7.99 US/$10.99 Can
There are those with dark plans for stolen
sacred remains that will alter the future of mankind.

SANDSTORM

978-0-06-058067-4/$7.99 US/$10.99 Can
Twenty years ago, a wealthy British financier
disappeared near Ubar, the fabled city buried beneath
the sands of Oman. Now the terrifying secrets of his
disappearance are revealed.

ICE HUNT

978-0-06-052160-8/$7.99 US/$10.99 Can
Danger lives at the top of the world . . . where nothing
can survive except fear.

AMAZONIA

978-0-06-000249-7/$7.99 US/$10.99 Can
There are dark secrets hidden in the jungle's
heart, breeding fear, madness . . . and death.

Visit www.AuthorTracker.com for exclusive
information on your favorite HarperCollins authors.

JR 0307

Available wherever books are sold or please call 1-800-331-3761 to order.

NEW YORK TIMES BESTSELLING AUTHOR

LAWRENCE BLOCK

HIT MAN
978-0-380-72541-0 / $7.99 US / $10.99 Can

Keller is your basic Urban Lonely Guy. He makes a decent
wage, lives in a nice apartment. Works the crossword puzzle.
Watches a little TV. Until the phone rings and he packs a suit-
case, gets on a plane, flies halfway across the country . . . and
kills somebody.

HIT LIST
978-0-06-103099-4 / $7.99 US / $10.99 Can

Keller is a pro at killing people for money. But the jobs have
started to go wrong. The realization is slow coming yet, when
it arrives, it is irrefutable: Someone out there is trying to hit the
hit man.

HIT PARADE
978-0-06-084089-1 / $7.99 US / $10.99 Can

Like the rest of us, Keller's starting to worry about his retirement. After all, he's not getting any younger. So he contacts
his "booking agent," Dot, and tells her to keep the hits coming.
He'll take any job, anywhere. His nest egg needs fattening up.

www.lawrenceblock.com

Visit www.AuthorTracker.com for exclusive
information on your favorite HarperCollins authors.

Available wherever books are sold or please call 1-800-331-3761 to order.
HIT 0607

 # 1 *NEW YORK TIMES* BESTSELLING AUTHOR

MICHAEL CRICHTON

STATE OF FEAR

978-0-06-101573-1/$7.99 US/$11.99 Can

In Tokyo, in Los Angeles, in Antarctica, in the Solomon Islands . . . an intelligence agent races to put all the pieces of a worldwide puzzle together to prevent a global catastrophe.

"EDGE-OF-YOUR-SEAT STORYTELLING."
USA Today

PREY

978-0-06-101572-4/$7.99 US/$11.99 Can

In the Nevada desert, an experiment has gone horribly wrong. A cloud of nanoparticles—micro-robots—has escaped from the laboratory. It has been programmed as a predator and every attempt to destroy it has failed. And we are the prey.

"TERRIFYING...IRRESISTIBLY SUSPENSEFUL."
New York Times Book Review

Visit www.AuthorTracker.com for exclusive information on your favorite HarperCollins authors.

Available wherever books are sold or please call 1-800-331-3761 to order.
MC1 0407

LET *NEW YORK TIMES* BESTSELLING AUTHOR

DENNIS LEHANE

TAKE YOU TO THE EDGE OF DARKNESS

Mystic River
978-0-380-73185-5
$7.99/10.99 Can.

Prayers for Rain
978-0-380-73036-0
$7.99/$10.99 Can.

Gone, Baby, Gone
978-0-380-73035-3
$7.99/$10.99 Can.

Sacred
978-0-380-72629-5
$7.99/$10.99 Can.

Darkness, Take My Hand
978-0-380-72628-8
$7.99/$10.99 Can.

A Drink Before the War
978-0-380-72623-3
$7.99/$10.99 Can.

Shutter Island
978-0-380-73186-2
$7.99/$10.99 Can

Coronado
978-0-06-113967-3
$24.95/$31.50 Can

Visit www.AuthorTracker.com for exclusive
information on your favorite HarperCollins authors.

DL 0707

Available wherever books are sold or please call 1-800-331-3761 to order.